That was what all the ⟨...⟩ her mum had come today. She had said she wasn't going anywhere, she was going to stay and look after Tommy, but she'd come to say goodbye to Jane. Jane was trying so hard not to cry, but she couldn't help herself. Was she being given away, and if so, who to? Who would want her? There had been a family in the next street to them that were put in the workhouse, and all the neighbours had cried and felt sorry for them because they'd heard the workhouse was such a terrible place. But they had all gone together. Would she be put in there all on her own?

Now she wasn't just frightened; she was terrified.

Alice bent down and gently kissed her on the cheek. 'I'm sorry . . . about your dad . . . and everything. Be a good girl an' always remember that I do love you.'

Jane wanted her mum to know that it wasn't her fault and that she loved her too, but she didn't know what to say. Alice straightened up and stood there looking at her for a few moments, then she pulled the bedclothes up round her, tucking the sheet beneath her chin, and turned and walked away, without saying another word.

Jane burrowed down in the bed, pulling the clothes over her head, and sobbed as if her heart was breaking.

A London Lass

ELIZABETH WAITE

SPHERE

First published in Great Britain in 2001 by Little, Brown
This edition published by Time Warner Paperbacks in 2002
Reprinted by Sphere in 2010

A CIP catalogue record for this book
is available from the British Library.

ISBN 978-0-7515-3208-1

Typeset by Palimpsest Book Production Limited,
Grangemouth, Stirlingshire
Printed and bound in Great Britain by
Clays Ltd, St Ives plc

Papers used by Sphere are natural, renewable and
recyclable products sourced from well-managed forests and certified
in accordance with the rules of the Forest Stewardship Council.

Mixed Sources
Product group from well-managed
forests and other controlled sources
www.fsc.org Cert no. SGS-COC-004081
© 1996 Forest Stewardship Council

Sphere
An imprint of
Little, Brown Book Group
100 Victoria Embankment
London EC4Y 0DY

An Hachette UK Company
www.hachette.co.uk

www.littlebrown.co.uk

Chapter One

South London, 1920

'DID YER SEE what's going on over at the Castle?' Jimmy Bradshaw asked as he and his mate Ronnie Brown approached the men grouped around the coffee stall which stood on the island in the centre of Tooting Broadway.

Wally Simmonds, manager of Tooting Markets, put his mug of tea on the counter, looked at the two lads and grinned good-naturedly.

'It's Saturday night, son, and turning-out time for the pubs usually means trouble of one sort or another.'

'But this woman's taken one 'ell of a bashing by the looks of 'er.' Sixteen-year-old Ronnie's voice held not only concern but a hint of fear as well. 'We saw 'er being dragged off by 'er hair.'

'Yeah, screaming blue murder she was.' Jimmy put his twopennyworth in; after all, he was older by two years and wasn't going to be outdone.

'All right, lads, I'll take a look.' Wally sighed as he picked up his mug and drained the last of his tea. He was ninety per cent sure that it would be Mickey Jeffrey having a go at his long-suffering wife Alice.

From where he stood outside Lyons tea rooms, Wally had only to look across the main road to see that the forecourt of the Castle pub was being cleared rapidly due to the presence of two policemen.

'Mickey must have scarpered pretty quickly,' he murmured to himself. 'Anyhow, I may as well go home down Selkirk Road, it's not much out of my way.'

Truth was, he had a lot of time for Alice Jeffrey; she didn't have much of a life. In a nutshell, she'd an eight-year-old daughter, a three-year-old lad, no regular income and persistent beatings from Mickey whenever he thought the world wasn't treating him right.

Wally crossed over the main road, walked a few yards and turned left into Selkirk Road. It was gone eleven but the street was well lit, and the pie and eel shop on the left and the fish and chip shop on the right were still doing a roaring trade. Young lads and even a few younger kiddies were sitting on the high kerbstone, their feet dangling in the gutter, eating their pennyworth of chips out of greasy newspaper or spooning eel liquor into their mouths from what was known as a penny basin, which consisted of mashed potatoes and a thick green soup. Meanwhile, their parents were inside the shops, seated at marble-topped tables having their supper off china plates. Loads of people were still about, of course there were; within yards of where he was walking there were four pubs which had just turned out: the Selkirk, the Fox, the Angel and the Castle.

Saturday night, and the locals were having what to most of them was their only weekly treat. Never mind that the landlord would be wanting his rent come Monday, this lot were living for the moment. Again Wally sighed; folk round these parts never seemed to look further than the nose on their face.

Could he blame them? Not really.

Two years ago, in 1918, when the Armistice had been signed, the wounded and the crippled had been left to fend for themselves, and those few men who had returned whole had long since given up looking for the land fit for heroes that they had been promised.

Why did he stay around these parts? Wally asked himself that same question time and time again. Too lazy to seek pastures new? No, that wasn't true.

He'd been born and bred in Garrett Lane, gone to school in Broadwater Road and then Defoe Road School for Boys. You could say he was one of the lucky ones, but maybe privileged would be a better word. His parents had met when they were in service, his mother a parlourmaid, his father a stable lad. It was the training in working with horses that his father had received that had gained him entry into a crack cavalry regiment when he'd answered Lord Kitchener's call to fight for his country.

A blessing in disguise, his mother had said, when a bad bout of pleurisy had prevented Wally himself from being called to the colours and sent to France.

His father had risen through the ranks to become a lieutenant. An office that was short-lived; he'd been killed in France on the Western Front in 1916.

The only good to come out of that whole episode was the fact that his mother received an officer's war pension.

It hadn't made them rich, but at least they hadn't wanted for the essential things in life. They had a neat little house, and they had each other. It had been enough. Though if the truth be told, since his mother had passed away two years ago, Wally had often admitted to himself that he felt the need of a woman in his life. Still, he was only twenty-one, and some day he hoped he might meet the kind of woman he could settle down with.

When he'd first left school, aged fourteen, he'd had high hopes of getting a job in Fleet Street; he'd always wanted to be a reporter. More than willing to start on the bottom rung, he'd have run errands, made the tea, whatever, but no such luck. Too many lads chasing too few jobs.

He'd been lucky to get taken on with the co-op that ran the markets. He'd started off as a van boy, up at four o'clock every morning and off with a couple of stall-holders to Covent Garden or Spitalfields to bid for fruit and vegetables. He'd learned to love the life. The noise was always deafening. The chaos of porters carrying great quantities of boxed fruit dashing about all over the place, while costermongers piled their push carts. By the time they were ready to go to the café for a hearty breakfast, they had to be careful how they trod, because the floor of the great hall would be littered with cabbage leaves and squashed tomatoes.

Now, seven years later, the fact that they had given him the title of manager didn't alter the fact that he was still a dogsbody. Apart from being responsible for collecting the rents, and having eyes out the back of his head where the barrow boys were concerned, he was also caretaker and nightwatchman all rolled into one. Still, there wasn't a trader that he couldn't call his friend, and by and large he was his own boss. Except for his Monday-morning call to the main offices, when if he hadn't the full amount of rent money, he'd have to have a very good reason as to why a certain stall-holder was falling behind in his dues.

The street door of number twenty-three was wide open, the light from the unshaded single bulb in the passageway streaming out. Wally heard a woman scream and he broke into a run.

It was worse than even he would have thought. Mickey

hadn't waited to get his wife inside the house; she was lying in a crumpled heap on the damp pathway that led up through the small front garden. Suddenly Mickey straightened up, took a deep breath and kicked his wife viciously in the stomach. He was laughing; a drunken beast he might be, but he was well aware of what he was doing. Again his leg was raised and his booted foot caught the side of Alice's head.

He was unfastening his belt when Wally reached him.

He heard the crunch of knuckles against bone as he shot his fist out and whacked it straight into Mickey's face.

'You . . . you . . . bastard.' Mickey was having a job to get his words out as he clenched his hand tight up to his chin and felt the blood trickle between his fingers.

Wally watched in horror as Alice struggled to get to her knees. Her moans were so pitiful, he felt he had to help her. Mickey blocked his way. Wally, being at least three inches taller and far more thick-set, could have swatted him like a fly, but for the moment that wasn't what was bothering him. Peering into the darkest corner of the front garden, he felt the vomit rise in his throat.

Janey and Tommy, Alice's two youngsters, were huddled together. Wally felt so sorry for them. Dare he interfere? At times little Jane was the sweetest child one could imagine. A baby face that would look great on an expensive china doll, clear blue eyes and soft silky hair that hung in natural ringlets to form almost a halo around her head and shoulders. But upset her and she had the temper of an alley cat. She was cuddling Tommy, her baby brother. Most folk thought of Tommy as an adorable child. His hair was several shades darker than his sister's, his face plump and dimpled, with the biggest dark brown eyes you could imagine. Both children were shivering; all they were wearing was very thin nightclothes, and they looked dirty and bedraggled.

With Wally's attention focused on the children, Mickey started his battering again. Having managed to get up on her knees, Alice was sent sprawling once more. Both the children winced as they heard the thud of their mother's head hitting the pathway.

Wally breathed a sigh of relief as the police van screeched to a halt. He hastened to put his arms around the kiddies and the three of them watched as two uniformed coppers pulled their father away from their mother. Mickey sealed his fate for the night as the policemen dragged him to his feet. He hadn't the sense to go quietly and did his utmost to boot one of them between his legs. He hadn't managed to raise his foot high enough, but all the same his boot made contact with the copper's shin, causing enough pain to ensure that some form of retaliation would soon be forthcoming.

Wally, Janey and Tommy watched as Mickey was practically thrown into the back of the van and the door slammed shut.

'I'll see to the kids.' Mavis Owen's voice was harsh as she stepped over the low fence that divided the two houses. 'Disgusting, ain't it, Wally? The way Mickey carries on, an' gets away with it every time.'

Wally heaved another great sigh, 'Living next door all these years, Mavis, you know more about it than I do. Right now, I think I'd better see about getting Alice indoors, though she probably ought to go straight to the hospital.'

'No, me mum don't never want to go t' St James'.' Jane's voice held a note of authority which belied the fact that she was so young.

By now Wally had bent and picked Alice up from the ground, cradling her gently in his arms he walked into the house.

Neighbours were standing at their doorways; it was nothing new for them to see Alice Jeffrey get a bashing, but it was a strange twist to see Wally Simmonds get involved.

'Best thing that could 'appen, if you ask me,' Hannah Watkins chuckled. 'I've lived all these years across the road with me front door facing theirs and I've seen so much of it. It's about time someone took Alice's side.'

'Who said anything about him taking sides?' John, her husband, asked. 'I'd say Wally will be sorry he came along when he did.'

Inside number twenty-three, Wally had set Alice down in a big shabby armchair, and his one thought was that she looked like death. Mavis had taken coats down from a hook on the back of the kitchen door and was helping young Tommy to put his arms into the sleeves, while Janey had already shrugged herself into hers.

'By God! Will yer look at her face, she'll 'ave a massive black eye come the morning,' Mavis murmured half to herself. 'Are you going to stay for a cup of tea?' she added, looking up at Wally.

'I'll put the kettle on,' Janey piped up. 'It won't be a minute.'

Wally glanced sideways at Mavis as Jane went through to the scullery, and remarked, 'That girl has an old head on her young shoulders, more's the pity.'

'Yeah, you're right there. Been a case of 'aving t' grow up. Ain't been an easy life for her so far, an' it don't look as if things are going to improve with time, does it?'

Janey came back into the room holding out a wet face flannel and a striped towel, and asked Mavis, 'Would you mind wiping me mum's face while I get the tea?'

Wally swore beneath his breath. This shouldn't be happening. A decent women knocked nearly senseless and an eight-year-old girl left to care for her. Mickey was probably sleeping off his drunken stupor in a warm police cell, and like as not they'd let him out first thing in the morning.

Then he had to quickly smother a grin. The thought had come to him that maybe, just maybe, the copper Mickey had kicked might have been mad enough to give him a good going-over. It would be no more than he deserved.

Janey brought in two steaming mugs of tea for Wally and Mavis, and a few minutes later she knelt down in front of her mother, saying quietly, 'I've made you a cup of tea, Mum, I've put loads of sugar in it.' As Alice struggled to sit up, she stared into her daughter's face, and what she saw there hurt her more than all the beatings that her husband ditched out.

Wally was at his wits' end to know what to do for the best, and Mavis had three children of her own next door to see to. Whatever they did tonight to help Alice and her children wouldn't make the slightest bit of difference to the way they lived.

They both knew that, though neither would admit it.

Chapter Two

JANE'S BABY FACE looked very different this morning. Her huge blue eyes showed she was in a temper, and with good reason, she would have told anyone who cared to listen.

Her dad was home. She could hear him shouting.

When finally she had got into bed last night she had said her prayers, remembering that her Sunday school teacher had told her that the dear Lord Jesus would always be there for her.

So why had her dad come home?

She'd wanted him to be sent to prison. And kept there, for ever and ever. Where he couldn't hurt her mum nor her. She'd told Nancy about the times he'd hurt her, and old Nancy had been ever so angry but all she'd said was, 'We have to make allowances for him.' What did that mean? No one ever answered that question. Sometimes she felt that she was the cause of all the things that went wrong for her father. She tried hard to keep out of his way whenever he was in a bad mood. She knew the signs. When he'd lost money at the bookmaker's. When the Labour Exchange had made him go after a job. Jobs he made sure he never got.

Helping out at the markets, touting on the racecourse, all for money in his hand, so her mum said, was all he was willing to put himself out for.

If he'd had a bad day, it was always Jane he picked on. If she were lucky she'd manage to slip out of the house and run up to Nancy, who lived in the end house of this road. Nancy was a smashing lady. Kind. Oh yes, kind to everyone. Short and dumpy, with a head of dark frizzy hair which Mum always said was Nancy's own fault because she was always burning it with hot curling tongs. You could always be sure of a kiss and a cuddle from Nancy, and even more to the point, something nice to eat, because she was ever such a good cook.

'I suppose I'd better go downstairs,' Jane muttered to herself.

'Sit up to the table, luv, I'm just making you a bit of porridge.' Her mother's voice sounded shaky and it was only when she turned round that Jane saw just how dreadful she looked. Her face was a mass of bruises; she had a big black eye, her lips were swollen and a patch of dried blood seemed to be covering her right ear.

'Oh Mum! You should be in bed.' Jane managed to get the words out before she burst into tears.

'It's all right, pet, really it is. Come on, sit down, Tommy's had his breakfast and he's gone next door to play with Mavis's lot.'

Jane sensed her father's closeness and knew she'd have to pass him to get to the table. She hung her head, making sure her eyes looked only at the floor.

Suddenly he lunged out at her, grabbing both of her arms and almost yanking her off her feet.

'You're a crafty little bitch, you are. It's you that's the cause of more than 'alf the goings-on in this 'ouse, an' I've just about 'ad enough of it. Bad enough I took yer mother on; didn't bargain for all the trouble she was bringing with 'er.' He flung her from him with such force that her right leg smashed against the side of the table and she wasn't able to stop herself from falling.

'Mick, Mick, you promised!' Alice beseeched him, her voice little more than a croak.

'Me promised? Don't come that old lark with me. What about you? You ain't exactly come across, 'ave yer? When did you ever bring so much as one pound note into this 'ouse? Go on, tell me that.'

'Oh Mick, you know I try. I take in washing, I do dress-making, or I did till you took it in your 'ead to smash me sewing machine.'

'Pennies, that's all. Yer said she'd never be a burden to me. Well let me tell yer, you an' she are a bloody great burden t' me day in day out. You could get out there an' earn a few quid a couple nights a week; most wives round 'ere do. But not you. Oh no. Too damned lah-di-da, or so you think.'

Alice ached from head to foot, felt tired out, beaten, but she made one more attempt to get her husband to see reason. 'Mick, that's not true. There's not a woman in this street that I know would do what you ask me to.'

Jane knew things were beginning to turn nasty again, and all she wanted to do was slip away from the room and out of the house. She'd almost made it to the door when her father took two strides and grabbed hold of her.

'You mind what you're saying, young lady. What goes on in this 'ouse is between yer mum and me. It ain't got nothing t' do with you. And certainly not the damn neighbours.

You got that?' He was still raging mad and gave her a hefty slap around her head as he let her go.

Alice was crouched up against the fireplace, the tears trickling slowly down her poor bruised face. What Mick did to her was bad enough, but what he did to young Janey went beyond cruelty. It was evil. How could she stop him? If she interfered, especially today, she'd more than likely make matters even worse.

But she had to do something!

She had allowed this situation to go on for far too long, and at this rate it was never going to get any better. She didn't have any choice now. She had to act before Mickey did something terrible.

Something they would all live to regret.

Jane dragged her feet but kept walking. She wished she knew what she could do to make her father like her. Well, not so much like her as be a bit kinder to her. She felt the side of her face with trembling fingers; it was stinging, and her head really hurt. Sometimes she managed to duck when she saw a blow coming, but this morning her dad had really caught her a hefty blow. Her mum had to suffer terrible things and it wasn't fair, because she was kind and gentle really. Though there were times when she wished Mum would stand up for her a little bit more. She could see what was happening, but she never did anything to stop it. There was the time that Tommy had knocked their dad's tobacco tin off the side of his chair and it had burst open, spilling all the tobacco over the lino.

It was me, Jane was ranting to herself, that got down on my hands and knees and did my best to scrape the tobacco into a little pile. Me dad never said thanks. He kicked me halfway across the room and I had a pain in my side for ages after that.

There was the time when her teacher had asked why she was limping so badly. She had thought about telling her the truth: that her dad had kicked her shin and stamped hard on her foot. But she'd tried that with Nancy and it hadn't got her anywhere. If Nancy couldn't help her, then no one could. So in the end she'd just said that she had fallen over.

She gave a sad little sigh. She couldn't walk any further, her head hurt so and her mouth was bone dry. She wished she'd had a drink of tea before she left the house. Turning off the main road, she stumbled on to Garrett Green, making her way to the bench that was set beneath a huge tree. Thankfully she sat down, lifting her legs up to stretch them out in front of her. Leaning back, she clutched her arms around her chest, wondering what she had done this morning to set her father off. She tried so hard, she really did. But there was no pleasing him, no way that she could think of to stop him clouting her. She had known all her life that he didn't love her. More than that, he didn't even like her. But why was he always so angry with her?

She knew her mum had seen her dad shake the life out of her this morning and then bash her round the head, but as ever she'd not tried to stop him. Though perhaps today Jane ought not to feel that way, because Mum looked so ill. Last night had been terrible, with Mum lying on the ground in the front garden, and Dad kicking her ever so hard.

It wasn't fair. Why couldn't he pick on someone of his own size?

Then she remembered. Mr Simmonds had whacked her dad in the face. Good job too. Perhaps that was why he was still in a bad temper today. But what did I do? Jane asked herself. Nothing, except try to keep Tommy warm. Her dad loved Tommy. She was glad about that, he was such a lovely little boy. Still, it didn't seem fair. Not all the time. She wondered what the difference was: why he was always so angry with her and never with Tommy.

She began to cry. Her leg hurt where she'd knocked it against the table, the side of her face was stinging and her head really hurt. She tried to think of nice things, like going to school; she liked her teacher a lot. Eating bread pudding that Nancy had brought out of the oven steaming hot and sprinkled with lovely brown sugar. She wished she could live with Nancy.

Her head drooped down on to her chest. She'd have to stay where she was for a while; she couldn't walk any further.

It wasn't long before this lonely little girl thankfully drifted off into a state of unconsciousness.

It was three o'clock in the afternoon and Alice was getting worried. Where the hell had her daughter got to? Mickey had just come back from the pub and the first thing she'd asked him was if he'd seen Janey.

'No I ain't, but I suppose it would be too much t' 'ope for that she's disappeared for good.'

'Mick, sit down. It's about time that we 'ad a talk. I know you did me a favour by marrying me when I was pregnant, but by God you've made me pay for it over the years. You use me as a punching bag whenever the mood takes you, and maybe I've only got myself to blame for that, but I think it's about time you laid off Janey.'

He'd had more than a few pints of beer and he stood there gently reeling, his face showing nothing but amusement.

'Aren't you afraid you'll hurt her real badly one of these days?' Alice's voice held a plea.

'Maybe she won't end up in the pudding club like you did if I knock a little sense into 'er now. Told me you were doing a neighbour a favour, minding 'er kids, when their father came 'ome an' raped yer. Nobody was daft enough to believe yer. Except me! Yer don't want yer daughter taken in like that, do yer? So it stands t' reason someone should knock a bit of sense into her. She might even thank me for it later on.'

Alice sighed heavily. 'The worst of it all is, Mick, I think you actually believe that. You've lied to yourself for so long.'

'Oh, so now you're telling me I'm too hard on you an' the kid?' Mickey said, visibly angry at being told a home truth.

'Too hard? *Too hard?* Do you ever bother t' look at her bruises, not t' mention how you leave me looking.'

'Don't be ridiculous. You ask for everything you get, and as for the kid, you should be grateful that I put a roof over 'er 'ead and food in 'er belly. She's a cheeky bitch, gets away with murder just because she looks like butter wouldn't melt in 'er mouth. You make 'er worse, all the time yer spend on those bloody curls an' telling 'er what beautiful big blue eyes she's got.'

'You're drunk, Mick. But not too far gone t' know that what I'm saying is the truth. I'm just really sorry that I held on to her. I was only just fifteen when I was raped, and not even sixteen when Jane was born.' Alice paused and stared at the state her husband was in. 'I should have gone into a home for unmarried mothers and let the baby be put up for adoption. Even leaving her on the steps of a church would have given her a better chance than she's had here. She doesn't deserve the life she has to lead, with you on at her all the time.'

Mickey wiped a hand across his face as if trying to pull himself together. 'If you're doing yer best t' make me feel guilty about her, don't bother. I've been pretty good t' that kid.'

'Really? You believe that?' Alice asked sarcastically. 'You give her a clump practically every day, but mostly you're dead clever. The worst you do to her can never be seen.'

'Don't know what yer talking about.'

'Oh, you know right enough! Like a few weeks ago when the poor kid couldn't sit down properly because you'd pinched her backside so badly. She didn't let on for days, and when I did find out she'd got a festering sore. Your fingernails had drawn blood and the dye from her navy-blue kickers had got into it. You're damned lucky she didn't tell her teacher about you.'

'Yer want t' mind what you're saying or I might just give you a taste of me belt, because I'm warning you, Alice, I'm master in me own 'ouse, always will be or I'll know the reason why. Jane knows she's a little bitch at times, an' she never answers back when I chastise 'er 'cos she knows she deserves it.'

'She's too afraid of you to argue with you, and you know it.'

Alice watched in wonder as Mickey took a quart bottle of brown ale from the dresser and poured himself a glassful. Talking to him was like pouring water over a duck's back. Seeing what he was doing to her daughter, day in day out, had made her begin to really hate him.

But not enough to stand up to him. She had done in the beginning and ended up black and blue herself. Now she cringed whenever he raised his hand to Janey and winced as she watched the blows rain. Yet she could never summon up enough courage to try and stop him. She hadn't the guts to do that.

In her own way she was as frightened of Mickey as Jane was, so she stood by and let it happen.

And for that she hated herself.

Chapter Three

LES BANISTER, THE local policeman, looked at his watch. It was seven thirty on this cold November night. Another hour and a half before he could report back to the warmth of the station. I deserve a fag, he said to himself. Drawing his tobacco tin from his overcoat pocket, he walked across the grass of Garrett Green, making for the wooden bench, all the while telling himself that he might just as well take the weight off his feet for a few minutes.

There was no one about to hear his gasp of horror when he realized that the heap of clothing that lay on the end of the bench was actually a small child. He shone his torch and cautiously moved the arm that was covering her face. Her long blonde curls were stained red and matted to her head. As far as he could tell, the bleeding had been coming from around her ear.

He talked to her, saying anything that came into his head, but got no response. For one terrifying moment he thought she must be dead. 'I have to get an ambulance,' he said aloud, and heaved a sigh of relief that not far away, on the main road, a green light shone over the doorway of a doctor's surgery.

He blew three long blasts on his whistle to summon assistance. With fumbling fingers he undid the buttons of his coat and swiftly but gently wrapped it around the small body, then stared down at her for a moment. How on earth did such a small child happen to be out on her own at this time on a winter's night? And more to the point, how come she was injured, because there was no mistaking that she was.

And badly so.

He heard footsteps approaching, turned and ran to meet his colleague. Shouting loudly, he gave his orders. 'Get to that doctor's surgery and tell them we've a badly hurt child here on a park bench and we need an ambulance.'

'Right,' the constable called back, sizing up the situation right away

'Thanks, mate. I'll stay here with the child.' As he retraced his footsteps he thanked God that professional people had telephones now.

The time that he sat holding the cold little hand and saying over and over again, 'You'll be all right, pet, you will, I promise,' were the longest minutes he had ever had to live through. He was allowed to ride in the ambulance with her. The ambulanceman had put an oxygen mask on her small white face and smothered her in blankets, but even he hadn't been sure at first that she was still breathing. On arrival at hospital she was placed on a trolley and rushed away, surrounded by nurses.

He felt dazed and bewildered as he made his way back to the station, where his sergeant was waiting to take his report. 'No name, no identification whatsoever?' the portly, red-faced officer asked in disbelief.

'No, Sarge. I felt sure someone would have reported the child missing by the time I got back here.'

'No such luck, son. Still, you sign off, get yerself a cup of tea in the canteen and I'll ring the hospital, ask them to let us know when the child is able to talk.'

'*If* she's able,' Les Banister said softly to himself. He was relieved to think that he had found her, but had he been in time? What if she had lain there all night? And the state she was in! God, he'd like to get his hands on whoever had treated a small child so cruelly. She could so easily have died.

When Jane woke up in the early hours of the morning, she began to cry. She didn't know where she was or how she was going to get home. If she was ever so late her dad would surely have a real go at her.

The nurse who had been sitting beside the bed got to her feet and, bending over the tiny figure, spoke softly. 'There, there, pet, no need for tears. You're safe and warm now. I'll just let Sister know you're awake and I'm sure she'll give you something nice to drink.'

'Please don't go, I don't know where I am.' Jane's fingers fluttered and the nurse took hold of her hand.

'You're in hospital and everyone is going to take such good care of you, you'll see.'

Jane managed to get the young nurse's smiling face into focus. She wanted to ask if her mum and dad knew where she was, but she was afraid. She tried to sit up but fell back; she was giddy, her head hurt so and the side of her face stung and felt funny.

'Try and lie still.' The nurse had seen her wince. Poor child, she had a concussion, and had suffered a terrific blow to her ear. The damage had not yet been assessed because there was still blood being drained from it. Also, the doctor had said he was appalled at the amount of bruises they had found on her body.

The sister came, raised her gently and held a feeding cup to her lips. Jane drank, then gratefully felt herself being lowered down against soft white pillows, and soon she closed her eyes and slept. The nurse went off duty and a young doctor came to watch over her. It worried him that she cried in her sleep, and as he stared at this young child's face he knew that she had been treated badly over a long period of time. There were questions that would have to be asked. But would they get any answers? Any true answers, that was. He had seen injuries like this before and very rarely were they the result of an accident. Something would have to be done to protect this child from further harm. But what?

It would be a wise man that could answer that question.

That same night, Wally Simmonds met up with Alice Jeffrey.

Having checked on all the neighbours, and Nancy in particular, and found no trace of Jane, Alice, now half out of her mind with worry, had been wandering the streets.

'Wally, you haven't come across Janey, 'ave you?'

'No, luv, I 'aven't, but surely she's not out on a cold night like this. An' look at you, you look 'alf frozen t' death, come on t' the coffee stall and I'll get you a hot drink.'

'Thanks, Wally, but I can't. I 'ave t' keep looking for 'er. I think she's probably afraid to come home.'

'You are going to 'ave that drink and I'll take no argument,' he said, taking hold of her arm very firmly. 'While you're drinking it you can fill me in on what has happened and we'll take it from there.'

'Sometimes I think Mickey has hated Jane from the day she was born,' Alice told him sadly, 'and yet she's so wonderful, a terrific kid, always trying to please everyone. So pretty, that's been more than half the trouble; she's been the little girl everyone fell in love with. Except Mick. I know he resents her and I do believe he's actually begun to hate her.' Then it all became too much for her and she started to cry.

Wally was very moved by her tears but he could do nothing except stand and stare at her. He had always had great admiration for the way this woman coped. He knew full well her life had never been a bed of roses, but he hadn't until very recently had any idea that Mickey might be ill-treating the little lass.

Holding out a steaming mug of cocoa, he insisted that she wrap her hands around the mug and sip it slowly. 'How long has she been missing?' he asked, his eyes blazing when he heard the truth as to why Janey had gone off.

'Since this morning, about half past ten or maybe eleven o'clock. It's not fair, Mickey is so jealous, it's mad really, she's only a little girl, and yet . . . all our troubles, no matter what, he lays the blame on her, says she's responsible.'

'We'll find her,' Wally said firmly. 'But first I think I'd better see you home, it's too cold for you to be out. Then I think I'll call in at the police station just in case she has been in an accident.'

'Oh my God! Let me come with you,' Alice implored him.

'No,' he said, even more firmly. 'You go home, wait indoors in the warm and I'll come and tell you the minute I find out anything.'

Sergeant Bolton was very relieved when Wally Simmonds put in an appearance and was able to tell them that he was a hundred per cent sure that the little girl the constable had found injured on Garrett Green was Jane Jeffrey from Selkirk Road.

'Can you tell me how badly she was hurt?' Wally asked, showing great concern.

'Not exactly, we haven't had a full report yet. The doctor did tell our constable that the child had concussion, two broken ribs and quite a bit of damage to her ear. However, I'm sure she's in good hands now and the hospital staff will take care of her.'

This statement didn't do much to reassure Wally. It had finally become crystal clear to him that Mickey Jeffrey not only knocked his wife about but his young daughter as well. He felt such revulsion that he had to clench his fists and make sure that he kept them to his sides. But with knowledge came the resolve to put a stop to it, in as much as he was able. No child should have to suffer at the hands of a no-good waster like Mickey.

Speaking quietly and choosing his words carefully, Wally made his suspicions known to Sergeant Bolton.

'My God!' the sergeant exploded. 'Has there been no one to protect her?'

'I think the mother lives in fear of her husband and feels if she intervenes it will only make matters worse. She did admit to me some time ago that her husband is not Jane's real father and that most of the time he not only resents her but hates her.'

'So he thinks that gives him the right to use his fists on the child? Come to that, how can a grown man hate a little child?'

'Who knows what goes on in the mind of men like Jeffrey?' Wally answered sorrowfully.

'Well I'll tell yer this, after this night and the facts that have been brought to our attention, he'll find things will be a damn sight hotter for him. Oh yes.' The sergeant paused, held out his hand to Wally and thanked him profusely for having come into the station. 'You leave this to me. You can rest assured he won't abuse that child ever again, I'll make it my business to see t' that. He'll be sorry for it, you mark my words. Whatever excuses that man comes up with for hitting her won't wash with me. He'll find this time it was once too often.'

Alice wasn't totally surprised when she answered the door to find a uniformed constable standing on her doorstep. As she listened to the policeman telling her they had found Jane and that she had been taken to St James' hospital, she felt emotionally and physically drained. She had reached the end of her tether.

'It's only me, Alice.'

Mavis Owen's voice was loud as she walked in through the back door. She stepped into the kitchen and was in time to see Alice doing her best to wipe away her tears.

'I saw the copper leaving. 'Ave they found Janey?'

Alice nodded her head. 'Yeah, it was a policeman on his beat what found her. She was lying on a bench on Garrett Green.'

''Ad she bin 'urt, d'you know?'

'According to the copper she was 'alf dead, would 'ave bin by morning if he hadn't come across her.'

'She 'adn't been in an accident, 'ad she?'

'No, I told you earlier when I went out to look for her, she was afraid t' come 'ome. As she tried to pass Mick this morning he gave her a right bash round the 'ead.'

'Good God, does he never let up? I think it a bloody disgrace the way he picks on Janey, and what about you? You don't look the picture of 'ealth. Look at the state of yer face. I wouldn't let my ole man treat me the way Mickey does you.'

Alice went to shake her head but winced as it started to throb again.

'Sit down before you fall down, gal, I'll put the kettle on. Any idea what set him off again this morning?'

'Well, a night in the cells didn't do that much for him, and I don't suppose they treated him too kindly. After all, he did kick one of the coppers on the shin . . .' Alice paused and did her best to pull her swollen lips into a smile.

'What's tickled you all of a sudden?' Mavis asked as she struck a match to light the gas under the kettle.

'I shouldn't be laughing, I know, but Mickey got more than he asked for in more ways than one last night.'

'Well go on, 'urry up, tell me about it,' Mavis chipped in.

'You know Wally Simmonds came along when Mick was bashing the life out of me. Well, I don't think he would 'ave interfered but for the fact that he saw Tommy and Janey shivering an' huddled up in the corner of the front garden, an' like any decent man would, he went to get to get t' them.'

'And?' Mavis said hastily.

'Wally punched him straight in the face. I didn't dare t' look too close this morning, but I'd lay money his nose is broken.'

Mavis crossed the room and gently put her arms around her friend. 'Damn good job too! Pity you ain't 'ad someone t' take your part long before this.'

'Oh, I don't think he was taking *my* part exactly; he was thinking of the kids more like.'

'If you say so,' Mavis grinned, 'but I'd never be surprised to 'ear that Wally 'as a soft spot for you.'

'Oh Mavis, don't say that! Ain't I got enough complications in my life as it is?'

Mavis laughed out loud at that, saying, 'We'll see.'

Five minutes later she brought two steaming cups of tea to the table and the two friends sat opposite each other, deep in their own thoughts. While Mavis sipped her tea and thanked God that her Joe had a regular job and that he wasn't a bad father to their three children, Alice was trying to reason with herself as to how she could carry on living with Mickey. What she had allowed to happen to Jane was nothing short of sheer wickedness on her own part. As to Mick: well, the police were involved now, so she probably wouldn't have any say in the matter.

She chided herself again: you should have acted before.

She sighed heavily. It was too late to turn the clock back now.

For most of the next few days, Jane slept fitfully. Her mother came to see her every day and tried to explain to the doctors that Jane's injuries had been caused by her continually falling over. They knew she was lying, but they sympathized with her and told her over and over what a sweet little girl her daughter was. The nurses would have done anything for Jane. She was so good. She cried, often, but only quietly, always sobbing beneath the bedclothes. She seemed so grateful for everything they did and sighed with pleasure when they gently gave her a bedbath and finished off by covering her with sweet-smelling talcum powder. She never had much to say, even when her mum was there. She just lay still, watching, sometimes sighing, but when she did smile it lit up her pretty face and tore at the hearts of those who attended her, making them ask, 'How on earth could anyone bring themselves to hurt such a dear little defence-less child?'

One afternoon her mother was very talkative. She told Jane that she must be brave, that where she was going would be a very nice place, so much better for her than coming back home.

'What do you mean, Mum? Aren't I coming home when the doctors say I'm better?'

'Well . . . not for the time being.' Alice was whispering. 'I have t' tell you that I won't be able t' see you for a while.' She got up from her chair and sat down gently on the side of the bed. With trembling fingers she smoothed the soft hair from her young daughter's forehead.

'You'll be with other children, it won't be so bad, I promise you it won't.'

'Why can't I come home? Where are you going, Mum?'

'Oh pet, I'm not going anywhere. I came today to say goodbye. It really is for the best that you don't come home.'

Jane struggled to sit up, her face showing the terror that was running through her mind. 'Where will I live, when will I see you, and what about Tommy?' With wisdom beyond her years, she knew that whatever happened to her from now on, the arrangements would not include her father.

'Please, darling, you're not to get upset.'

A nurse who was hovering near by felt she wanted to scream out: 'She's not to get upset! What do you expect her to do?' The child's headache seemed to be a lot better but her poor little ribs were still strapped up with tape and still no one knew for sure how much damage had been done to her ear. Now here was her mother quietly telling her they weren't going to have her home ever again. All the staff knew that the relieving officer had been in touch with the lady almoner of the hospital and that the police had been involved. The outcome of it all was that the father was to be charged, if and when they found him; for the moment he had thought it best to disappear. And the little girl was being taken into a council home.

'Do you mean it, Mum, I'm not coming home, not ever?'

Alice didn't answer. She hung her head, fighting her own tears.

Jane needed no telling that her father didn't want her. Did her mother not want her either? Suddenly she felt very frightened. Was this all happening just because her father didn't like her? Perhaps now her mum had had enough of her as well. Could that be right? After all, she'd heard Mum say to Nancy that Janey was the cause of all the trouble.

And when she thought about it, her mum had never stopped her dad from hitting her. She'd never helped her, and now she was telling her she couldn't come back to live at home and that she wouldn't be seeing her for a while. So in other words, thought Janey, she really doesn't want me and is getting rid of me.

That was what all the talking was about. That was the reason her mum had come today. She had said she wasn't going anywhere, she was going to stay and look after Tommy, but she'd come to say goodbye to Jane. Jane was trying so hard not to cry, but she couldn't help herself. Was she being given away, and if so, who to? Who would want her? There had been a family in the next street to them that were put in the workhouse, and all the neighbours had cried and felt sorry for them because they'd heard the workhouse was such a terrible place. But they had all gone together. Would she be put in there all on her own?

Now she wasn't just frightened; she was terrified.

Alice bent down and gently kissed her on the cheek. 'I'm sorry . . . about your dad . . . and everything. Be a good girl an' always remember that I do love you.'

Jane wanted her mum to know that it wasn't her fault and that she loved her too, but she didn't know what to say. Alice straightened up and stood there looking at her for a few moments, then she pulled the bedclothes up round her, tucking the sheet beneath her chin, and turned and walked away, without saying another word.

Jane burrowed down in the bed, pulling the clothes over her head, and sobbed as if her heart was breaking.

Chapter Four

SISTER WALKER HELD out her hand to Mrs Elsie Rogers, a
child welfare worker from Sussex who had become involved
in this case. She was not only thoroughly pleased that it was
this woman who had come from the children's home to pick
up Jane Jeffrey, but intensely relieved. The poor child had
suffered enough. It had torn at her heartstrings and those
of her nurses as they'd listened to Jane's small, breathless
sobs become uncontrollable after she had watched her own
mother walk away from her. That drama had taken place
over two weeks ago. Jane had hardly spoken a word since.
Much as she would dearly love to keep the child here, where
she was safe, Sister Walker knew it was impossible. A hospital was not what Jane needed now.

But if anyone could console the child it would be Elsie
Rogers.

Widowed at an early age and having no children of her
own, Elsie had given her life over to caring for children who
were placed in the care of the authorities. She was a remarkable woman with a sweet smile and piercing blue eyes that

seemed to see everything that went on. She kept her finger on every situation and did her best for each and every child.

Elsie had visited the hospital twice in the last fortnight to discuss the arrangements that the court had ordered for Jane Jeffrey. But she hadn't expected the child to be so frail-looking, nor so upset.

'Has she been told that I'm coming for her today?' she queried.

'Yes,' Sister Walker answered softly, feeling that never before had she been invovled in such a sad case. 'She's all ready, waiting for you in my office . . .' She hesitated. 'You won't believe how sweet she looks; most of the staff clubbed together and bought her a coat. You could have shot peas through the one she was wearing when she came to us.'

They walked the corridor in silence, and when Sister opened the door to her office Elsie Rogers stepped in first. 'Hello, Jane,' she said solemnly. 'Remember I told you I was coming for you today? We're going to travel by train, and then when we get to the right station there will be a lovely surprise waiting for you.'

Jane made no reply; she merely looked at Sister Walker, her eyes pleading to stay here in the safety of the hospital where, for the first time in her young life, she had felt wanted and safe; even more than that, she'd felt everyone in the whole place had loved her.

Elsie was staring at the child, and what she saw tugged at her heartstrings. Janey did look so sweet, almost unreal, dressed in a blue coat that reached the top of her well-worn buttoned boots. Her little matching hat had an upturned brim that showed off the fair ringlets hanging down to her shoulders.

'My, my,' she exclaimed quietly. 'Haven't the nurses done you proud? You really do look a very pretty little young lady.'

Jane wasn't used to being spoken to so kindly, and the colour rose in her cheeks, which only served to made her look even more doll-like.

Sister Walker had great difficulty in swallowing the lump in her throat, which was threatening to choke her. 'Come along, pet, there's a lot of people who want to say goodbye and wish you well.'

Jane didn't speak but walked slowly out into the corridor, stopping within an arm's length of the nurses and doctors who were standing in a group.

Sister watched her hesitate, and when the first nurse put her arms around the child she saw her eyelids close and the tears trickle down from beneath them. 'Oh, don't, Janey, don't cry. For God's sake, don't cry, you'll set us all off,' she murmured.

When finally all the goodbyes had been said, the young doctor who had been in charge of her throughout her stay picked Jane up and wrapped his arms about her. His action was very gentle, and he held her as if she were fragile and could easily break. The kiss he placed on her cheek was tender, and there was a tremble to his lips as he said, 'Be happy, Jane, and if you ever need us, you come back here and find us.'

Elsie Rogers looked around. There was no suitcase, only a brown paper carrier bag that held a nightdress, washing things and two picture books, all of which had been provided by the staff. Outside the main entrance a taxi was waiting to take them the short distance to the railway station.

Jane stared out of the rear window until she could no longer see the mass of waving hands. She had no idea where she was going or what kind of reception awaited her. Just one thing she was sure of. She had never before been treated with such love and kindness as she had received whilst in

St James' hospital. She looked into Mrs Rogers' eyes; they looked kind, but that didn't tell her much, so she looked down at her feet so that the lady wouldn't see just how frightened she really was.

After the quietness of the hospital, the railway station was alarming. A porter opened a carriage door for them, and having assisted Mrs Rogers up the high step, he lifted Jane and set her down safely within the carriage, saying, 'It isn't every day I get to see such a pretty little girl.'

That was twice already that someone had told her she was looking pretty. For an instant Jane smiled the smallest smile. Elsie Rogers was pleased; the smile had made such a difference to that pinched little face. She wanted to do her best to keep this child from further hurt, and everything she wished for Janey showed in the way she took her in her arms and held her. Jane looked up at her, half afraid that she had imagined something, and yet she didn't know exactly what. Suddenly she realized with amazement that this lady actually cared what happened to her!

And from that moment a bond was established.

Settled in a corner seat, Elsie undid the ribbons of Jane's bonnet, held out her arm and nestled the child in close to her side.

With a great swoosh, several jerks, and a lot of steam, the train pulled out from the station. Where were they going? Who exactly was Jane going to live with? Would she ever see her mum again? And how about little Tommy? It was she that mostly looked after him. Was he wondering where she was? Would he miss her? So many questions and no answers. And when Jane heaved a little sigh, Elsie hugged the child tighter and kissed the top of her head.

Safe for the moment in these kind and caring arms, all the fighting and arguing, the slaps and the punches and the disappointment that had lately been inflicted on her didn't seem quite so bad. And whatever happened when they got where they were going, she knew with wisdom beyond her eight years that she had found a true friend in this lady who was sitting beside her, holding her gently but safely.

Jane missed the spectacle of the changing scenery, because hardly had they left the soot-riddled buildings of London behind than she had fallen fast asleep.

No matter, Elsie mused to herself as the train rattled on into Sussex. The trees outside the window were a mass of bare branches, but the fields were fairly green, and there were plenty of beautiful black-and-white cows and shaggy sheep to be seen. Had not Jane fallen asleep she would have been utterly enthralled by the countryside. There was no doubt in Elsie's mind that the child had never been far from the city of London, and she had made it her business to know that she had never experienced the joys of a family holiday.

When the notes on this case had first been handed to her, she had felt utterly helpless. Sorry for the mother, married at sixteen and already breast-feeding a baby of only a few weeks old. The poor lass had grabbed at straws. Turned from her own home because of the disgrace she had brought on her hard-working but God-fearing father, she'd had no choice but to accept the offer of marriage to a man ten years older than herself.

Reading between the lines of the report, written by the relieving officer who had been appointed to supervise this case, Elsie had uttered to herself, 'By God, the lass didn't know what she was letting herself in for!'

But the real victim in this nasty affair had been the child herself. Although the woman had gone on to give her husband a son, whom he apparently adored, he had never let her forget that she had come to him with another man's child. Never once, it would appear, did he take into consideration that the mother had been little more than a child herself, raped by a brute of a man that the courts had sent to prison for two years' hard labour.

Still, Elsie sighed softly, God works in a mysterious way his wonders to perform.

Having been asked for help because of the difficulty her colleagues were experiencing in placing the small girl, she had agreed to read the case history. No stone had been left unturned, but the fact was that every charity-owned children's home within the London boundary had been full to capacity.

It was then that Elsie had called upon two dear friends who had been a tower of strength when she herself had needed comfort.

Dorothy and Richard Stuart were an elderly couple, quite comfortably off, who since retiring had devoted most of their spare time to good causes. It was through them that she had come to know of the charity that went under the name of the Guardians of the Poor, and of the children's home set in Sussex of which the Stuarts were directors.

She firmly believed that if it were necessary for a child to be taken from its parents, for whatever reason, or if a child were to be orphaned with no relatives to be held responsible for its upbringing, there was no better place for that child to be sent than Winchelsea Lodge.

She had come to understand that, with only a few exceptions, the staff at the home did not regard their work as a mere job but as a vocation. When Elsie herself had been widowed after only eighteen months of what had been a truly happy marriage, she had gone to pieces, ranting as to why she was not only widowed but childless.

When Richard Stuart had suggested that she take a post as house mother at Winchelsea Lodge, it had taken her some time to enjoy the job, because it often involved her in court cases, some of which made her feel so helpless. And even more time to realize that she had been called by God to be of service in special work and in special conditions all to do with underprivileged children.

It had been her salvation.

It had also been a great relief when Richard and Dorothy Stuart, having listened to her account of the ill treatment of Jane Jeffrey, had agreed to put it to the board that the child be given a place at Winchelsea Lodge.

Making soothing noises, Elsie now gently shook Jane until she was wide awake. 'Only a few more minutes and the train will be pulling into our station. Sit up so that I can put your bonnet on.' Jane yawned and gave a gasp of utter surprise as she looked out of the window to see nothing but fields, with not a building in sight.

The train slowed its speed down to a crawl and slid along the platform. A large sign in the centre of the platform proclaimed that they had arrived at Rye. The day was very cold, but a weak sun was shining and it did a lot to lift Jane's spirits as she held Mrs Rogers' hand and walked along the short platform towards a funny-looking man who was dressed differently to anyone she had ever seen. He was wearing a corduroy jacket, a bright waistcoat and a highly coloured neckerchief, and grinned down at her as he held open a rickety wooden gate. Ted Grimshaw was a big, bluff man, his face puffed and red from drinking too much cider. He'd lived in the village of Winchelsea all his life, and although he had several irons in the fire when it came to making a few bob, he was never too busy whenever the staff at the children's home asked him to help out.

Jane was struck dumb with astonishment when the jolly man indicated that she was to put her foot on to a step, take hold of a hand rail and heave herself up into an open carriage that had a huge horse standing between its shafts. She was thrilled at the prospect of riding in this horse-drawn vehicle, but looked shyly up at Mrs Rogers to gain her permission before she put her foot on the high step.

Elsie Rogers couldn't help herself: she threw back her head and roared with laughter. 'Oh Ted,' she said, clutching at his arm, 'isn't the look on Jane's face a picture to behold?'

Ted agreed that it was, his gaze observing every detail of this frail-looking little girl. 'Let's be 'aving yer, missus,' he said as he caught hold of Elsie's arm and helped her into the carriage.

Once settled in the front seat, Ted flicked the reins and the horse moved forward. As they went down the narrow cobbled high street, Jane looked at the houses and shops in utter perplexity. They were nothing like the buildings where she came from. Some of them were so crooked they looked as if they were falling over. Many didn't even have proper roofs; they were thatched, but Jane didn't know that. She was still staring wide-eyed at the small, funny-shaped windows, most of which had red and green banners stretched above their doorways wishing their customers A HAPPY CHRISTMAS.

A postman on a bicycle went whizzing by, shouting, 'Morning, Ted, see yer t'night.' Two kindly-looking elderly women, each carrying a wicker basket, stood on the narrow pavement, and as the carriage drew near they each raised a hand in salute and called out a greeting to Ted and Mrs Rogers.

'See you both soon,' Elsie Rogers called back over her shoulder as they passed by.

How come everyone seemed to know each other and was so friendly? Jane was asking herself.

At the bottom of the main road, Ted steered the horse to the left. They were now passing alongside what looked like a river, with many different kinds of boats moored along the bank. Mrs Rogers bent her head and whispered, 'We are only two miles from the sea; what you are looking at is Rye Harbour.'

When Jane made no reply, she added, 'Where you are going to live is a place called Winchelsea, and it even has its own beach. Come the summer, you and all the other girls will spend many a happy hour down by the sea.'

Jane had no idea as to how she was supposed to react. She had never seen the sea. At school they had read about it, and there were some pictures of seaside places pinned up on the wall in the main hall, but to be told that not only would she be able to see it soon, but would spend days on a beach . . . It couldn't be true. Not really.

Soon it became a bumpy ride. Jane didn't know where to look next, there was so much to see. Holding tightly to the hand rail, she twisted from side to side as the horse clip-clopped through the country lanes.

Then, out of the blue, they were approaching a huge crowd of people, and the sight and sounds had Jane reaching for Elsie Rogers' hand.

'It's all right, pet, what we're looking at is the pre-Christmas horse fair,' Elsie laughed.

Horse boxes were lined up at one end of the field. There were a few horses on show and several lovely little ponies. Farmers, trainers, breeders and owners milled around. At the other end there was a fair. Jane knew all about that, because on bank holidays her mum had often taken her and Tommy to the fair on Clapham Common. Here, there were gaily painted gypsy caravans and lots of stalls.

'Buy a sprig of lucky heather for the young lady, missus?'
A dark-skinned young woman with hair the colour of a raven
and a beautiful curly-haired baby in her arms ran beside
their horse and cart.

'Course I will.' Elsie Rogers grinned as she fished in her
handbag to find a couple of pennies.

Smiling broadly, showing a gold tooth, the young gypsy
reached up for the coins and handed over the lucky sprig,
saying, 'Thanks, missus. Gawd bless yer, an' you too,
missy.'

Elsie gave the purple heather to Jane and, watching the
delight on the child's face, felt it had to be a good omen.

They left the noisy scene behind and Jane remained quiet,
deep in thought, until Ted turned the horse into the yard
that led up to Winchelsea Lodge.

As if it knew they were almost home, the horse neighed,
scattering a flock of chickens and hens and making two dogs
bark.

Ted turned his head, and there was a triumphant gleam
in his eye as he said, 'I live over there, missy.' He pointed
to a cottage some way away. 'Matron up at the lodge gives
out the jobs, but maybe you'll get t' come down 'ere an'
gather up the hens' eggs from time t' time.'

Elsie laughed. 'Give her time to settle in before you have
her working, Ted.'

Jane was having mixed feelings. She had seen live chickens before, because one of their neighbours had kept a
couple in his back yard. But there were an awful lot of them
here, and she didn't know about going amongst them to get
at their eggs. Besides, there were those two dogs. Ever so
pretty they were, their silky coats all black and white, and
from where she was sitting, high up in the cart, they were

all right. But to go near a dog! Oh no, she couldn't do that. Dogs frightened her.

When Ted Grimshaw finally lifted Jane down, she couldn't have described how she felt, not even to herself. Everything that had happened today was becoming too much for her to take in, and at that moment she would have given anything for her mum to appear, put her arms around her and say, 'Come on, Janey, I'm going to take you home.' If that were to happen, at least she would get to see Tommy. He had to be wondering where she was after all the time she'd been away.

A sob rose in her throat and she shuddered as she tried hard not to cry.

Rye railway station she had thought looked like a castle. A huge great red building with ever so many windows and such a lot of nice grounds around it. Now, as she stared up at Winchelsea Lodge, she knew she had never before gazed on such a lovely house, but the whole of the outside looked so big and so different. It wasn't made of bricks; it had been built with what to Jane looked like huge stones.

Elsie Rogers sensed the child's confusion and gave her a moment to get her bearings. Then, taking the small hand within her own, and without saying a word, she drew her forward and felt Jane's grip tighten as they walked side by side up the wide stone steps. At the top she had to let go of Jane's hand because it took all of her strength to push open the heavy oak front door.

Janey couldn't believe the length of the entrance hall, nor the roaring fire that was burning in the wide fireplace. 'Cor, look at that,' she exclaimed out loud, pointing at the high window set in the far wall. The wintry sun was shining through it, causing its gentle blues and reds to fill the hall with colour.

'That's really lovely, all those colours,' she murmured.

'It is beautiful, isn't it?' A soft voice had come from behind her, and Jane turned quickly. What she saw was a kind of nurse, but not quite like the nurses who had looked after her in the hospital. Dressed in a navy-blue dress with long sleeves and a white collar and cuffs, Lillian Cooper wore sensible low-heeled lace-up shoes and dark stockings. Above average height, she had short shiny dark hair and deep brown eyes, and looked just what she was: capable and efficient. If asked, the powers-that-be would all agree that she managed Winchelsea Lodge and its occupants just fine.

'It is known as a stained-glass window,' she told Jane, then paused. When no reply came, she said, 'You must be Jane; we are very pleased to have you staying with us. I am what is known around here as Matron.' Lillian's voice was full of fun as she bent her knees and looked into Jane's pale face, adding, 'I shall see you later, and we will all do our best to see that you are happy here.'

Still Jane hadn't uttered a word.

Elsie Rogers nodded to this confident, kind woman as she straightened up, and holding out her hand she said, 'Come along, Jane, we have to go up this big staircase to get to where you'll be sleeping.'

Jane took the outstretched hand and Elsie gave the small fingers a squeeze of reassurance.

The first-floor landing was broad and long. There were three bedrooms, the doors to which were propped open, showing that each held six single beds, three on either side of the room. Elsie passed the first two, but at the entrance to the third she stopped and ushered Jane inside. 'The middle bed on the right will be yours for now,' she smiled. Beside each bed stood a tall locker, and she was about to tell Jane that she could put her things away in what was to be hers when she remembered that there was no case to unpack.

'Take your coat and hat off, Jane,' she said softly, doing her best to conceal her embarrassment. Removing a padded coat hanger from the narrow cupboard, she took the coat from Jane and hung it up for her. 'I'll show you where the bathroom is. You can wash your hands and then we'll go back downstairs.' Glancing at her watch, she added, 'We shall just be in time for tea.'

So many wonders! A great big white bath set on iron claw feet had pride of place in the centre of the room, and a toilet with a polished wooden seat was set in the corner. What was more, there were two taps fixed to the end of the bath. Surely you didn't just turn them on and water came out into the bath?

'There is also a toilet next door if the bathroom is occupied, and another downstairs near to the eating quarters,' Mrs Rogers quietly told her.

Three toilets. All inside the house! This place must belong to someone very, very rich!

Back downstairs, through a huge kitchen, and there was the eating quarters. Three long tables and about thirty girls, mostly older than herself, all smiling a welcome at her. At a nod from Matron, a girl seated about halfway down the first table rose and came bustling to where Jane was standing. Tall, fat, with fair hair tied back into two short plaits, Connie Brown was all smiles.

'Jane, this is Connie. She will be around at all times to look after you and show you the ropes,' Matron smiled.

Although neither girl made a move to put out a hand or take a step towards the other, their eyes met and held. 'We'll be friends, you'll see,' Connie whispered as they walked side by side to sit at the table.

Jane lowered her eyes and bit her lip, wondering if this Connie really meant what she said. Not many people had ever wanted to be her friend. At least not for long. Once they discovered the terrible names her dad called her, or heard him hollering and swearing, they never spoke to her much. Not even at school.

Still, her dad wasn't here, was he?

Connie, being fourteen years old, felt Jane's doubts, and once they were seated side by side at the table she said again, 'I'll be your friend, you'll see.'

'I . . .' Jane's voice was barely more than a whisper, 'I hope so.'

Having eaten a slice of bread and jam and a rock cake, and drunk a mug of milky tea, they were all ordered to stand before filing out and returning to their allocated jobs.

'I've already been told that you are to be with me, at least for the next few days,' Connie told Jane as she half pushed her through another door. 'Normally I work outdoors – well, most of the year I do – but as it's getting near Christmas there's not a lot that can be done. Ground is too hard. Still, makes a change.'

Jane counted. There were six other girls in this sitting room besides herself and Connie.

'We've all got some needlework to finish,' said a fresh-faced young lady with creamy fair skin, red hair and huge green eyes that looked as if they were laughing. 'But you will be excused, Jane. There are plenty of books on the shelves over there; find one you like and go sit by the fire.'

Jane squirmed. She didn't know what to say. Sensing this, the redhead said, 'I'm Fran, short for Frances, and I'm captain of this team. There are four in the house; you'll be told which one you'll be in when Matron decides to give you a badge.'

Jane couldn't take her eyes off this Fran, who was easily the prettiest girl she had ever seen.

Connie tugged at her arm. 'Come on, I'll see you settled with a book before I start on my work.' When the choice had been made and Connie was about to turn away, she hesitated, then, seeing Jane look so frail and vulnerable, bent over the arm of the chair in which the younger girl was sitting and spoke softly. 'There's no need to be so frightened, really there isn't. By an' large this is a great place to be sent to. Mind, not everyone is as nice as Fran, and when it comes t' some of the staff they're not all of the same kind nature as Matron. But you'll find out for yourself who you can trust, and like I said, I'll be around whenever you want me.'

Everything was beginning to overwhelm Janey. It was all too much. And Connie's kindness broke the dam. Pulling a handkerchief from up her sleeve, she nestled right into the corner of the winged armchair and held the cotton square tightly across her eyes while she quietly cried her heart out.

Later, with all her tears spent, she rubbed hard at her eyes and stared into the fire. Standing to the side of the hearth was a large tapestry, mounted on a polished wood screen. A colourful peacock was the centrepiece, surrounded by lovely flowers and greenery. It was so real-looking that Jane was tempted to lean forward to smell and even touch the small petals. Nancy did a lot of needlework and knitting, selling her finished articles on Tooting Market. Jane had often watched her sew, but her work wasn't anything like this. While she was fascinated by it, she was equally sure that this screen must have taken a very long time to make.

Frances O'Brien came to the side table to fetch a new reel of cotton. Seeing the look of intense awe on the face of this new little girl, she knelt down beside her chair.

'Every stitch is a work of art, isn't it?' She spoke softly.

Janey nodded her head.

'The sisters come here every Wednesday and they are responsible for work of that kind. You could join one of their classes if you think that's what you'd like to do.'

Jane raised her eyebrows. 'I couldn't do nothing like that!'

'How do you know if you've never tried?' Fran was laughing as she spoke. 'I've spent many a happy hour being taught how to patiently sew smaller tapestries than that one. You get to use fine silks and wools in every colour of the rainbow. Anyway, we'll see. If you don't like your book, have a little sleep. Connie will wake you up when it's time for supper.'

Jane's first hot meal at Winchelsea Lodge was an eye-opener. A hot meal for supper was not something she was used to. The shepherd's pie with rice pudding to follow absolutely filled her up. Connie told her it was the only time of the day when all the girls and staff sat down together, and that when everything was cleared away prayers would be said. Jane had been startled to see how many of them there were. Forty-two all told, Connie informed her.

At eight o'clock, along with nine other girls, the youngest in the home, Jane climbed the stairs, undressed and got into the strange single bed. She wanted her mum. She wanted her to cuddle her and to kiss her good night. Not that she ever did if her dad was at home at bedtime. She wanted to say good night to Tommy, to feel his chubby little arms round her neck. Oh, she wanted to be at home.

Suddenly five small voices were calling out, 'Good night, Jane. God bless you.'

In a tight voice she managed to answer, 'Good night,'

before she tucked her head down beneath the bedclothes. Then, in the darkness, the questions came flooding back. Why was she here? Why hadn't she been able to go home when she came out of the hospital? Why didn't her mum want her any more? Was she to stay in this home for ever and ever?

The day had taken its toll. She was too tired even to cry.

At last her eyelids began to droop and merciful sleep took over.

Chapter Five

THE VERY NEXT day Jane was initiated into the more normal routine that would be her life for the foreseeable future. She was also quick to learn that not everything in Winchelsea Lodge was going to be as nice as it had been during the first hours of her arrival.

Woken at seven o'clock, she washed and dressed in a room that was totally different to the main bathroom in which she had washed her hands yesterday. This room was sparse and cold. A line of metal basins stood in a long zinc-lined trough, with cold-water taps placed at three-foot inter-vals and slabs of hard yellow soap held in racks above.

Jane shivered, standing barefoot and wearing only a clean pair of navy-blue knickers which she'd found laid out with other items of clothing on the foot of her bed. She washed her face and neck, then dried herself using a harsh towel that had to be shared with the girl standing next to her. Watching the other girls, she saw that they were cleaning their teeth with a toothbrush which they dipped into a bowl containing a grey powder. When told to do the same by a girl standing opposite her, Jane found the taste absolutely horrible.

'You'll get used to it, and by the way we do get hot water on bath nights,' Connie whispered.

When Jane had brushed her teeth, the older girl helped her to put on a vest, then a fawn jumper and over that a thick brown pinafore dress. Black woolly stockings held up by a piece of white elastic, and a pair of black plimsolls completed her outfit.

'They haven't got any shoes small enough for you at the moment,' Connie informed her.

Breakfast, at a quarter to eight, consisted of thick oatmeal and a slice of fried bread.

From the top table Mrs Rogers watched Jane carefully as she ate her breakfast. She looked so small, the youngest in the home at the moment, and she was such a shy child. Or perhaps a better word would be withdrawn. In some respects she seemed very frail, yet in other ways there was a quiet strength about her, and a knowing that belied her age, and then there was the cautious way she had of approaching people. Connie Brown was a good choice for the task of taking Jane under her wing. She had been orphaned at the age of ten and had been at the home ever since. She was a friendly girl who chafed a bit at the restrictions of Winchelsea Lodge and dreamed of going out into the big wide world.

'Normally we'd be getting ready to go to school as soon as breakfast is over.' Connie grinned at Jane. 'But we've broken up for the Christmas holidays. It's not all good news though,' She added when she saw Jane smile. 'Some of us have to attend classes here. Only those in their last year, nearly sixteen, are excused; they have jobs to do.'

'So will I have to go to a classroom?'

'Yes, you will, but first I've been told to take you to Matron's office.'

They walked down the long entrance hall and stopped outside a door marked OFFICE, where Connie turned to leave, saying, 'I'll see you at lunchtime.'

Jane was wondering what was going to happen to her now as she stepped into Matron's office.

'Did you manage to get any sleep?' Lillian Cooper asked, smiling, doing her best to put Jane at her ease.

'A bit,' Jane answered quietly.

Why did the child look so frightened? There were a great number of questions Lillian would have liked to ask, but it was too soon for her to do such a thing. Instead she said, 'We are putting you in the blue team. Frances O'Brien is the captain, and you must have made a good impression on her yesterday, because she particularly asked to have you.'

Jane stood silent, her eyes downcast.

'I thought you'd be pleased. Didn't you like Frances?'

Jane looked confused. 'Yes, but . . . why have I got to be in a team? An' why must I go t' school?' The words finally came out in a rush.

'All children have to go to school. Don't you want to learn?'

'Yes, an' I like my own school an' my teacher.'

Lillian Cooper took a long, slow breath, wanting to choose her words with the utmost care and not upset Jane more than was necessary.

'You are going to stay here with us for a while, and of course it would be too far for you to travel every day to attend your old school.' She smiled warmly at Jane, 'We're very pleased to have you.'

'Oh,' was all Jane said.

Matron waited. She knew the hard part was yet to come.

Suddenly Jane blurted a question out bluntly: 'How long am I going to stay here?'

There was a pause while Matron again weighed her words carefully, never taking her eyes off Jane's sad face.

'Your mother isn't well. You know that, don't you?'

Jane nodded, then again blurted out, 'But she'd be all right if me dad didn't keep hitting her.' Realizing what she had said, she flushed a deep red and covered her mouth with her hand. Several moments passed before she added, 'I didn't mean t' say that.'

'Never mind, Jane. A doctor has seen your mother and he's going to be taking care of her from now on. But . . . your mum thinks you will be a good deal happier staying here with us. Besides, you'll have lots of other girls who will want to be friends with you.'

Jane took her time considering what Matron had told her. Then, drawing in a deep breath, she said, 'I'm never going home, am I?' Her big blue eyes looked straight into Lillian's.

The question was so direct that Lillian knew she could not lie to this frightened child. It took her a while to form an answer.

'I honestly don't know. I don't think your mum does either. Maybe you will when things get better at home.' It was as honest as she could make it without telling the girl that it was out of her mother's hands and that it was the authorities who would make the decisions as to what happened to her from now until she reached the age of sixteen.

In an effort to ease the child's pain she said quickly, 'Jane, you must never forget that your mother loves you. You know that she does, don't you?'

Jane nodded silently. Then, a second later, she said, 'I think she does . . . sort of . . . though she never . . .' Her eyes filled with tears as she remembered all the times her mum had watched her dad hit her. Later Mum would always say, 'I'll kiss it better,' but kissing hadn't made it better, had it? And Alice had come to the hospital to say goodbye. Why hadn't she said she was taking Jane home? She hadn't seen Mum since then. Was she ever going to see her again? Does she even know where I am? she wondered. It was hard to say whether she still loved her mum, but if not her, who else was there for her to love?

Finally she whispered, 'I love her too, and Tommy.'

Matron had read in the notes that Jane had a younger brother, but now was not the time to go into that. The child had more than enough complications to cope with as it was.

'Come along,' she urged, rising from her seat behind her desk. 'I'll take you along to the class you will be in for the next few weeks until we can sort out what standard you are up to and find a suitable school for you to attend.'

Matron held her hand as they walked, which was a great comfort to Jane, and she was very reluctant to let go as a classroom door was opened. There were ten girls in the class. Jane was startled as they all got to their feet, and even more mixed up when the teacher said, 'One by one, starting at the back row, introduce yourselves to our newcomer.'

Peggy . . . Lizzy . . . Hilda . . . Mary . . . Jean . . . Pauline . . . Maggie . . . Doreen . . . Ann . . . Kathleen.

Jane was by now thoroughly flustered. Was she supposed to remember all their names?

Matron said a few words to the teacher, then, having patted Jane on the head, she took her leave, saying, 'Miss Paterson will take care of you.'

Jane wasn't too sure about that!

Miss Paterson was a formidable sight. She was a big woman, with mousy-coloured hair cut short like a man's.

She wore a heavy tweed skirt topped by an equally heavy Fair Isle twin-set, the outfit finished off with grey lisle stockings and heavy brogue shoes

'So you are Jane Jeffrey,' Miss Paterson barked. 'How old are you?'

'Eight,' Jane mumbled.

'Speak up, girl. And I'd say you're almost nine, seeing as how your papers say you were born on January the first, 1912.'

Jane couldn't have said whether that fact was true or not. Birthdays had never been a source of celebration at home.

'Turn around.'

Jane did as she was told.

'Not too bad. Quite neat really,' Miss Paterson said kindly, in a much softer voice.

Jane was about to give a sigh of relief when the bark returned, making her jump.

'My goodness, this hair is really dreadful.' Miss Paterson lifted a few strands of Jane's long blonde hair and let it run through her fingers, grimacing as she did so.

Jane was aware that her hair was not looking its best. The nurses had washed it gently because of her bad ear, and the night before she left the hospital one of them had done it up in rags, just as her mother had loved doing, so that her ringlets had looked really pretty. But the journey had helped to tangle her curls, and though Connie had made an attempt at brushing them while they had been in the washroom this morning, time had been short and a monitor had told them to hurry up.

'No matter,' Miss Paterson stated. 'When class is finished for the day I personally will see to your hair.'

Jane saw the girl sitting nearest to her wince. She kept her eyes low as she made her way to the vacant desk that was allocated to her. She didn't like the sound of Miss Paterson saying that she would personally see to her hair.

Come to that, she didn't like Miss Paterson very much either.

The lesson went quite well. Much better than Jane had imagined. Miss Paterson was pleased to learn that she could do joined-up writing and was able to recite her times-tables.

At the end of an hour, the rest of the girls were told that they could leave the class, but Jane Jeffrey should remain behind. Miss Paterson held tightly to her hand as they went out through the front door and down the stone steps. 'You see those three sheds over to your right?' she said to Jane, pointing with her forefinger. Jane nodded. 'Well, they are the toilets you will use when working or playing outside.' They went on past the lavatories and stopped outside a much larger and more solidly brick-built building. Miss Paterson pushed open the door.

Inside a man in his shirt sleeves was sitting at the far end of a table, with a smallish woman with a head of thin white hair at his side. The two of them were apparently sorting out a pile of clothing.

The door closed with a slam behind Jane, making her jump slightly. Then Miss Paterson pushed past her, saying, 'I'm told an assignment of clothing has arrived. This is our latest arrival, Jane Jeffrey. I thought you might like to meet her, she badly needs to be kitted out.'

'Oh!' The exclamation had come from the man, and he repeated, 'Oh! Well, it would 'ave been nice, Miss Paterson, if you'd given us a bit of notice. We 'aven't got 'alfway through the 'amper yet.'

'Still, needs must when the devil drives,' the small woman said, getting to her feet and smiling at Jane. 'Did you bring any clothes with you at all, my dear?'

'Do they ever?' Miss Paterson cut in before Jane had a chance to reply. 'She needs from the skin outwards; gymwear can wait for the time being.'

Having by now sorted out the situation in her own mind, Jane spoke up. 'I've a lovely brand-new coat. The nurses at the hospital bought it for me and it wasn't second hand.'

The man rose slowly to his feet, all the while staring at Jane. Then he pushed a chair towards her, saying, 'Sit you down, my love, my missus 'ere will fit you out, you've no need to fear, an' as for being second hand, you wait and see. We get clothes given to this home which come from some of the finest families in the land.'

Jane was surprised at how soft and kind his voice sounded.

'I'm Patrick Carter, and that's me wife, Emma. We're always about somewhere, 'cos we live in a cottage down by the gate, so if ever you need us, you won't have far t' look.' He bounced his head with almost every word, as if to emphasize that he meant what he was saying.

'You're a bit smaller than most of the girls we have to deal with.' Emma Carter spoke quietly as she began sorting things out of a great big hamper. She nodded towards Miss Paterson. 'What d'you think of this?' she asked as she took out a navy-blue raincoat. 'It does have a very thick lining, so it might do her for school.' She laid the coat across the table, and Miss Paterson looked at it, feeling the material between her finger and thumb.

'It will have to be shortened quite a bit, but it is a very good quality,' she said eventually.

'Well, we'll only turn the hem up, we won't cut it, then it can be lengthened again as she grows,' Emma Carter said, nodding from one to the other now. 'Come along, child, try it on.' When she saw Jane in the coat she looked pleased, even though the hem was touching her ankles. 'Yes, my dear,' she murmured. Then, falling to her knees, she pinned up the hem. 'Now that's better. That's much better. What do you think, Miss Paterson?'

The teacher looked solemnly at Jane and agreed, adding, 'It really is good quality.'

Jane took the coat off and it was handed to Mr Carter, who drew lines round the hem with a piece of tailoring chalk.

Next two skirts were brought out. One of them was far too big, but a navy-blue one was deemed to be fine. Two blouses followed, which Jane was told would be suitable for school, and a jumper and a cardigan. 'There's plenty of warm underwear over at the house, in the cupboard on the first floor.' Emma Carter spoke more to herself than to anyone in particular.

Miss Paterson seemed pleased with the result and was preparing to lead Jane away when she turned her head towards Patrick and asked, 'No chance of any footwear, I suppose?'

'I was just glancing at the child's feet. Did she arrive wearing those plimsolls?' Patrick asked, although he suspected that he already knew the answer.

'No, she has a pair of boots but they've seen better days. Plimsolls were all Matron had that would fit.'

'Um . . .' Patrick grunted. 'Umpteen of the lasses could do with a decent pair of boots or shoes, but as you know, it's what we get least of. We've nothing for her, even to be going on with. But I'll tell you what, send her boots over an' I'll do what I can to repair them.'

'Thanks, Patrick,' Miss Paterson said quietly.

Jane's feelings were mixed as she wondered just how long she was supposed to be staying here. All these different clothes they were giving her! And as for this Miss Paterson!

One minute she was jumping down your throat and the next she was being ever so kind.

As if to prove a point, Miss Paterson turned to Jane now, saying, 'Come along and let's see what I can do about that hair of yours.'

Patrick Carter placed an arm around Jane's shoulders. She smiled up at him, but his face was straight. And what he said next Jane was to remember for the whole of the time she would spend at Winchelsea Lodge: 'I meant it, lass: if and when you need a friend, or just feel like a chat, you come and find me or me missus.'

Miss Paterson nodded, first to him and then to Emma, then turned and led Jane quickly from the room.

Once back inside the main house, Jane was ushered into what appeared to be a cloakroom. A chair was pulled forward and she was told to sit down, then Miss Paterson flicked a towel around her shoulders, tucking it in all round her neck and under her chin. When Jane saw that she was holding a comb and a pair of scissors, her face crumpled.

Miss Paterson held her by the shoulders as she explained quietly, 'It wouldn't do to let you keep this long hair. No child is allowed to. We haven't the time to keep it clean, let alone tidy.'

Jane felt so sad. Her hair was the only thing that made her look pretty. It made people take notice of her. Besides, what would her mum say when she saw her without her ringlets? But then a thought struck her. When was her mum likely to see her? Never, probably. So what difference did it make anyway!

There was dead silence in this small room for a moment, and then Miss Paterson got to work.

Head down, eyes glued to the floor, Jane watched as the long, fine, silky strands of hair fell around her feet. The towel was whipped away and she felt the soft bristles of a brush go around her neck, then Miss Paterson said, 'All done. There's a mirror on the wall over there. Go take a look at your new self.'

Her face looked smaller, clean and white, as if she had just washed it. What hair she had left was straight, barely touching her ears. She ran her hand around her neck. It felt cold, and utterly bare.

Her mum wouldn't recognize her.

But then she'd already worked that one out. Her mum wasn't likely to see her, was she? Jane was no longer her responsibility.

Chapter Six

THERE WAS LIGHT streaming from all the windows at the front of the house as the crocodile of girls walked up the steps to the front door.

They had all taken off their woolly hats and unwound the long scarves from their necks, and were trying to take in the effect of the surroundings. The huge Christmas tree had been standing in one corner for two days. Now decorated with baubles made by the girls themselves from silver paper, it looked beautiful.

The hall, too, looked lovely, adorned by paper chains and with holly draped around the top of the picture rail.

'So you've all come back now everything is almost finished,' a big booming voice called from the far end of the hall. 'Well, at least it will save me getting up and down these steps; some of yer come an' hand the holly up to me.' Ted Grimshaw was perched halfway up some standing steps.

Elsie Rogers turned her gaze to Jane, who was standing with a look of amazement on her face. Elsie, along with two other members of staff, had just taken the girls to a carol

service in the local church. She had watched Jane throughout the entire service and had come to the conclusion that
this was probably the first time in her young life that the
girl had experienced the true meaning of Christmas.

When Matron came down the stairs it was to a babble
of voices all exclaiming how wonderful the decorations were
looking.

A cluster of girls were handing all sorts of greenery up
to Ted Grimshaw, and when he almost overbalanced and
was saved by several pairs of hands grabbing at the steps,
the whole room seemed to rock with laughter. Ted, wiping
his hands down his apron, said, 'I think I've earned a drink,'
before muttering, 'You'd think with all the females in this
house one of them would be capable of making a man a
cup of tea.'

With laughter rumbling in her throat, Lillian Cooper
didn't answer him for a moment, then she said, 'Well, by
the time you've finished off up there I shouldn't be a bit
surprised if hot drinks and even mince pies aren't laid out
on the table for everyone to partake of.'

To herself Matron was saying, 'Oh, I hope each and every
girl that is here in my care has a happy Christmas. And all
my staff. They work so hard, never seem to let up.' Then
she smiled broadly. Their cook was a gem, even if she did
rule the kitchen with a rod of iron. These past few days she
had come up trumps. With almost a full week ahead during
which there was to be no schooling, she would have her
work cut out feeding this lot. It would be a happy time,
though. Lillian would make it her business to see that it
was. Fifty per cent of the girls here had come from broken
homes and the rest had either lost their parents through
tragic circumstances or been abandoned. The board of directors had been generous in making an additional allowance

this year, and she and her staff had between them decided as to how it should be spent. There was not enough money to go mad, but each child would receive a small present and a stocking, which would be hung on the end of their beds on Christmas Eve.

'Clear a space,' Nellie, the cook, called out, coming into the hall carrying a heavy tray. She was followed by Daisy and Minnie, her two assistants.

Willing hands poured tea, and there was hot milk for those who preferred it. Slices of Madeira cake and hot mince pies were being handed round by the senior girls. Elsie Rogers was still watching Jane. She loved to see the different expressions of surprise and sometimes delight which flickered across the child's face. During the short time Jane had been at Winchelsea Lodge there had been a marked improvement. She didn't jump now when spoken to, neither did she back away from physical contact. Elsie gave a short laugh as she listened to what Ted Grimshaw was saying to the girl.

'These pies are as good as my Maggie makes. Must be Christmas, 'cos they don't often feed me when I'm working up here.'

Stepping closer, Elsie said, 'He does go on, doesn't he, Jane? You know we wouldn't starve him, don't you?'

Jane smiled happily. 'I think he's only teasing, don't you, Mrs Rogers? He likes coming up to the house really, he told me he does.'

Ted looked a bit embarrassed and mumbled, 'Suppose I'd better go an' do me own clearing-up if I want it done properly.' Then, turning to Jane, he said, 'Me an' me missus has been invited up here for tea on the great day, so I'll see you then if not before.'

A while later they were all saying goodbye to Ted as he pulled on his overcoat when the door bell rang and Matron called out, 'Whoever is nearest please open the door.'

Frances O'Brien stepped forward and quickly called out, 'There's two woodmen here, Matron, they say they have a load of logs to deliver.'

'Well I never,' Matron was heard to mutter. 'I certainly wasn't expecting them, but never the less they are so welcome. Ask them to come in.'

In all, six sacks of logs were brought in and stacked to the side of the great fireplace. When one of the woodmen casually remarked, 'Did you know it has started to snow?' girls turned their faces to each other and then there was a general rush to the windows. It was only four o'clock in the afternoon, but already the night was drawing in. The white flakes were floating silently down, turning the paths into a white trail and decorating the bare branches of the trees in a Christmas magic all of their own.

'May I be allowed to know who has so generously sent us this most welcome gift?' Matron asked after she had seen that both men were handed a big mug of tea and a hunk of Cook's Madeira cake.

'Don't know as how we can answer that, mam, 'cos we wasn't informed.' The taller of the two men scratched his head before adding, 'But we can tell yer that we loaded up the sacks ourselves from Mr Stuart's grounds, and after that it were himself that asked us if we'd make the delivery.'

Lillian looked across to where Elsie Rogers was standing and they both nodded knowingly. Their thoughts were running along the same lines. What great friends were Dorothy and Richard Stuart, and such good benefactors to the occupants of Winchelsea Lodge.

One way and another it was going to be a very nice Christmas.

* * *

The next seven days were an eye-opener to Jane. Spending Christmas in the happy safety of Winchelsea Lodge, it was as if she had been transported to a different world. If only Tommy could be here to share it with me, was her constant thought. She no longer asked herself if or when her mother was going to come and take her home. She had been rejected by her family. It was only too plain that she was unwanted by them. Her thoughts did often run to dear old Nancy, who had been like a grandmother to her. Not that she knew much about having grandparents; only what the girls at school had told her. In fact she couldn't remember her father ever having mentioned his parents. She had had a gran, her mother's mum, and she had been real nice, but she had stopped coming to the house a long time ago and her dad had told her that Gran had died. What puzzled Jane was that her mother wouldn't talk to her about her gran. She had stopped asking questions about her, because Alice got ever so upset.

Even though Christmas had been such a happy time, Jane had missed her brother Tommy. How she would have loved to have shared with him all the things that she had been given. Wished that he could have seen the big Christmas tree, been there when they toasted chestnuts on a long-handled shovel over the big log fire. How he would have laughed when the chestnuts popped and jumped off the shovel. She hoped that he too had had a nice time.

She had been fast asleep when the church bells had rung in the new year.

She was woken up by cries of 'Happy birthday, Jane.'

Sitting up and rubbing her eyes, she took the small crepe-paper-wrapped parcel which Connie was holding out to her and stared at it in disbelief. 'Go on, open it up,' Connie urged her. The wrapping tore away easily to reveal a small comb and a pale-blue enamel hairbrush with an edging of silver paint.

As Jane sat turning both items over and over in her hands without saying a word, Connie asked softly, 'Don't you like them? Your hair will grow again soon and I thought they would be useful.'

'Oh,' was all that Jane uttered, but Connie could hear the sob in her voice. It took a couple of minutes before she was able to say, 'I think they are so lovely. Thank you, Connie, for buying them for me.'

'That's what birthdays are all about. Friends always give little presents,' Connie reassured her.

'Not to me, nobody ever did before,' Jane said sadly.

'Well, today will be different, you'll see. So get up quickly, we don't want to be late, not on the first day of the year.'

It was a day Jane would always remember. There was a card signed by all the girls and members of staff, as well as one from Matron and one from Mrs Rogers. Cook said she was saving her surprise until tea-time, and it turned out to be a huge sponge cake with nine lighted candles. When it was time for Jane to blow out the flames of the candles she had to have help, because her big blue eyes weren't able to focus properly. They were filled with tears.

Then, with the new year eight days old, Jane set off with ten other girls all under the age of twelve to start her first day as a pupil at Lion Street School for Girls in the old town of Rye. The school was a collection of solidly built one-storey stone cottages. Collectively they had the appearance of being a church. There was no rule as to uniform, but it had become normal for all the girls to wear blouses and a gymslip, and on Jane's first day she looked no different from any of the others who attended the school, thanks to the efforts of Patrick Carter and the sewing ability of his wife Emma.

The classroom was not at all like the one Jane had been used to in London. It was heated by a round stove. At regular intervals, even while a lesson was in progress, the caretaker would enter and feed the stove with coke, then make sure that he replaced the guard that stood around it. After prayers had been said and hymns sung, Jane watched as small bottles of milk were placed around the base of this stove so that they might thaw out on this frosty morning. Then, at playtime, each girl was given a bottle of milk to drink, absolutely free. Milk had been available at her London school but only if a child had a halfpenny to pay for it. Which Jane had seldom had.

During the morning she was given an exercise book, on which she was told to write her name, plus a pencil, a rubber, a pen and two pen nibs. There was an ink well in the top right-hand corner of her desk. The tall girl who sat next to her leaned across and said, 'It will cost you dearly if you lose any one of those things.'

Jane was puzzled. She had no money, so how would she be able to pay? She decided that she had better take very good care not to lose a single one of them.

As time went on she was taught other things rather than just lessons. Each class took it in turn to clean the main hall. Some pupils washed the windows while others dusted and polished the pews. All cleaning cloths then had to be washed and hung out on a line in the yard behind the main building.

Jane's school terms became reasonably happy. She was a bright pupil, quick to learn, but was given no advantages.

Scholarships and suchlike were not for children who lived in charity-run homes. She had to take a lot of ribbing from local children, who never let her forget that she had no proper family. But at least she had the comradeship of the other girls who were in the same boat as herself.

And so the pattern of her next five years was set.

She settled down at Winchelsea Lodge and became very adapt with a sewing needle, taught by the Sisters of Mercy from the Church of England, who gave their services free to the girls of this home every Saturday afternoon. It was Jane's ambition to start and finish a fire screen as beautiful as the one that stood in the hearth of the small sitting room. She would do it before she left. She'd made up her mind on that. Some girls left the home when they reached the age of fourteen; that was, if they were lucky enough to find employment that offered them accommodation as well. Others found employment but still returned daily to the home, using most of what they earned to pay for their keep. No one, however, was allowed to remain under the care of the home after they reached the age of sixteen. It was from then on that a girl was on her own.

Over the years, Jane was to become part of many a tearful goodbye. The worst was the day that Connie Brown walked through the front door to live her life in the outside world. She had kept her promise to Jane and had been her friend, a fact that was greatly appreciated by Jane, who realized that in the beginning it was Connie who had made life a whole lot easier for her, cushioning blows that otherwise would have floored her.

Jane tried hard not to think about the day when she herself would no longer be allowed to stay at Winchelsea Lodge. She never heard from her mother, not so much as one letter, but she still thought of her. Especially when the lights were turned off at night and she lay in her narrow bed and no one came to kiss her good night. There weren't many days that she didn't think of her brother Tommy. What school was he going to, and what kind of a life was he leading?

As to her father . . . She still had the odd bad dream when she was at her wits' end to know what to do to please him. These dreams became less frequent, but the terror he caused her was still there in the back of her mind.

Mrs Rogers had long since told her that her father had got over the trouble he was in with the police, and she had firmly assured Jane that he had not been sent to prison. So was he still at home? Did her family still live in Selkirk Road?

As Jane neared her fourteenth birthday, Elsie Rogers made her report to the Guardians of the Poor. In her view, she told them, Jane was still shy, but not so withdrawn now. Over the years she had learned to trust those she lived with. Strangers were a different matter. Especially males. The only two men that Jane really trusted were Ted Grimshaw and Patrick Carter. She had grown into an attractive girl, though she herself did not seem to sense it. No one could accuse her of being vain. She still wore the second-hand clothes that were given to the home. Not a single letter or a parcel had she received from her parents in all the time she had been at Winchelsea Lodge, yet she never complained. It was Elsie's considered opinion that Jane Jeffrey was still far too insecure to be turned out of the home to fend for herself.

At the end of her report she added a reminder that Jane was entirely without family or any known relatives who would offer her a home. She also stressed that were Jane to be allowed to stay on at Winchelsea Lodge for a further two years, she felt sure the girl would do any task asked of her, and do it willingly.

It was a month before Matron received the official letter.

The board's written decision was that Jane be allowed to stay on at Winchelsea Lodge for a further two years. During that period she was to work as an assistant to Nellie Matthews, the cook, who was reaching the age when she needed full-time help. Two local girls from the village were employed on high days and holidays, and though only paid a few shillings they were still a drain on Matron's expenses. Jane would work in return for her board and lodging.

Those two years were to stand Jane in good stead for the rest of her life.

Nellie Matthews liked Jane, and the feeling was mutual. Therefore Nellie shared her knowledge, taking the time to teach Jane not only how to cook everyday substantial meals, but also how to make a little go a long way. She taught her too how to make bread and cakes that would cost a fortune if bought at a baker's shop.

The two years passed all too quickly. There wasn't a person, male or female, associated with Winchelsea Lodge who wouldn't be sorry to see Jane leave.

The thought of leaving the safety of the home and all the friends that she had made had Jane feeling really sick as she sat facing Matron. Did she but know it, Lillian Cooper wasn't feeling all that good about it either, but her hands were tied and there was nothing she could do. As Matron, she was trying to convince herself that Jane's time spent here at Winchelsea Lodge had been a godsend to the child. She had been fed, given warmth and shelter. But much more than that, she had been taught to value her own worth. She had been loved and had loved in return. The skills she had learnt while under this roof were endless. She had no worries that Jane wouldn't be able to work and earn her own living. It was the fact that no one had ever laid claim to her in the entire seven years she had been here.

Loneliness was the biggest problem Jane was going to have to contend with. And what could possibly be worse than that?

Heaving a sigh, Lillian sat up straight and, using her Matron's voice, began: 'Well, Jane, a lot of loose ends to tie up. First, Mrs Rogers has found you a place to live. It is in Chestnut Grove in Balham. The trustes have voted to pay your first month's rent to give you a chance to find a job and get on your feet. They will also be giving you six pounds, which should be enough to tide you over until you receive your first week's wages.'

The colour had drained from Jane's face, and Matron felt she couldn't bear to look at her. Meanwhile Jane had just about grasped what she had been told. First week's wages? Where was she going to work? Who was going to give her a job?

'I don't want to leave here.'

It was a cry for help rather than a statement, and it tugged at Lillian's heartstrings.

'I do understand, Jane. The very fact of going out into the world must seem terrifying to you. But you are grown up now. You'll have Christmas with us and then start the new year off as a sixteen-year-old. You know we aren't allowed to keep any girl here after they reach the age of sixteen, which if you think about it is only fair. There are so many young girls who need our help, just as you did seven years ago.'

'Why do I have to go and live in Balham?'

'Most of us thought it best to let you go back to a neighbourhood near to where you lived the early years of your life. Balham is not too far from Tooting, and more than likely, once you get settled, you might even look up old friends and relations. You can't have forgotten everyone.'

Jane felt she wanted to scream. No, she had not forgotten, but then again she didn't want to be reminded. Her family had made it quite clear that they wanted nothing more to do with her, so why should she go seeking them out?

Matron felt she had to try a bit harder.

'There are so many things that you can do. You'll go along to the Labour Exchange, have a talk with the people there, and I'm quite sure they'll have no difficulty in finding you a job. Think about it, Jane. You'll be earning money of your own. Meeting girls your own age, making friends.'

Jane stared at her, her eyes brimming with tears.

'What you're telling me is I'm old enough to be taking care of myself. That I should be out there earning a living, making my own decisions. Well, Matron, I know you're right. I am old enough. But it doesn't feel like it. I just don't know how I'll cope.'

It would have been hard to tell which of these two females were feeling worse at that moment.

Jane left Matron's office feeling she was carrying the worries of the world on her shoulders. She had so much to sort out in her mind. When I first came to Winchelsea Lodge I was in a terrible state, terrified, she reminded herself, but this is ten times worse. She had learned to feel safe here. Everything she needed had been provided, plus love from kind, caring people, and suddenly all that was to be cut off.

From now on she had to fend for herself. Find new friends.

It was a daunting thought, but she knew with utter certainty that whatever happened in the future, she would never find better friends than she had at Winchelsea Lodge.

Chapter Seven

MRS ROGERS AND Jane stood side by side on Rye railway station, staring into space for what seemed an eternity. For Elsie Rogers speech was almost impossible; she was too choked up. For seven years she had watched this child grow, seen her become more confident and less frightened. I know I should never have got myself involved so heavily, she was telling herself. But at the same time she was asking how anyone could have resisted the pinched face of the small child she had picked up from that London hospital seven years ago. Especially someone like Elsie herself! No husband, no children of her own; what else was to be expected? There had been many a sad story that she had had to deal with since she had become implicated in court cases. But never a one where she had felt the child was so vulnerable.

Jane broke into her thoughts by saying, 'Matron said I'm old enough to take care of myself, and I told her it doesn't feel like it.'

She sounded like a small child again, and Elsie couldn't

stop herself from taking her into her arms and holding her close.

Several minutes passed before she could bring herself to say, 'Jane, I'll always be there for you. I shall treasure my fire screen, and every day, when I look at the neat stitches that you learned to do, I shall think of you. We'll write to each other, and meet as often as possible.' She meant what she said. She wouldn't just cut this girl off as a job well done. Jane had become a whole lot more than just a case number. There was a bond between them that had come about through love.

The screech of a whistle announced that the train was coming down the track. Time for one last long, lingering hug.

The train stopped. Someone opened the door of the nearest carriage and Jane, carrying a mackintosh over one arm, an attaché case and two brown paper carrier bags climbed the high steps. She dumped everything down on a seat and went to stand at the window. She wasn't sure that she believed that Mrs Rogers would keep in touch with her, but she dearly hoped she would.

The idea that this might be the last time she would ever see this dear friend – for that was what Mrs Rogers had become over the years – was something that she just did not want to think about.

Jane managed to smile and lift her hand to wave, and when finally the train gathered speed she sank down into her corner seat and buried her head in her hands. All she could think of was what she was leaving behind her: safety, warmth, friends, food and clothing. The enormity of what she was going to have to face suddenly hit her, and out loud she murmured, 'God help me!'

Then, taking a grip on herself, she said, 'There may be

many things that I'll be sorry for in the future, but I'll never be sorry that Mrs Rogers came into my life and made it possible for me to be taken into Winchelsea Lodge.'

Jane came out of the railway station and stood in Balham High Street feeling at an utter loss. So many people. So much noise. Everyone in such a hurry. Old men and women, young women with babies in prams, even they were all rushing along. Each and every person, except herself, seemed to have someone to talk to and somewhere to go.

She caught sight of herself in a shop window and realized that she not only felt different, she *looked* different. Thanks once again to Patrick and Emma Carter, she was well turned out. She was wearing a dark-grey skirt that was perfectly straight, the hemline finishing just below her calves. The jacket was a work of art. A darker shade of grey, it had been very much too big for her the first time she had tried it on, but armed with a pad full of pins and a tape measure, Emma Carter had gone to work.

'Don't make her look like a flapper,' Matron had pleaded as Emma nipped the jacket in at the waist.

Jane had seen pictures of flappers. Some girls managed to get hold of magazines, and these were handed round so often that they became dog-eared, especially the fashion pages. They did, however, give the girls an inkling of what was going on in the big world.

The material of the jacket was quite thick, but seeing as how this was January and some days were bitterly cold, Matron had herself provided a thick, long-sleeved jumper in the most cheerful shade of red. Jane loved it. It went so well beneath the grey jacket. As a special treat Jane had been allowed to have her hair cut in a ladies' hair salon in Rye. Though it had been kept short during her stay at Winchelsea

Lodge, the blonde assistant who had seen to it this last time had been very encouraging.

Having washed it with real shampoo, she had remarked on the beautiful natural colour of Jane's hair: no longer quite so fair, but a rich shade of dark gold. Jane had been astounded at the finished result. It was still cut short at the back, but the young lady had used the length at the sides to finger-pinch it into waves that covered Jane's ears.

Elsie Rogers had sighed deeply when first setting eyes on the new Jane.

'She's no longer a little girl, is she?' she had commented to Matron.

And the answer had been: 'No indeed, they are so young when they arrive here, but how the time flies by.'

Well, this won't do, Jane chided herself, and so she picked up her attaché case and started walking. She knew from the drawing that Mrs Rogers had given her that Chestnut Grove was only a few minutes' walk from the station. A tram stopped in the middle of the road; the destination board on the front said TOOTING BROADWAY. It awoke such memories from the back of her mind that for one crazy moment she was tempted to get on that tram, go to Tooting and try to find her mother. She had no idea if Alice still lived at the same address, let alone if she would be glad to see her should she turn up on the doorstep after seven years.

She found Chestnut Grove and was surprised at the spacious houses with their own large gardens. This area was nothing like Tooting! At least not how she remembered it. There were no children playing in the street and no women standing gossiping on the doorsteps. These properties looked as if they belonged to very rich people. Tall, with high windows and massive front doors. Surely the folk who lived in this kind of house did not rent out rooms. She glanced again at the slip of paper. 'Walk on down past the field that is used as a park, cross over and you'll find a blind alley in which there are only four houses. The one you are looking for will be the last one on your right.' Mrs Rogers had certainly been explicit.

Having found the house, Jane let out a sigh of relief. 'Oh, it does look nice,' she murmured. It was a much less impressive building than those she had just passed, and for that she was grateful. The windows were sparkling and the lace curtains were starched and pure white. She opened the gate, walked up the path, which had evergreen shrubs on each side, and rang the bell. In no time at all the door was opened and a neat little woman in a hairnet, wearing carpet slippers and a wraparound pinafore, was saying, 'I watched you from my sitting room window, thought for a moment you weren't going to come in. I had been notified to expect you today, you must be Jane Jeffrey. I'm Mrs Forrester, come along in.'

The hall smelt of lavender and furniture polish. There was a gate-legged table on which stood a bronze plant pot with an aspidistra in it, and underneath the pot a white lace crocheted mat had been placed. The narrow stair carpet was held in place by brass stair-rods so shiny that it almost dazzled Jane to look at them.

Jane decided her new landlady was a pleasant, very clean, very proper lady.

'I'm afraid the only room I had vacant is right at the top of the house,' Mrs Forrester said, as she motioned for Jane to follow her.

'Has Mrs Rogers found you a job?' she asked, pausing for breath when they reached the first landing.

'No . . . not yet . . .' Jane said apologetically.

'What kind of work are you going to be looking for?'

'Anything I can get,' she answered honestly. 'I hope they will have something for me at the Labour Exchange.'

'I'll get me hubby to save his evening paper for you. You never know, you might find something in there.'

'Thank you, I'd be very grateful,' Jane said as they reached the third floor.

'Anyhow, there's one thing you've not got to worry about: your rent's paid up for a whole month. That's a blessing, isn't it?'

Jane nodded her head in agreement and was rewarded by a smile from her new landlady.

The room Mrs Forrester showed her into was low-ceilinged and had only two very small windows, but it was cheerfully furnished and seemed cosy, and on looking round, Jane found it to be surprisingly large. There was a narrow single bed, covered with a patchwork quilt, a wickerwork armchair that held two blue cushions, and a low chest of drawers on top of which stood a two-burner gas cooker, a saucepan and a tin kettle. Placed at an angle was a black iron-framed gas fire, beside which stood a gas meter.

'I have put a shilling in the meter,' Mrs Forrester said. 'That will keep the fire going for this evening, and after that you must put your own money in.' Seeing Jane's worried look, she quickly added, 'It does take pennies if you haven't always got a shilling to hand.'

Jane thanked her, though she wasn't feeling very thankful at the moment. Then, turning round, she saw that Mrs Forrester was holding open the door of a cupboard. Inside, a rail ran from side to side holding four coat hangers, and below it were several shelves.

'I hope you will be happy here, lass. You'll find a few bits and pieces of china there, in that small cupboard on the wall,' the landlady said warmly. She had decided that all

Mrs Rogers had told her about this girl was true. She was quietly spoken, clean and tidy, and very polite, and she didn't look as if she was going to be much trouble. Mrs Forrester liked having the rent from the rooms she let, it made a difference to both her and her hubby, but she never wanted to get involved in the comings and goings of her lodgers. If once she started to feel sorry for this young girl – because by the look of her that was all she was – who knows where it would end.

Shaking her head, she made for the door, saying over her shoulder, 'I forgot t' show you where you'll wash. If you'll come back down to the next floor I'll give you a couple of towels and point out which rooms you share the bathroom with.'

Back in her own room, Jane placed the two towels on a shelf in the cupboard, then plonked herself down on the bed.

For several minutes she just sat there, staring at nothing in particular. She couldn't ever remember feeling so lonely. She wanted to cry, but she stopped herself, muttering aloud, 'What good would it do? No one is going to help me. From now on I am on my own and the quicker I get used to the idea the better off I shall be.'

With a heavy sigh, she opened her attaché case and hung her one dress and one skirt up on the rail, placing her underwear, two blouses and a cardigan on the shelves. She had certainly left Winchelsea Lodge with a lot more than she had gone there with.

Daylight was gradually creeping through the curtains and Jane was thankful that the first night was over. She had tossed and turned, going over and over in her mind what she might do. She decided there weren't many options. Top of the list was to find a job. The very thought scared her half to death.

Washed and dressed, she realized she was starving. There wasn't a thing to eat in her room, and not even a spoonful of tea with which to make herself a cuppa. She had heard people moving around and her first attempt to use the bathroom had been unsuccessful because the door was locked.

'That's right.' She was muttering to herself again, for who else was there for her to talk to? 'If you want to eat and drink from now on, you have to go shopping.' Mrs Forrester had said there was a corner shop if she turned right at the top of the road, but she hadn't felt like going out again last night. Now she'd have to; it was either that or starve. God! Going into a shop to buy food, and she'd have to find a dairy if she wanted milk! That was something that had never even entered her head!

By eight thirty she was in Balham High Street. Passing a café, she sniffed, and although she was frightened of spending too much of the money she had been given, she couldn't resist. As she opened the door, the heat hit her. The whole café seemed full of steam, though she could see at a glance that several men were seated at the tables. After hesitating for just a moment, she made her way to the counter and ordered a cup of tea and a bacon sandwich.

'Large tea?' the man who owned the place asked. He was a stocky man in his fifties who was thinking that this young lady was very different from his usual customers.

'Yes please.' Jane smiled her answer.

From a huge brown enamel teapot he filled what looked like a pint pot with scalding strong tea and pushed it across the counter, saying, 'Find yourself a seat, I'll bring your sandwich over when it's ready.'

Jane lingered over the food, enjoying every mouthful, then

finally drained the remains of her tea and went back to the counter to pay her bill.

'That'll be eightpence,' he told her, watching with interest as she produced a florin from her purse.

Giving her her change he held on to her hand much longer than was necessary. He felt sorry for her; she looked frightened, and he wondered why.

'Please could you direct me to the Labour Exchange?' Jane asked.

Ah! So that was it. She was new to these parts and needed a job. 'Course I can, my luv. I'll come to the door and point you in the right direction.'

Jane was grateful. She felt very much better for having eaten something, and it was right what Matron had told her: there were some kind people around who would help her if she could only pluck up enough courage to ask them.

There weren't many applicants in the exchange, and within a quarter of an hour Jane found herself in a wooden cubicle, sitting opposite a middle-aged woman whose hair was dragged back from her face and twisted into a tight bun, which made her look a lot more stern than she probably was.

So many questions! But Jane knew she had to answer them truthfully because she badly needed a job. From her bag she pulled out a letter that Lillian Cooper had had the foresight to write.

'This will explain where I've been living and tell you something about me.' She spoke quietly as she leaned across the counter and handed in the letter.

There was complete silence as the lady clerk read the page and a half of Matron's neat handwriting.

'Hmm. Going to be a bit difficult to place you!' she muttered when she had finished. Then, pulling a long, narrow wooden box in front of her, she quickly ran her fingers through the endless cards that it contained. Only two cards had she pulled out by the time she reached the end of the box. She cleared her throat before settling back in her chair and saying to Jane, 'I've only found two possibilities. The first is for the Sunlight Laundry, in the bag-wash section; then again, maybe not, you don't look particularly robust, and at the end of the day it would mean heaving sacks of damp washing back on to one of their delivery vans.'

Jane looked as bewildered as she felt. She'd never heard of a laundry that did bag-wash! The lady clerk picked the second card up.

'This client is requesting a maid of all work.' She smiled knowingly at Jane. 'That title could cover a multitude of jobs. But I think we'll give you a green card and send you along for an interview. It states that interviews are given between two and three o'clock. It's a big house just off Wandsworth Common, you'll have plenty of time to find it.'

Jane was twisting her hands in her lap and her eyes were lowered.

'Well?'

The one word, barked at her like that, made her jump. 'I'm sorry, I was listening,' Jane said.

'Well, answer me. Are you willing to go along for an interview?'

Doesn't seem as if I've got much choice, was what Jane felt like saying. Instead she softly said, 'If you think I will be suitable.'

'That's for the employers to judge. I'll make you out a card, and to be on the safe side I think you should take this letter along with you. Matron Cooper has been very explicit and it will save you a lot of explanations.'

Once outside the Labour Exchange, Jane decided to take her time and walk towards Wandsworth Common. It was still only a little after eleven o'clock in the morning and the day stretched endlessly before her. Once again she looked at the people in the street, all well wrapped up against the biting-cold wind, hurrying along, no doubt anxious to get home where more than likely someone would be there to greet them. Just watching them made her feel so lonely; yes, that was the word, lonely.

She was sixteen years old. On her own and feeling lost.

She sighed heavily, pulled the belt of her mackintosh more tightly around her waist and slowly began to walk. Thoughts were going round and round in her head, What on earth was she doing here? She knew no one. In fact she couldn't think of a single soul to whom she could turn. Why was she so alone? For almost nine years of her life she had had a mother, father and brother. Sometimes she hadn't been exactly happy, but that didn't seem to matter so much now. At least then her mother had loved her, and Tommy had been such a lovely little boy. Then, almost without warning, she had become the responsibility of the Guardians of the Poor.

Again she asked herself why.

Not that she wasn't grateful to them. Oh, she was. Life had been good at Winchelsea Lodge, once she had accepted the fact that her family had turned their backs on her. But now, no matter which way you looked at it, the same thing had happened all over again.

She agreed with Matron that it wouldn't be fair to let girls stay on in the home once they reached the age of sixteen. Not when there were so many other youngsters needing protection.

But being right didn't make it feel any better for her.

If only she had someone to talk to. It felt rotten to have been turned out. As if, once again, folk were saying, we've done all we're going to do for you. You're on your own from now on. For the second time she had been abandoned. Was that the word? Or was rejected a better one? What did it matter? It all boiled down to the same thing.

No one really wanted her.

When she found the address that was written on the green card, the house was nothing like she had expected it to be. This was a huge building made of red bricks. Not friendly and warm-looking like Winchelsea Lodge. Silly thing to say, but to her it looked cold. It was so plain, no bow windows. Just three large, straight windows on each side of the front door. The second-floor windows were smaller than those on the ground floor, but even these looked enormous. The top row of windows were quite small and Jane guessed these to be the attic rooms, probably only used for staff. The roof was made up of grey slate tiles, with huge chimney pots rearing up almost as if they were turrets on a castle.

A brass plaque on the outside wall noted that the trade entrance was round to the left.

'I suppose I'd better use that door, seeing as how I'd not exactly be classed as a visitor,' she murmured aloud. Then she stood still and added, 'This is getting to be a bad habit, talking out loud to yourself.'

She found a flight of flagstone steps leading down to a heavy oak door that held a black painted lion's-head knocker. Having raised it and knocked quite hard, she stood well back, doing her best to stop her teeth from chattering. It wasn't so much that she was cold, just plain scared as to what would happen next.

A couple of minutes passed before she heard a bolt being

shot and the door was opened. Standing there was a gentleman with a thick head of white hair. She knew he had to be a gentleman by the good suit he was wearing and the leather shoes he had on his feet.

Without a word, Jane handed him the letter that Matron had so thoughtfully provided and the green card which she had been given at the Labour Exchange.

He glanced only at each side of the card but did not remove the letter from its envelope. He didn't speak for a moment but stood looking her over, then said, 'Have you been in service before?'

'No, sir. Well, not exactly.'

'Either you have or you haven't,' he said, but the voice was amused and Jane felt herself relax just a little.

'If you would kindly read the letter, sir, it will explain things properly.'

He laughed. 'Well then, if we are going to do things properly, I had better introduce myself.' He paused, glanced again at the card, then said, 'Miss Jane Jeffrey, I am Mr Harris. You had better come in.'

As she followed him down a short passage, her first impression was how dark and cold the house was. The first room they entered was obviously the kitchen. It was only half as big as the one she and Nellie had had the run of at Winchelsea Lodge, yet she was pleased to see that the black-leaded range was much the same, with a huge oven to the side and on the top lots of space for kettles and pots and pans. Then, having found that she was smiling to see that a good fire was roaring away in the grate, she chided herself: don't run away with the idea that they'll let you do any of the cooking even if you do get the job. Maid of all work it said on the card. And, as the clerk had half insinuated, that would probably mean that she'd be doing all the hardest and dirtiest jobs that nobody else would stoop to.

'Sit yourself down there.' Mr Harris pointed to a high-backed wooden chair

When she was seated, he stood in front of her, removed the letter from the envelope and read it. 'You've never worked with a family.' It was an observation, made more to himself, and Jane gave no answer. He pursed his lips, half turned away from her, then, quickly swinging back to her again, said, 'You might as well meet the lady of the house, but never let it be said that I didn't warn you: she's not the most even-tempered person you'll be likely to meet.'

Jane swallowed deeply and stared at him. She was surprised when he quickly added, 'It's my sister I'm talking about. Her husband died two years ago, and having just returned to England after working abroad for five years, I made the mistake of coming here to live with Marjorie.'

Jane was even more taken aback now. Should Mr Harris be talking to her like this?

He must have read her thoughts, because he said, 'Sound ungrateful, don't I?' Then he muttered a few more words, but he now had his back to her so Jane didn't quite catch what he said. He half smiled. 'Take your coat off and I'll take you upstairs, you can at least judge for yourself.' Then, as an afterthought, he asked, 'Could you do with a cup of tea?'

Jane didn't know how to answer. She hadn't had a thing since she left the café early this morning. The walk had been far longer than she had expected and every now and then she had sheltered in a shop doorway to get out of the biting wind. So yes, she would love a really hot cup of tea, but it didn't seem right for her to say so.

Mr Harris was no fool. He watched the different expressions flick across the young girl's face and quickly said, 'Of course you could, and so could I. And seeing as how Cook is lying down, we can lay claim to her kitchen.' Whilst saying all this he had been walking round the room, gathering cups and saucers from the dresser, and before very long he had not only made the tea but had produced a Victoria sponge cake from the larder.

They ate and drank in silence, but somehow Jane now felt very much at ease with this strange but friendly gentleman.

'Would you like another slice?' he asked, at the same time sliding a wedge of the sponge cake on to her plate.

She looked at him and they both laughed as he said, 'The strawberry jam inside is very nice, isn't it? I think I will have a second piece too.'

Then, with their plates cleared and their cups drained, he said, 'Well now, I think I'd better go and see if Mrs Bonneford will see you.'

In his absence Jane felt the silence. Winchelsea Lodge was never this quiet. It always rang with the sound of children's voices and laughter. Oh yes, there weren't many days when laughter wasn't heard, and how she was missing it!

A short while later the kitchen door opened and Mr Harris came back into the room and beckoned to her. He led the way down the dark passage and up a narrow flight of uncarpeted stairs into what she presumed was the main entrance hall.

Now this area was cold! There was a stone floor with just a couple of rugs placed one each side of a big round table. There was a fireplace, a huge one with a marble surround, over which hung an enormous gilt-framed mirror. How long since a fire had been lit in that grate? Jane was asking herself. Many a long day, she decided, because there were no dead ashes, just dust. In fact everywhere she looked could do with a good clean-up.

Mr Harris was crossing the hall now, and Jane followed him up the staircase. Halfway up, she stopped to get her bearings. It was a beautiful staircase divided into two, with one flight branching off to the left and the other to the right. She had never before seen anything like this.

They had reached the first landing now, and what a difference!

Mr Harris opened a door and stood back, allowing her to enter the room first. Her breath caught in her throat. It was a beautiful room. Light, airy and best of all warm. And why wouldn't it be, for a brilliant log fire was crackling away, sending sparks flying up the chimney. The furniture was old, but even at first glance Jane knew that whoever was responsible for keeping this part of the house clean was doing an excellent job. The chairs and sofas were all the same colour, a kind of dove grey, with cushions and curtains being pale blue. The carpet on the floor was so thick that Jane felt her feet would sink in it. She was still standing just inside the doorway and hadn't noticed there was a woman sitting near the window, until the lady rose and turned to look at her.

Just looking at her face was a surprise, because if, as Mr Harris had said, she was his sister, then she must be years older than he was. She could easily have been mistaken for his mother!

'Marjorie, this is Jane . . . Jane Jeffrey.'

His manner and even his voice sounded stiff. Not at all like the friendly gentleman he had been when they were downstairs in the kitchen.

'I gave you the letter to read, it tells you quite a lot about her.' He stepped right back as he finished speaking, as if he wanted to get out of his sister's way.

'How old are you?' The words were said sharply. But then everything about this lady seemed kind of sharp. Her mouth was small, her face long and thin, her nose pointed. The nicest thing about her was her hair. It hung loose down her back, long, jet black and very silky. Oh, her clothes were also beautiful. A long pale-lilac dress with a soft loose matching coat that was left unbuttoned to reveal the embroidery adorning the hem of both dress and coat.

'Sixteen.' Jane got the word out eventually.

'Sixteen what?' Sharp words again.

Jane was puzzled, almost frightened, and she made no answer, but dropped her gaze to stare at the floor.

'When you speak to me you will address me as madam. So what you should have answered was, "Sixteen years old, madam."' Now she had a finger stretched out straight, pointing at Jane, and she added, 'Or you could use my title, which is Mrs Bonneford, do you understand?'

'Yes . . . madam.'

'That's better. They haven't taught you much, this home where you've been cared for for the past seven years.'

It was a long time since Jane had lost her temper, but right now she was very tempted to answer back. However, as she bit her tongue, she turned her glance to see that Mr Harris was gently shaking his head at her and half smiling. That kind gesture was enough to put the brakes on.

And then she was glad she hadn't been cheeky, because suddenly the lady smiled and said quite nicely, 'Well now, we know where we stand, don't we? I'm still not sure that you are up to doing the rough work that will be required of you, but we'll give you a month's trial. Can you start straight away? Would you like Mr Harris to show you where you will be sleeping?'

Panic bells were ringing in Jane's head. She hadn't referred to him as her brother, only as Mr Harris. What did that tell her? And again, if she were to give up the room in which she had only spent one night and things did not work out here, where would she go? It would be like burning her bridges.

'Please . . . madam . . .'

'Well, girl, what is it? Didn't the Labour Exchange tell you the hours, and that the wages are six shillings a week paid monthly, and on top of that all your food will be provided?'

'Yes, they did . . . madam, but it's about the room. Arrangements were made for me, at least for the time being. I only moved in yesterday and my rent has been paid for a month.'

'That's no problem if it's what you prefer. Just remember you have to be here by seven o'clock in the morning.'

'Yes, madam, thank you.'

As she said those four words, Jane felt, at least for the time being, that her fate had been sealed. She should be feeling grateful. She had a job and all her meals would be provided. So why were her lips trembling, and why did she still keep getting the urge to cry?

'Very well, you can start the day after tomorrow; that will give you a little time to get yourself sorted.' Mrs Bonneford turned from Jane and glanced at her brother.

'You can outline the tasks we shall expect her to do, and fix it up with Ada about her uniform, her day off and suchlike. Oh, and by the way, give her sixpence to pay her tram fare back to her lodgings. Can't expect her to walk, it will be quite dark soon.'

Jane was flabbergasted!

That woman certainly was a mixture!

Out on the landing, they had moved away from the door before Mr Harris stopped and, looking her straight in the face, said, 'My sister can seem very kind at times, and at others she will appear hard. Just remember, whatever her mood, she very rarely allows anyone to be fully aware of her true colours.' He stared at her for a moment longer before starting down the staircase.

Jane shook her head.

Now what was she supposed to make of that?

Chapter Eight

BY THE TIME Jane was back in Balham High Street, it was gone four o'clock. Mrs Bonneford had been right: already it was almost dark. She longed to get back to her rented room and light the gas fire, for it was not only cold now, it was actually snowing. But before she could turn her footsteps towards Chestnut Grove, she had to tackle the problem of buying some food. She didn't think she was likely to find a dairy around these parts, but there were several grocery shops. The first one to hand was the Home & Colonial. Having taken a deep breath and pushed open the heavy door to the shop, she knew immediately that she had made a wise choice. The man who stood behind the polished wooden counter was in his forties, thin, with a balding head and a waxed moustache on his upper lip, and he was wearing a navy-blue and white bibbed apron.

His welcoming smile and enquiry as to how he might help her went a long way towards making Jane feel a little more secure about what she was going to purchase.

'Please,' she began, but then had to clear her throat before saying, 'May I have a quarter of a pound of tea and . . . do you sell milk?'

He looked curiously at this slight young lass who seemed almost at a loss for words. In the normal way of things he would have asked a customer which type of tea she preferred. But not in this case. He sensed the girl was not used to shopping and he placed a packet of the most popular tea on the counter before saying, 'No, miss, I'm sorry, we don't stock fresh milk. We leave that to the dairyman, who does two rounds during the day, but we do sell condensed milk, Funnels is a very good make,' he added, placing a small blue and white tin beside the the packet of tea.

Jane thought that would do very well – Nellie always kept condensed milk in the cupboard as a standby at Winchelsea Lodge – but then a thought struck her. Would there be such a thing as a tin-opener in her room? Well, she'd soon find out, wouldn't she?

'Can I get you anything else, miss?'

Jane felt she would have like to say, yes please, something for my dinner, but she didn't dare, so she said, 'Just some crackers and a small piece of cheese, please.'

While she watched the man cut into a huge round of Cheddar cheese, using a very thin wire with a wooden handle on each end, her thoughts were running along the lines that at least she had found herself a job without too much trouble, and that from the day after tomorrow she would have her food provided and wouldn't have to worry about what she was going to buy or how she was going to cook it.

'May I suggest a small pat of butter?' The enquiry broke into her thoughts.

'Yes . . . Thank you.'

Now he smiled at her and made a great show of dipping his two wooden butter platters into a bowl of water. He eased a small amount of butter from a large mound and deftly shaped it into a neat round, then pressed what looked to Jane like a silver letter-opener against the pat that he had formed. Laying the pat of butter on a sheet of greaseproof paper, he held it out for Jane's inspection.

He was rewarded by a wide grin. For in the centre of her butter was the impression of a perfect Scotch thistle.

'Will that be all?' The grocer smiled back at her, and when she nodded her head, he totted up the five items and told her the total was one shilling exactly.

Jane offered him half a crown and he gave her one shilling and sixpence change. As he did so, another thought came to her mind. She quickly held out the sixpence and, with her cheeks flushing red, blurted out, 'Please could you spare me six pennies.'

He took the sixpence from her cold fingers and his heart went out to her. His fears were confirmed when she said, almost beneath her breath, 'I need them for the gas meter.'

The grocer was so touched, he did something he did not normally do. Picking up the brown paper bag in which he had packed her few bits of shopping, he came around to her side of the counter and held the door open for her.

When she said, 'Thank you very much,' he answered her, 'You're more than welcome. Good night, miss.'

He did not turn and go straight back into his shop, but leant his head forward and watched as Jane, head down, battled her way along the high street. He shivered, for the snow was coming down so thickly now that it blotted out everything only a yard or so in front of him.

'My God!' he muttered to himself. 'Me wife and I have a lot t' be thankful for. On a night like this, that lass is going home to crackers and a bit of cheese, and how long will her six pennies last in a gas meter?'

Life wasn't fair, he mused as he closed the shop door.
It really wasn't.

Jane was frozen to the bone by the time she walked into the
house in Chestnut Grove. Mrs Forrester waited while she
stamped the snow from her shoes before asking, 'How did
you get on today?'

Jane untied her scarf, which she had been forced to tie
over her head to keep her ears warm, and rolled it into a
ball. She was frightened it might drip on to her landlady's
polished lino, because it was sopping wet where the snow
had soaked through.

'I got a job,' she said, her teeth chattering. 'I'm to be a
maid of all work in a big house near Wandsworth Common.'

'I don't much like the sound of that,' Mrs Forrester said,
pulling a face. 'Do they want you to live in?'

'Yes, they did. But as they were taking me on a month's
trial, I said I would prefer to stay here in my room, seeing
as how the rent has been paid for me.'

'You've a good head on your shoulders, lass, that was a
wise decision. Don't do to burn yer bridges till you've
crossed over.'

While talking, Jane was edging towards the stairs. She
didn't want to stand here talking, not that it wasn't nice
and warm in the hall, but her legs were aching and she really
wanted to make herself a cup of tea.

Reaching the second floor, she noticed the door to the
bathroom was wide open, so she went in, closed the door
and took off her mackintosh, which was soaking wet. She
shook it over the bath and hung it up behind the door.
Then, having used the toilet, she went on up to her room.
Two minutes later she was back down with her tin kettle,
which she half filled from the cold tap over the washbasin.

Back upstairs she struck a match, lit one of the jets on the small gas stove and placed the kettle on to boil. Now another match had to be struck and held against the flimsy gas mantle in order to give herself some light in the room. With a third match she lit the gas fire, thinking to herself: at this rate my six pennies aren't going to last for long. Only now could she close the door to her room, because she no longer needed the light from the gas jet on the landing to shine in and allow her to see what she was doing.

Now, one cup and saucer, one plate and a knife, and was there . . . She fumbled around at the back of the small drawer, and heaved a great sigh of relief as her fingers closed around a metal tin-opener.

Thank God she wouldn't have to drink her tea without any milk!

One thing she was determined on: as soon as she had eaten her biscuits and cheese, she was going to get into bed. At least there she would be able to stretch her legs out and hopefully get warm. She was feeling very tired now, exhausted in fact, yet in an odd sort of way she felt she had achieved a lot today. Despite all her misgivings she had found herself a job. Whether she would suit her new mistress was another matter!

She'd have to wait and see, wouldn't she?

It was midday before Jane decided to venture out. She had sat near the window of her room for more than an hour. Sitting down, she couldn't see below into the street, but she did have a good view of house tops, and in the distance the spire of a very old church rose high towards the grey sky. The snow lay thick, making everything seem not only a brilliant white but silent. Dead silent from where she was sitting in this top room all on her own.

Having wrapped herself up warmly, she came down the stairs and let herself out of the front door without seeing a soul.

She was going to be very brave and very extravagant!

She was going back to the café where she had had breakfast yesterday, and she was going to buy herself a hot dinner.

Oh, the pavements and the roads were treacherous. It must have frozen after the snow had stopped falling, and folk were having a job to keep upright, because every surface was so slippery. With difficulty she made it to the café, but as she opened the door she stumbled and actually fell in through the doorway. There was no shortage of men to help her; they left their food and came to her aid. Her right leg had buckled under her and was hurting badly as these kind, willing hands did their best to help her to her feet and on to a chair.

After a few minutes in which she took several deep breaths, she went to rise and go to the counter, but when the proprietor who had been so kind to her yesterday called out, 'Sit where you are, I'll bring you over a large tea,' she obeyed him without a murmur. Minutes later, he handed her a mug of tea and said, 'Let me 'ave a look at that leg,' and she made no protest as he straightened out her leg, lifted her foot and placed it on a second chair.

'Your shoes, that's the trouble, just look at this one.' He flapped the sole of her shoe, which had broken loose from the upper. 'You ought t' be wearing boots on a day like this,' he muttered, shaking his head and slipping her shoe off her foot at the same time. 'I'll see what can be done about this.'

'What? . . . Oh, thank you.'

'Were you intending to have something to eat?'

'Yes, I was. To tell you the truth,' her voice dropped to a whisper, 'I'm ever so hungry.'

'Well you've come to the right place. We've two specials today, me missus 'as gone mad. You can 'ave toad in the 'ole, or steak an' kidney pudding.'

Jane's mouth watered as she quickly said, 'May I have the steak an' kidney pudding, please?'

The proprietor went off grinning to himself and taking Jane's shoe with him.

She sipped at her tea. If it had been anywhere else that she had slipped because of her shoe she would have been embarrassed, but this café owner was a very nice man. Footwear had been a problem the whole time she had been at Winchelsea Lodge. Only once had she ever had a brand-new pair of shoes, and that was in the summer when she had been twelve years old. Even then they hadn't been real shoes, just sandals.

The tea was great, much stronger than she was used to, but it was warming her through right down to the soles of her feet. She let her mind wander.

If this job did turn out to be any good she knew what she was going to buy as soon as she had managed to save enough money. A pair of boots. Yes, a brand-new pair of boots!

Her dinner was placed in front of her and she ate every morsel. It reminded her a bit of the big stews that they used to have at Winchelsea Lodge, which made her long to be back there. At this moment she would have given anything to see Mrs Rogers again. And how about Matron? Just a glimpse of her hurrying down the stairs but never in such a hurry that she hadn't got time to smile and give a cheery wave. A sight of any of the other girls would be so nice. What were they all doing at this moment? At least they had company, which was a lot more than she had.

Would she ever get used to being lonely?

'Good girl,' the café owner said as he picked up Jane's

empty dinner plate. 'Now, what would you like for yer pudding?'

Jane was flustered by the question. She hadn't intended to have anything else to eat because she didn't want to spend too much money. There was at least four weeks to go before she would receive any more. And then only if she lasted that long in this new job.

'Look, lass, the price of the dinner is one an' tuppence, and that includes yer cup of tea and a pudding, so you might as well 'ave the lot,' he told her, sensing straight off that she was counting her pennies. 'There's college pudding an' custard, or apple pie an' custard.'

Jane hesitated, then, seeing he was smiling broadly, she too smiled and quickly said, 'I would love some apple pie and custard, please.'

When he came back and placed a bowl that was brim full in front of her he casually remarked, 'By the way, Sid the totter has just come in our back gate; he buys an' sells everything, 'as a scrap yard not far from here. As luck would 'ave it, he saw me trying t' mend your shoe and said he took on board several items from one of the big 'ouses this morning an' he thinks he's got a pair of button-up boots that might just fit you.' He saw the embarrassed look that came to Jane's face and added quickly, 'That's if you ain't too proud to . . .'

He didn't have to finish the sentence, because Jane was clutching at his hand and doing her best to tell him how grateful she was.

She was in no hurry to go out again into the bitter weather. She took her time eating the apple pie, savouring every mouthful, and it was nearly half an hour later when from behind the counter the café owner beckoned for her to come and join him.

'I'm Harriet, his wife.' A thin woman who was standing at the door of a large kitchen nodded her head towards the proprietor. 'And if he ain't told yer already, he's Jack. Come in, come in.' The woman was bending towards Jane, her face showing a great big smile. 'Sit yerself down . . . Aw lass, I forgot you've hurt yer leg an' you've only got one shoe on.'

Harriet hurried to give Jane a hand as she hobbled further into the kitchen and sat down on what appeared to be the one and only chair. Then she nodded towards a man who looked so very much like herself that Jane thought they must surely be brother and sister. 'Sid 'ere 'as found that pair of boots, if yer want to try them on.'

Sid was a weedy-looking man, red-faced, with thinning grey hair, but as he caught Jane's glance he gave a such a nice smile that she at once felt at ease. ''Ere yer are, me dear,' he said in a true cockney accent, holding aloft a pair of brown boots that to say the least looked as if they could do with a jolly good cleaning. Before Jane had the chance to say a word he was on his knees in front of her and very gently easing off her remaining shoe. His hands were grubby but they worked swiftly as he loosened the long laces of one of the boots, pulled back the leather tongue and helped her to put her foot inside. Then he did exactly the same with the other boot.

'Can yer stand up, gal?'

Jane did just that, and as she waggled her toes about inside the boots she grinned. 'Oh my goodness,' she said beneath her breath, 'they feel gorgeous. The lining is so soft and warm.'

She took a few steps, and Sid, Harriet and even Jane herself laughed. It was obvious the boots were at least two sizes too big for her small feet.

'Never mind that,' Harriet said, and pulling a dresser

drawer open she rummaged inside for a few minutes and came up with two inner soles. They were not a matching pair but what did that matter! Jane wouldn't have cared if one had been green and the other sky-blue pink.

'They won't make that much difference,' Sid said mournfully.

'Hold yer 'orses, you. Time I've given 'er a pair of Jack's socks to wear, she'll manage all right. I'll find a real thick pair and she can lace them boots up nice and tight. And you, me lad, can set to and give 'em a damn good clean.' This last remark was fired straight at Sid, who was looking very pleased with himself.

Jane couldn't believe it. She looked from one to the other and did not know what to say. She was smiling. For the first time since she had left the safety of Winchelsea Lodge, she was talking to people who were acting as if they had known her for a long time; as though they really cared about her. And that was a very good reason for her to be smiling.

'Well now, what are you going to do with yourself for the rest of the day?' Harriet put the question kindly to Jane, and when the answer was slow in coming she added quickly, 'Jack has mended your shoe, but it won't stand up to this weather, and Sid will be a little while cleaning up yer boots. Would yer like t' stay here an' give me an 'and? I can let yer 'ave the lend of me fluffy slippers. And I'll find yer a pinny.'

Jane looked anxiously at her benefactor and very quietly said, 'You don't have to do all this for me.'

'No, I know we don't, gal, but 'ave yer never 'eard it said what goes round comes round? Who knows when me or Jack, or even Sid, come t' that, is gonna need an 'elping 'and?'

'But Sid . . .' Jane hesitated at having used the man's

Christian name, 'he hasn't told me how much he is selling the boots for.'

''Ave you decided to stay here for a while and get stuck in on that sink full of dishes?' Harriet asked, pointing a finger towards a wooden draining board piled high with dirty plates.

'Well . . . yes.'

'Then we'll call it payment in full.'

At that moment Jack put his head round the door and was more than pleased to see that his missus and this little waif and stray that they seemed to have taken under their wing were laughing happily together.

For the rest of the day, Jane stood with her hands deep in soap suds washing an endless stream of crockery that kept coming from the café. Yet she was happy. Happier than she had been for the past two days.

Sharp at three o'clock she was ordered to sit down. Two huge toasted teacakes and another large tea were set in front of her, and this time she ate in the kitchen with Harriet for company. All Jane could think of was that she had landed on her feet.

She wouldn't have any need to go shopping today. She'd eaten more than enough to keep her going until tomorrow, when she would start her new job.

It was getting dark and the snow was starting to fall again as Jane said goodbye to her benefactors. She looked down at her now well-shod feet: shiny brown leather boots, high boots that came right up her leg to just below her knee, with a double row of buttons and laces which criss-crossed from one side to the other. A few yards on she turned her head quickly and glanced over her shoulder, and who was still standing in the doorway of the café but Jack and Harriet. Until yesterday she had never set eyes on either of them.

Now, because of their kindness and generosity, she had been well fed and kept warm all day, and was walking away wearing a pair of boots that would have taken her a whole year of Sundays to save up enough money to buy.

And to top that, her feet were warm inside because she was wearing a thick pair of socks that had belonged to Jack.

Unbelievable, wasn't it?

Life was strange.

Even funny, if you stopped to think about it.

Chapter Nine

IT WAS A nervous and subdued Jane that knocked on the heavy oak door at ten minutes to seven in the morning. She had lost the sparkle that had come so readily to her eyes yesterday.

'I'm Clemmy Morris.' A big-boned, wide-shouldered girl spoke in a friendly voice to Jane as they walked down the dark passage. 'I'm really pleased that you're starting here today. We've been without below-stairs help for three weeks now and a lot of the heavy work has fallen to me.'

That statement didn't do much to cheer Jane up. If this big girl thought the work was heavy, how was she herself going to cope?

The kitchen door was pushed open and the heat hit Jane immediately. She felt so thankful. She had left Chestnut Grove at five minutes past six and by the time she'd got here she was frozen to her very bones.

'This is Mrs Stratton, Cook to most of us in the house,' Clemmy said as she took Jane's mackintosh and hung it up in a cupboard. Mrs Stratton looked the typical cook:

short, dumpy, with a big bosom and rosy cheeks.

'Suppose yer could do with a cup of tea,' Cook said, and without waiting for an answer she pushed a big cup across the scrubbed tabletop, then, turning swiftly to the fireplace, took up from the hob a big enamel teapot. The tea in the pot must have been boiling, because it spluttered out of the spout as she poured it into the cup. Then she handed Jane a sugar basin, saying, 'Help yerself, you'll need to fortify yerself before you go upstairs to see 'er ladyship.'

As Jane sipped her tea, she was thinking that Mrs Bonneford had mentioned that it would be a person named Ada who would see to her uniform. It seemed that there were quite a number of people working in this household. She wondered how many family members there were besides the missus and her brother, Mr Harris.

'You won't get your uniform until Mrs Daniels comes in tomorrow,' Clemmy said, getting to her feet and indicating that Jane should follow her. 'She's left you an overall which will serve you for today.'

Seeing Jane hadn't quite understood, Clemmy explained: 'Ada Daniels is a widow. She comes here twice a week to do the washing and the ironing, sometimes three days if there are visitors staying in the house. I was told to set you on cleaning the main hall as soon as you arrived, so I'll show you where the the cleaning materials are kept.'

Jane followed Clemmy through the dark passageway, up the uncarpeted stairs and into the dreary-looking cold hall. She was certainly being thrown in at the deep end, was what she was thinking as she donned a dark-brown coat-like overall and wondered where she should start. The first thing she would have liked to do was light a fire in that massive hearth, but she supposed that was too much to ask for.

* * *

It took Jane a full week to get into the swing of things, and each day the tasks she was given seemed to be harder and dirty than the previous ones. From the minute she arrived in the morning until she left in the evening she was on the go all the time, with the exception of the thirty minutes allowed for her lunch. Her one consolation was Mrs Stratton, the cook. Though she presented a rough exterior and a loud voice, they covered a heart of gold, or at least they did where Jane was concerned. She put in front of Jane meals that were fit for a king. She also saw that there was a kettle of hot water at the ready so that Jane could have a good wash before she left for home.

Jane did most jobs without a word of protest. After all, she had known before she came here that she was to be a maid of all work. Yet her first task each morning was one that stuck in her gullet.

She had to attend Mrs Bonneford in her bedroom, which meant lugging a huge can of hot water all the way up the main staircase, then pouring it into a china bowl which was placed on a side table in order that her mistress could wash herself while remaining in bed. Meanwhile, Jane emptied the slop pail before going about whatever other tasks had been allotted to her for the day.

Then, when Clemmy blew a whistle, she had to come back up the stairs and carry the now dirty water back downstairs. All right, she was getting paid to do these tasks. But the fact was that Clemmy, being Mrs Bonneford's personal maid, was in the room all the time, always in full uniform: neat black dress, white starched apron and cap. Sometimes she would walk beside Jane in her drab grey uniform as she struggled either up or down the stairs with the water can, but never once did she offer to take a turn at carrying it.

Jane hadn't seen very much of Mr Harris, but the few

occasions they had met had reinforced her impression that he was a kind man. A true gentleman. Whereas his sister had never once uttered the words 'thank you'.

It was on the Thursday of the second week that Jane began to feel she was being asked to do too much. The minute Ada Daniels had arrived she had put what she called the white washing in to soak while she lit the fire beneath the copper. Then, calling for Jane to help her, they had dragged the long tin bath into the outhouse and all the coloured things had gone into that, together with a handful of soapflakes that had been grated off the big bar of yellow soap.

'All right, Jane, I'll manage nicely on me own now, you get yerself back indoors. I'm sure you've more than enough t' cope with.' Ada Daniels spoke kindly, for her heart went out to this young lass who she felt was being put upon rotten. Still, so far the lass seemed to be coping pretty well. But wait till the missus lost her temper. If Jane should be anywhere near when that had happened, then Gawd help her. The missus in a temper was not a pretty sight. In fact, if it were left to me, Ada was thinking, I'd say outright she should be put away in an asylum for some of the terrible things I've seen her do over the years. Jane walked thankfully back into the house. She was working in a bedroom on the first floor, doing her best to remove a stain from the carpet and not making a very good job of it, because she thought it was red wine which had probably been spilt the night before and allowed to soak in. Just as she had straightened up to take a breather, that was when she heard the scream and the commotion that followed.

She let it pass over her head and got on with what she was doing. Until she heard three sharp blasts on the whistle and knew she was being summoned.

Ada Daniels had slipped on the cobbles and banged her head hard and hurt her back.

Mrs Bonneford, dressed in full finery, stood several feet away from Jane and stared at her with a very odd smile on her face. Her weird expression had Jane feeling something was about to happen. It wasn't that she was afraid of her mistress. But she certainly was wary of her. Whenever Mrs Bonneford spoke directly to Jane, which wasn't very often, her words were always sharp, and although Jane tried to tell herself that it was just the woman's way, she knew it wasn't. She treats me like dirt and that's the truth of it, Jane admitted to herself.

'Jane, hurry and finish what you were doing and then take over from Ada. The washing has to be done, come what may, so don't be making any bones about it.' All this was said quickly before Mrs Bonneford made a dramatic departure from the room.

Jane just shook her head. This woman could not be civil if she tried.

She didn't think she would ever come to like her mistress.

As if reading her mind, Mr Harris, who had been standing behind his sister, said, 'Don't let her get to you. If she thinks she's got you cowed, she'll always be on at you.' He paused and smiled broadly at her as he added, 'But somehow, Jane, I think given the chance she might find she's met her match in you.'

Jane didn't answer, because if she had said what was really going through her mind she would surely have been shown the front door there and then.

Having been told by Cook what needed to be done, Jane got started.

Using the big ribbed wooden board, she scrubbed and then boiled the entire mass of washing that had been put in to soak. The steam from the copper was awful as she leant over, using a thick stick to lift each item out of the boiling water and then drop the next lot in. Every now and again she had to get down on her knees, open the little door at the base of the copper and feed into it more kindling in order to keep the water at boiling point.

Her hair was stuck to her head, her clothing to her body. She wasn't damp, she was soaking wet!

Now for the next stage, and by God, she murmured, that was the worst of the lot. Outside in the yard, especially after the heat of the outhouse, it was freezing cold. But it was out here that the great ugly-looking mangle stood. She took the oilskin cover off and stared in horror at the enormous wooden rollers and the mighty iron handle that she had to turn and keep on turning in order to squeeze all the water from the washed linen. It should be a job for two people, Jane was thinking to herself, as she did her best to fold the sheets and feed them between the rollers. 'God knows how I'm going to get this lot dry,' she muttered out loud, and nearly jumped out of her skin when Mr Harris's voice answered her.

'I've got a couple of lads coming in from the gardens to put up some clothes lines, one here in the outhouse and two in the big shed. I'll also get the gardener's wife to come and help you peg them up.' He patted her shoulder, saying, 'You've done a good job,' before turning and going back towards the house.

Jane sighed heavily. That was kind of him, yet it hadn't made her feel much better. Why? Because Cook had been out to tell her that Ada had been taken home on one of the carts because she couldn't straighten her back and so she wouldn't be turning up for work for some time.

When finally Jane left the house that evening, her legs

felt they could hardly carry her and every bone in her body ached.

Cook had said, 'Good night, luv, see yer tomorrow.'

Tomorrow! That held a lot of promise. A huge mountain of damp washing that would need to be ironed, and there wouldn't be any prizes for guessing who would get the job.

At ten o'clock the following morning, Jane was in the outhouse, and she didn't know how she was still standing on her feet. She had had an awful night. Before going to bed she would have given anything to have lain in a hot bath, but she had no idea how to work the geyser in the bathroom. She had put a shilling in the gas meter in her room and hung her clothes on the back of a chair because they had still felt so damp. That hadn't done much to improve things; the room had merely become very steamy.

It had taken a real effort to get herself to work this morning, and Cook had kindly said that she could tackle the ironing in the kitchen. That was fine. Heating the flat irons on the range, it was quite a pleasant task. But, feeling nicely warm, she had to make regular trips to the outhouse in order to fold the linen and bring it back into the house. Outside it was still freezing, and the outhouse was not only very cold but thoroughly damp.

Now she couldn't understand what was happening to her. It felt as if a tight band was wrapped around her chest and that two or three hammers were beating away inside her head as she moved the flat iron backwards and forwards across the surface of a linen sheet.

Clemmy had taken Mrs Bonneford's breakfast up on a tray some time ago, and although she was half expecting it, Jane jumped when she heard the shrill whistle.

She up-ended the iron on the corner of the range and

limped out of the kitchen, dragging herself up the stairs and into her mistress's bedroom. Mrs Bonneford was sitting up in bed, a pale-pink bed-jacket trimmed with swan's down draped around her shoulders, but it was Clemmy who said, 'You may remove the mistress's tray and bring the hot water up now.'

Going towards the bed to lift the tray from the bedside table, Jane glanced at Mrs Bonneford's face. The look on it was one of sheer disgust.

Jane took a step backwards, looking down at herself. Oh my goodness! she thought. She had forgotten to remove the sacking apron she had tied around herself in order to keep her body from coming in direct contact with the damp washing.

'How dare you come into my bedroom dressed like that!' Mrs Bonneford's voice was loud and harsh.

They stared at each other for a moment. Then her mistress was screaming at her: 'Get out, you're little more than a slut. Go on, do as I tell you, get out.'

Jane was so flustered, she dropped the tray.

The clatter it made was deafening. All hell was suddenly let loose.

Mrs Bonneford was using her fists to beat on the bedside table, emphasizing every word. Jane was pleading that she had come quickly in answer to the whistle and hadn't thought to get changed.

Mrs Bonneford would have none of it. 'Who do you think you are talking to, girl? I knew we should never have offered you employment. Dragged up, that's what you've been, in a home for unwanted children, but even they turned you out.'

How she got out of the room Jane never knew. She stood at the top of the stairs, blinded by tears, and didn't know how she was going to get down them. What that awful woman had said was so hurtful. She had not been dragged up. Everyone at Winchelsea Lodge had loved and cherished her. And from them she had learned about decency and kindness, dignity and courage. They had become her family. She *had* been wanted. They had truly loved her.

She tried to take a deep breath but the pain in her chest was too much.

She must get back downstairs. She lifted a foot, but her leg was so stiff she failed to find a step. She was going forward, falling, tumbling, and then suddenly she didn't care.

She felt her body go limp and then there were no more aches or pains.

Cook had heard her fall and came running immediately. She knelt beside her on the floor, trying hard to get her to open her eyes, to say something.

It was a few minutes before Jane did open her eyes. Cook breathed, 'Thank God,' as she touched the girl's face, but was troubled when she felt how dry and hot her cheeks were.

'You'll have to go home, Jane, no one can expect you to work, not the state that you're in,' she was saying when, looking up, she saw that Mr Harris was there.

'Let's get her up and into the kitchen,' he said, putting his hands under Jane's shoulders and endeavouring to get her up on to her feet.

'Is she going t' be all right? What ever happened upstairs? I could hear the mistress shouting from down here. Hadn't we better call a doctor?'

Jane was too dazed and too tired to even bother to answer.

Finally they had got her into the warmth of the kitchen and settled into a big armchair, which Mr Harris had drawn up close to the range. 'Cook, make her a hot drink and put lots of sugar into it. I'll be back as soon as I can.' At the doorway he paused, saying, 'Make sure she drinks it.'

When Cook offered Jane a cup of hot chocolate, she couldn't even hold it. She was shaking from head to foot. She felt so ill, but it no longer mattered to her. She was tired. All she wanted was to go to sleep and she didn't care if she never woke up again!

Cook supported her with one arm as she held the cup to Jane's lips.

'Come on, dearie, sip it for me, it will help to make you feel a whole lot better.'

Jane did her best to smile, but at this moment she couldn't think of a single thing that would make her feel any better.

She closed her eyes and slept.

She wasn't even aware that a doctor had bent over her and confirmed Mr Harris's fears by saying, 'This young lady has influenza and should be put to bed straight away.'

Cook cried as she listened. Too much had been asked of the lass!

'We can't keep her here.' Mr Harris voiced the words out loud.

Mrs Stratton had every sympathy with him. There was no need for him to explain further. If he were to attempt to keep Jane here and attend to her needs, he would be answerable to his sister. And the good Lord knew what that would mean. His own life would be made intolerable. She had seen it all before!

But that didn't alter the fact that Jane did have to be put to bed.

Mr Harris was shrugging himself into his overcoat and had reached for his hat before he spoke. 'I'll walk along to the corner and flag down a cab.' Then, seeing the astonishment on Cook's face, he heaved a great sigh and asked quietly. 'Do we have any alternative?'

Slowly she shook her head.

'Well, I'll give the cab driver her address and tip him enough to see her to the door.'

Cook heaved up her bosom and was about to say something when Mr Harris held up his hand and again spoke in little more than a whisper. 'Whatever it is you are thinking about me can't make me feel any worse than I already do. So, please, wake her up, get Clemmie to help you put her coat on, and between you get her to the back door.'

Cook woke Jane very gently and tried to get her to take a few more sips from her hot drink. Jane had neither the the desire nor the strength to swallow. She looked ill and her eyes were glazed . . .

'I have to get out of this house,' was all she managed to croak through dry lips.

Cook held her hand when she and Clemmie finally got her to the door. Looking at Jane sadly, she said, 'I wish there was some way I could take care of you, but if I lose this job I've nowhere to go. I will say one thing, though, you're well out of it here. You'll get better and find a much better job. You will, you'll see. Goodbye, lass.'

Jane did her best to squeeze Cook's hand.

She was too emotional to say anything.

Chapter Ten

WHEN THE CAB drew up at the corner of the street, it was raining hard, more like a freezing sleet and was still bitterly cold. Jane struggled to put one foot in front of the other. Only a few yards and she would be home. She tried to fix her eyes ahead; she had to get into the house.

The sight of Mrs Forrester coming towards her, holding a big umbrella, was enough to reduce Jane to tears.

It was to be many days before Jane realized just how good a friend her landlady had turned out to be.

Not only had Mrs Forrester helped her up the stairs, undressed her and got her into bed. She had also packed a hot-water bottle on each side of her, fed enough coins into the gas meter to keep it burning continually, and sat with her throughout the night. Jane had been delirious the whole time, shouting unintelligibly and muttering about things and people that Mrs Forrester had no knowledge of. The girl was running a high temperature, there was no doubt about that, and the landlady had been at her wits' end, not knowing what to do for the best. The minute it was daylight she had urged her husband to fetch a doctor.

The doctor had suggested that poultices be applied to Jane's chest and back at regular intervals, and had left a bottle of horrible bitter-tasting medicine to be given three times each day. It had been an almost impossible task to get Jane to swallow even a few drops; as Mrs Forrester spooned it into her mouth, it dribbled down her chin.

It was now the third day and Jane did not seem to be improving. Mrs Forrester decided she could not bear the responsibility on her own any longer. What if the child should die? Her own question frightened her. As soon as the doctor walked through the front door, she handed him a sheet of paper on which she had written the address of Winchelsea Lodge and the name Mrs Elsie Rogers.

'Please,' she begged. 'Will you get in touch with her? It was Mrs Rogers who came here and inspected the house and who paid a month's rent in advance for Jane. I do feel she should at least accept some of the responsibility.'

'Calm down, Mrs Forrester,' the doctor urged. 'You've coped remarkably well. Done your very best. Over and above the call of duty, I would say. So yes, you leave it with me.'

She offered him her heartfelt thanks. It would be a relief to have someone else involved in the girl's welfare.

Elsie Rogers did not waste any time. It was late in the evening of the same day when she appeared on Mrs Forrester's doorstep.

'How is she?' Elsie asked gently, fearing the worst, because she could tell from the look on Mrs Forrester's face that Jane couldn't be any better.

'Come an' see for yourself. I'm at me wits' end. I just can't think of anything else that we could do for her.'

But even that statement did not lead Elsie to expect to find Jane looking so dreadful. In these few days the illness seemed to have really taken its toll. Her face was grey, her cheeks sunken, and she was burning hot. As the two woman leant over the bed, the front door bell rang.

'It's all right, my husband will answer that,' Mrs Forrester said, straightening up. 'More than likely it is the doctor, he said he would call back this evening.'

Minutes later the bedroom door was pushed open and Mrs Forrester was making the introductions.

Elsie Rogers was greatly relieved to see the doctor, and murmured how grateful she was that he had contacted her. She was still so upset over the way Jane looked that she scarcely noticed what he was doing.

The two women stepped back from the bed, and it was some time before the doctor turned his attention to them. 'Her temperature is still very high, and she is dehydrated,' he told them, his face showing a dismal expression. 'I'm afraid you already know what I'm going to say . . . don't you?' he said, sounding deeply sympathetic.

'Please . . .' Elsie Rogers could say no more. She covered her face with her hands, for the moment too upset to cope. When she had composed herself she looked at the doctor seeking for him to reassure her.

He understood only too well. 'There isn't any thing else that I can do,' he said honestly. 'I will see if I can get her into a hospital, but the chances are very slim. This influenza has spread so quickly, there are not enough beds. All you can do is try to keep her temperature down by bathing her forehead with wet cloths, and if only you could get her to take liquids, as much as you can get her to swallow, that would help a great deal.' His tone was kind, but he didn't feel he could lie to these women.

He stayed a while, talking to Mrs Forrester while Elsie was already applying wet cloths as he had recommended.

Then, as he was taking his leave, he asked, 'Have you contacted her parents?'

Elsie sighed. 'I've reason to believe that I am the only person who really cares about her, but come tomorrow I will try to track down members of her family.'

Tomorrow may be too late, was what he was thinking, but what he actually said was, 'I wish there was more I could do for her . . . and for you . . . I can see how distressing this is for you.'

'For the last seven years I've been involved in her life, and to tell you the truth I've come to look upon Jane as the daughter I never had. There isn't anything that I wouldn't do for her.'

There was no answer to that, and the doctor felt utterly helpless as he followed Mrs Forrester down the stairs.

It was a long and lonely night for Elsie Rogers. She sat quietly by Jane's side, speaking softly to her, forcing water between her dry, cracked lips, making sure that the cloths on her forehead stayed wet and checking her pulse from time to time. And finally, as the morning light crept in, she felt that Jane was almost gone.

Mrs Forrester brought a tray of tea and offered to stay with Jane while Elsie went to the bathroom to freshen up. She also suggested that Elsie use her bedroom to try and get some rest. Elsie accepted the first offer but refused to leave Jane for any length of time.

At four o'clock that afternoon the doctor came again. The atmosphere in that big attic room was already one of despair, but as the doctor examined Jane she moaned and stirred uncomfortably, as though she were in pain. When he had finished, he straightened the sheet across Jane's chest, turned to the two women and gave them a weak smile.

'One can only marvel that she has hung on so long,' he said. 'Really it's remarkable. Has to be put down to the fact that she is so young, and that her physical condition is so good. But,' he sighed heavily, 'I have to say that she is nowhere near out of the woods yet. Not by a long chalk, I'm afraid.'

Two more days passed without much change

Elsie Rogers had given in to Mrs Forrester's plea and taken herself off for a walk. It was the first time she had been out of the house since her arrival. Having written three letters, she took this opportunity to post them. The most important was to Lillian Cooper, explaining why she had not yet returned to Winchelsea Lodge and urging Matron to use every power she had to trace Jane's mother and make her aware of just how ill her daughter was.

It was on her return, as she leant over the bed, that she heard Jane whimper. Then, quite suddenly, 'I'm so thirsty,' she muttered, in a voice that sounded ravaged.

'Oh, Jane, I'll get you a drink straight away,' Elsie said soothingly. She couldn't stop the tears from trickling down her face as she held Jane's head a little way off the pillow and placed a glass to her lips. The relief was overwhelming as Jane managed to swallow a few sips.

'Who are you?' Jane asked in a hoarse, ragged voice as her head rested once again on the pillow.

'Everything is all right, Jane. It's me, Mrs Rogers,' Elsie said, humouring her.

'Oh,' Jane murmured, sounding puzzled. Then she closed her eyes tiredly. 'No you're not,' she whispered. 'I haven't got her any more.'

These last words were spoken so sadly that they tugged at Elsie's heartstrings. She understood what was going through Jane's mind, but she couldn't let her continue to believe that once again she had been abandoned. She had to convince her that she was in safe hands. That there were people who cared very much about her and what happened to her. 'Everything is going to be fine,' she told her quietly. 'It is me. I'm here, and I'm going to stay here until you are really fit and well.'

Jane opened her eyes again.

'I don't believe you . . . Mrs Rogers said I had to be on my own,' she said, thrashing her arms frantically. Then she closed her eyes yet again, almost burying her head in the pillow.

The fact that Jane did not recognize her scared Elsie, but at the same time she felt pleased and relieved that at least the girl was able to mutter a few words.

When Mrs Forrester was told the good news, she urged Elsie not to celebrate too soon.

'But she is back with us,' Elsie insisted. 'It's just that her poor eyes are so sore she can't see properly and her mind hasn't yet grasped what has happened to her.'

'Well, she certainly seems to be a whole lot more peaceful. Maybe she'll sleep for a while now. Best thing that could happen if she does,' Mrs Forrester said, not wishing to dampen Elsie's hopes.

It was late afternoon of the next day when the doctor came again. He beamed at Elsie Rogers as he told how amazed he was at the vast improvement there was in Jane.

'How do you feel?' he asked the girl.

'Terrible,' she whispered.

'Of course you do,' he laughed. 'You're going to feel weak for some time to come, young lady, but you are going to be fine,' he reassured her. 'You're going to have rest, though, sleep a lot if you can and drink plenty,' and with that he held a glass of water to her lips, and this time her hands went around the glass and she held it and took several sips.

'Thank you,' she said, smiling wanly up at the doctor.

'I think it is these two ladies that you should be thanking. They've done a great deal more for you than I have.'

Elsie went to the top of the stairs with the doctor, closing the bedroom door behind her. 'What can we expect now?' she asked.

'Well, as you can see for yourself, she's as weak as a kitten, she won't recover that quickly,' he answered her honestly. 'She'll be surprised herself when she first tries to put a foot to the floor. She'll have to be patient, it will take time.'

'I understand,' Elsie said gratefully, racking her brains as to what provision she could now make for Jane's welfare. She shook hands with the doctor and walked slowly back into Jane's room. She looked down on this young girl she loved so much; she was sleeping, looking little more than a child. If Elsie had her way she would bundle her up in blankets, take her back to Winchelsea Lodge and look after until she was truly well and fit again. But that was not possible. The home belonged to the Guardians of the Poor, and they had already done their best for Jane, as they did for every child who came within their care. To single Jane out for preferential treatment would not be allowed. Yet there had been no response from Lillian Cooper about Jane's mother, or indeed any other living relative, so who, apart from Elsie herself, was there who would be willing to accept responsibility?

She could find no answer to that question.

She stayed two more days, until she was quite sure that Jane was out of danger. Then, very cautiously, she approached Mrs Forrester and asked her if she would be able to provide meals for Jane until she could fend for herself.

'My dear, that's the very least I can do. I'll take her on

willingly,' was the quick response, and Elsie heaved a great sigh of relief. 'Really, I mean it. I know you have to get back to your work, but please, rest assured I won't let her want for anything. At least for the time being, I promise you, I will do what I can for Jane.'

From her own pocket Elsie left enough money to cover Jane's food and toiletries, and she also passed over another month's rent for the bed-sitting room. When these arrangements had been completed, she stood up and held out her hand. 'I know Jane will be all right with you, but if she should slip back or seem at all unhappy, you will let me know, won't you? I'll be back just as soon as I can.'

'Jane will be fine now,' Mrs Forrester said with a warm smile. 'I promise. We've surely become good friends by now, good enough for you to trust me.'

'Of course.' Elsie returned the smile. 'I really don't know how to thank you. I shall always be grateful to you.'

'I keep telling you, no need for thanks. You just go back to you job and try not to worry, or else it will be you who is looking for somewhere to live.'

Elsie held out her arms. It was a special moment as the two women who had hardly known each other before Jane had been taken ill thought back over the nightmare of the past days. They hugged each other in silence, relieved, knowing how near they had come to losing Jane. A minute or two later they each had to wipe tears away from their eyes, but they were smiling as they did so.

'I'll just go back upstairs and have half an hour with Jane before I set off,' Elsie said from the doorway of the Forresters' comfortable living room, thinking how lucky she had been when looking for a room for Jane. This landlady had proved not only to be very kind, but a friend in need.

Poor Jane had been rejected by her own mother but had

had what Elsie hoped were several happy years at Winchelsea Lodge. To be turned out on her own to face an unknown world seemed so unfair. And yet somehow Jane had survived.

But what now?

Elsie sighed deeply, her heart aching, as she put her arms around Jane to say goodbye. The girl looked desperately unhappy, but not nearly as unhappy as Elsie herself was. She felt so responsible and at the same time so helpless.

'Bye-bye, Jane,' she said again, in a voice filled with regret.

Jane felt her knees wobble as Elsie let go of her. She had to sit down; all she could think of was that once again she would be on her own, and the prospect of having to find another job was absolutely terrifying.

'I'll see you again just as soon as I can,' Elsie said from the doorway.

Jane managed to raise a hand and wave, but words were beyond her.

All the way back to Winchelsea Lodge, Elsie could think of nothing other than what was to become of Jane. Whichever way she turned it over in her mind, there was no simple answer.

Life for Jane was going to be anything but easy.

Chapter Eleven

'I'VE BROUGHT YOU a nice piece of fish for your lunch,' Mrs Forrester said, looking carefully at Jane, knowing her suspicions had been correct. She was looking really mournful. 'I said to me 'usband, it's not a bad day, if we wrap up well we might take Jane for a short walk this afternoon. You've been cooped up here long enough and I got the idea you might be feeling lonely.'

'I was,' Jane confessed sheepishly. 'I just can't seem to get used to the idea that I have to live on my own. I suppose you think I'm daft.'

'Of course I don't,' she said, setting the lunch tray down in front of Jane, pulling a chair up next to her bed and sitting beside her. 'For years you've been living in a community of young girls, it's only natural that you're going to miss them all. It was like throwing a non-swimmer into the deep end of a swimming bath when they sent you out all on your own. If you don't feel like going out just yet, will you come downstairs every day and sit in our front room? At least there you can see people going by and tradesmen making their deliveries. What d'you say?'

'Thank you,' Jane said gratefully. 'I'd like that, and perhaps tomorrow we can go for a walk.'

'Well, eat your dinner,' Mrs Forrester insisted, removing the plate that covered the meal, 'and when I come back for the tray you can come downstairs with me.'

And so began a pattern that was to put new heart into Jane and help a great deal towards her recovery.

As Jane's strength returned, her mind turn to her everyday problems. She had been told that it was Mrs Rogers who had settled her immediate money matters, which left her feeling under an obligation and determined to do something about it as soon as possible.

With so much time on her hands, her thoughts had turned to other subjects. Most importantly of all was her family. If they still lived in Tooting, she was only a penny tram ride away. Should she visit? Would they be pleased to see her? She hoped her mother would be, but as to her father, she wasn't at all sure. She was a coward, she knew that much. They say absence makes the heart grow fonder, she mused. Would that apply in her father's case? There was only one way to find out what their reaction might be!

And wouldn't it be lovely to see her mum and Tommy? He'd be a grown lad by now. Her last thought before she fell asleep that night was that her mind was made up. She was going to do it.

It was just turned ten o'clock the next morning when she alighted from the tram at Tooting Broadway.

Nothing much had changed. For a moment she stood still on the pavement, comparing her surroundings with those of Rye and Winchelsea. Women were out doing their shopping, barrow boys were shouting their wares, the streets was strewn with litter and the smell was vastly different. There was a strong wind blowing, but it wasn't coming fresh off the sea.

She crossed the road and walked until she came to Selkirk Road. Down past the pie and eel shop, the fish and chip shop on the other side of the road, the oil shop where she had so often gone for paraffin and candles for her mother. Now she was passing the turning that led to Graveney Road and on past several houses until she reached number twenty-three, the house in which she had been born.

Her heart was beating nineteen to the dozen as she looked at the front gate, which was hanging on only one hinge. The paintwork of the front door was badly scarred, as if someone had tried to kick it in. The curtains at the windows were tatty and the steps, which her mother had always kept so white, hadn't seen hearthstone in many a long day.

It took a great deal of courage, but eventually Jane went down the path and lifted the knocker. The door was opened by an adorable little boy whose hair was a mass of golden curls. 'Is . . . your mummy in?' Jane asked bending her knees to be on his level.

'Mum, a lady wants yer,' he shouted back down the passage.

A young, tired-looking woman appeared, holding a baby in her arms. 'Yes, what is it?' she asked.

'I've come to see Mrs Jeffrey, but . . . it doesn't look as if she still lives here.'

The young woman stared at Jane for a moment, then said, 'I ain't never 'eard of her. I've lived here for four years and it was a Mrs Chapman that moved out when me an' me 'usband moved in. Sorry I can't 'elp yer, I've got t' go,' and with that she tugged at the boy with her free hand and kicked the front door shut.

Nancy! That was the thought that came into Jane's head, and she clung to it as a drowning man would cling to a piece of driftwood.

Last house in the street, she repeated to herself over and over again as she walked the length of Selkirk Road.

She had to knock three times before the door was opened. Then she was looking at an enormous body that almost filled the narrow passageway, but she couldn't believe this was her dear friend Nancy, because she hadn't remembered her being this size. The face was the same, though. 'Thank God,' Jane murmured, then the words came tumbling out. 'Nancy, oh Nancy, I am so pleased that you're still here.'

The woman was bending forwards, her huge breasts almost bursting out from her blouse. She tugged her cardigan more tightly around herself and stared hard at Jane. 'Is it? It can't be . . . Is it you, young Janey? In the name of God! It is.'

The next minute she had her arms round Jane and was holding her tight, not saying a word, just holding her close.

Now she was pulling Jane into the house and closing the door behind her.

'Come in. Come on, lass, come in.' She was now using both her hands to haul Jane along the passage and into a room where a young woman sat beside the fire with two crying children beside her and a baby on her lap.

'Be quiet, you kids,' Nancy bawled at them, and they all looked towards Nancy and Jane.

Now their mother got to her feet, lifted the baby on to her hip and, with a sweep of her hand, pushed the two boys across the room. Then, turning to Nancy, she said, 'I'll get out of yer way now you've got a visitor, I'll see yer later.'

'They live upstairs,' Nancy said by way of explanation. 'Worst day's work I ever done when I let me rooms to that tribe. But never mind about them just now. What about you? Sit yerself down an' I'll get yer a cup of tea.'

While Nancy busied herself out in the scullery, Jane sat still and took stock of her surroundings. This living room was bringing back such memories! The same faded wall-paper, damp patches in several places, crowded with large furniture. Then suddenly there was a banging and a shouting coming from overhead. Foul swear words were being hurled. Jane shuddered. Hurtful memories came flooding back. She felt she knew exactly what was going on up there.

There would be the young mother, who hadn't looked very clean, trying hard to cope with three children; probably the eldest of them wasn't even four years old. The father was in a temper from the sound of it, lashing out in desperation, feeling useless because five of them were living in two rooms.

Nancy came back with a steaming cup and handed it to Jane. 'Shut yer ears t' that lot,' she said, raising her eyebrows and nodding towards the ceiling. 'She's nineteen years old, already worn out 'cos that last baby never stops crying day or night. Her 'usband's a local lad, Ron Berry. Used t' be a decent lad; at least he married her when she found she was in the family way. His parents ain't badly off, took them in first off, but things went from bad t' worse and when he lost his job and just 'ung about the 'ouse all day they chucked 'em out. Can't say I blame them. Poor Ron only 'as t' lay his trousers on the end of the bed and she's pregnant again.'

She stopped talking, let out a great belly laugh and put her plump arm across Jane's shoulders. 'Now, how about telling me what's been 'appening to you all these years, 'cos yer know, I've never forgiven yer mother for going off the way she did without so much as a goodbye.'

Jane smiled weakly. 'I went to the house first. I was hoping my mum and dad might still be living there, and I did so want to see Tommy. When did they move?'

Nancy plonked herself down on to a chair and rested her elbows on the table before she said, 'Drink yer tea and I'll fry yer a bit of breakfast in a minute, when I get rid of some of these.' The last statement referred to a couple of mugs and a few greasy plates that were lying on the table. All the time thoughts were running through her head that were making her feel terrible. Surely someone must have told this poor lass what had gone on in her so-called family? Suddenly she raised her head and looked straight at Jane. 'Ain't you 'ad any contact with yer mum at all since the authorities put you away?'

'No, Nancy. Not a word. I did write a couple of times when I first went to Winchelsea Lodge, but I never had a reply.'

'Well, lass . . .' Nancy considered for a moment. 'I hate t' think that I've got t' be the one to set yer straight, but it don't seem like there's anyone else in line for the job.' She lumbered to her feet. 'I'll get you another cup of tea before I start.' She placed a hand on Jane's silky hair, adding, 'You've grown into such a beautiful young lady, very much like I remember yer mum looking when she first came to live here.'

When Jane had drunk her second cup of tea, she looked to where Nancy had seated herself and said, 'You were going to tell me about my mother.'

Nancy turned her head and looked towards the fire, saying, 'I'm trying to decide where to start.' Then, wetting her lips, she went on, 'I suppose first off it's best if I tell you, Mickey Jeffrey was not your father.'

The silence in the room was deafening.

Nancy heaved a great sigh before beginning again. 'That's

the reason he saw to it that you were never given any favours. In fact he was downright mean to you. Well, now you know why he acted as he did, not that that's any reason to make excuses for him. He knew when he married yer mother what he was letting himself in for. Yer mum was pregnant by another man.'

Jane didn't look at Nancy. Was she troubled by what she'd just heard? Difficult to say really. At the moment relief might be a better word. At least the knowledge went a long way to settling so many unanswered questions.

''Twas a long time ago, I know, but yer mum paid over an' over again for something that was not her fault. During the time when Mickey was going heavy on the booze, he led her a dreadful life.'

From the odd things that Jane could remember from her early childhood, she knew that her mother had indeed led a terrible life: bleak, without love or even affection; in fact it always seemed as if she lived in fear. But of what, Jane had never known. Now at least she had some idea. She closed her eyes tightly and her fingernails dug into her palms.

'It's no good, lass, I can't stop now,' Nancy said reluctantly. 'There's so much more you need to know, and like it or not, it seems that I 'ave t' be the one t' do the telling. There's no way of wrapping it up. Are you all right?'

Jane just couldn't bring herself to look at Nancy. In her mind's eye, she could imagine the beatings her mother had taken, and now she realized that it was because Alice had given birth to her that her husband had been so cruel to her.

Nancy waited for an answer but there was none forthcoming. She thought that Jane looked as if she were overcome with weariness and sadness. I have to tell her the rest, she decided sadly. Heaving her bosom high, she took a deep breath.

'About a year after you was taken away, young Tommy was admitted to the Grove 'ospital. He died three days later. Scarlet fever, they said it was.'

Nancy paused, giving Jane time to take in the terrible news that her little brother was no longer alive.

'Your mother was distraught. Mickey was calm enough until after the funeral, and then he let fly. Oh my God! What he did t' yer mother doesn't bear thinking about. She almost died. In fact, when the ambulancemen arrived they thought at first she was dead. She never came back to this street . . . but from what I've learned since – an' maybe it's only hearsay – it was Wally Simmonds that took her out from the 'ospital. What I can tell yer, lass, is that neither of them 'ave ever been seen in these parts from that day t' this. I've 'oped an' prayed that the pair of them 'ave made a new life together somewhere an' at last yer mother may 'ave found a bit of 'appiness. God knows she deserves it.'

In these last few minutes Jane felt she had lost everything.

Her young brother dead! It was more than she could bear. Tommy . . . oh, she had loved him so much. And he had loved her. She had felt she was on her own before now, but always at the back of her mind was the fact that somewhere she had parents and a brother. Now even they had been taken away from her.

Her father had never been her father! That fact didn't worry her too much. But she was never going to be able to see her beloved brother ever again. Her mother had been beaten half to death and no one knew where she was now.

If she hadn't been sitting down, she would have fallen down. She felt weak and slightly sick.

She leaned her head back against the chair. It began slowly, the tears just welling up in her eyes and dropping

down from her lashes on to her cheeks. Then like a swollen
river it became a torrent. She fell forward, buried her face
in her hands and sobbed as though her heart was breaking.

Nancy let her be.

She emptied the teapot and stood it on the hob; she'd
make a fresh brew later. Then, bending down, she took a
hearth brush and swept the loose ashes under the grate
before turning once more to the table and the sad figure of
Jane. She's nothing but a slip of a lass, she thought sadly,
and she must be feeling that the whole world is against her.

'Aw, lass,' she whispered, taking one of Jane's hands
between both of her own and squeezing it gently. 'I wish it
'adn't 'ad t' be me what told yer all this. I'm gonna get us
a bit of a meal now, but before we leave the subject I want
yer to listen to me. Will you do that?'

Jane sniffed and raised her head. Her bright-blue eyes
looked straight at Nancy and the sadness in them tore at
Nancy's heartstrings. What I wouldn't give to be able to
make life a lot easier for this young girl, she said to herself.
They say God makes the burden to fit the back: well, all I
can say is he got it bloody well wrong in her case. Still barely
more than a slip of a girl, she's had more troubles in her
young life than most kids have had hot dinners. And what
can I do about it?

The answer was not a lot, and sadly that was the plain
truth of the matter.

Nancy lumbered off towards the scullery again and came
back with a wet face flannel. Gently taking Jane's face in
one hand, she washed it, all the while softly murmuring:
'It's been a rough old morning for yer, 'asn't it, my love?
But I want you to remember that you're welcome here each
an' every day that yer feel like coming. Wasn't it always t'
me that yer ran when yer dad . . . sorry, lass, yer know what

I mean . . . when Mickey was in a temper? Well, I'm still here an' always will be for yer.'

With a clean towel she dried Jane's face, and her voice was low when again she began to talk. 'There's one thing yer mum did tell me after you went away, and that was that she thought she had done the best thing possible for you. I know for a fact that she lived in fear that Mickey would do you a terrible injury one day. And as things turned out, she wasn't far wrong. She took her time making up her mind, yer know. It wasn't an easy decision. It almost broke her heart to let you go. In the end it was only after she had been told that the home you would be sent to was a very good one, and the folk that ran it had assured her that you'd be well cared for. I saw yer mum the day she came back from saying goodbye to you at the 'ospital, an' believe me, she was in a terrible state. Was it true that the people in the home were good to you?'

Jane nodded her head slowly. 'Yes, that's perfectly true. And you know, Nancy, you're the first person I've heard talk about my mother in all these years. I know now that she did do what she thought was best for me at that time. What I can't understand is why she didn't keep in touch.'

Nancy didn't answer for a moment. She had heard rumours, but that was all they were. She had no way of knowing if there was any truth in them. So all she said was, 'Maybe she was still very ill when Wally Simmonds took her out of the 'ospital. Don't know exactly where they went: some say to Australia, others say Canada.'

Still looking at each other, they both held out their hands and, taking hold, Nancy said quietly, 'Give yerself time, Jane, get some order into your life, and then perhaps you can start making a few enquiries.'

Nancy bustled about frying sausages and making mashed

potatoes, but when she put her head round the door and saw that Jane had slipped down in the armchair and was fast asleep, she sighed thankfully and placed their two dinners in the oven.

Food could wait, she decided. Sleep would do the girl far more good.

It was late in the afternoon as Nancy stood on her doorstep watching Jane walk away. They had talked for ages. She knew all about the disaster of Jane's first job, and hoped and prayed that she'd have better luck next time.

When Jane reached the corner of the street she turned round to see that Nancy was still standing there waving to her. 'I'll see you again soon,' Jane called loudly.

For answer Nancy nodded enthusiastically.

You can't go by appearances, Jane was saying to herself as she walked towards the tram stop. She'd learned that much today. Nancy might still look a bit untidy, and she was most certainly very fat, but beneath all that she was still the loving, caring person Jane had known as a child.

At least there was one person who was still there for her.

Chapter Twelve

THERE WERE TIMES during the next three weeks when Jane felt she was never going to be able to find a suitable job. She had been taken on at the Merton Box Factory, but after only three days they had told her she wasn't quick enough and not to come back.

If it wasn't for the fact that she had Nancy to call in to for a chat, she didn't know how she would have filled her days. It seemed most of the jobs on offer were for secretaries, but shorthand and typing lessons had never been available to children who were being educated by the Guardians of the Poor.

On her way home from another fruitless trip to the Labour Exchange, her mind was on money matters. Mrs Forrester had turned out to be such a good friend. Each and every day now she insisted that Jane have her evening meal with her and her husband. That was all very well, and Jane was very grateful, but it could not go on for ever. There was also the matter of the rent. It was about time that she stood on her own two feet, but how or when she was going to be able to do that she had no idea.

When she reached home to find Elsie Rogers standing in the hall talking to Mrs Forrester, she was overwhelmed with joy. Having been hugged and listened to a hurried whisper, 'Can't wait to tell you some really good news,' Jane was filled with excitement. No matter if she hadn't seen Mrs Rogers for a few weeks or merely a couple of days, it was always the same. Relief and a feeling of being loved.

Today was no exception.

Hardly inside Jane's room, Elsie could contain herself no longer. 'I'm staying the night here and tomorrow I am taking you to see a beautiful house where I am almost sure a job is waiting for you.' She blurted the words out.

'Oh, really?' Jane managed to mutter. Thinking, I've had one experience of working in a big house and I didn't come off too well. Then she smiled and leaned forward to kiss Elsie's cheek. 'You always manage to put in an appearance when I need you most. I have a lot to tell you but I'm not too sure about this job, even if it is in a beautiful house. Where is it?'

'Hold your horses,' Elsie laughed. 'Let's have some tea and then we can talk to our hearts' content. By the way, it's an early night for you because we have a car coming for us tomorrow. The driver will be here by eight o'clock and we must be ready.'

Now Jane was really intrigued. She had so much to tell and so much to find out.

Talk they did. Until a very tired but very excited Jane climbed into bed.

Even Mrs Forrester was impressed as she stood in her doorway and watched as a uniformed chauffeur held the door of his shiny black car open while Jane and Mrs Rogers settled themselves in the back seat. Jane's feelings were mixed.

Having told Mrs Rogers the sad news that Tommy had died and that her mother had disappeared, probably with Wally Simmonds, she had been heartened by being informed that there were ways and means by which people could be traced. With a firm promise from Mrs Rogers that she would do everything in her power to help, Jane had brightened up. Now her worry was where were they going and what kind of job was facing her when they got there.

As the scenery changed and London was left behind, Jane's mood ran from eager to impatient, at times excited, and finally, as she felt the area was strangely familiar, worked up. She knelt up on the back seat and stared out of the window before saying:

'Mrs Rogers, our chauffeur has just driven through Rye!'

'I thought you might notice once we hit the cobbled high street.' Elsie laughed loudly.

'But surely we're not going back to Winchelsea Lodge, are we?'

Jane half wanted to be told that yes, that was where they were going, but the other half of her was very apprehensive. It would be such a wrench to see the dear place and all her friends, knowing that it could only be for a fleeting visit.

'No, Jane, we've already passed the road that leads to Winchelsea. The next village on our route will be Peasmarsh and the one after that is Northiam. The house we are making for is about halfway between the two.'

When they had set out, a thin mist had masked London, but now they were in Sussex the sun had come out and the countryside was really showing signs of spring. There were new-born lambs in the fields and Jane stared at them, her face showing how delighted she was.

Now the car was turning into a wide lane.

'Nearly there. Are you all right?' Mrs Rogers asked her.

'Yes, I'm fine,' Jane smiled. 'I'd almost forgotten how lovely the countryside can look.'

'A good view of the house is just coming up,' Elsie said as the car turned a corner.

Adelaide House stood in front of them, tall trees to either side. The sun reflecting light from every pane of the many windows gave the impression that the whole house was glowing with warmth. The chauffeur brought the car to a halt in front of this magnificent house.

They crossed the numerous flagstones in silence. The massive front door under its stone arch was already standing open. A tall, grey-haired gentleman waiting at the top of the entrance steps smiled a greeting, saying, 'Good morning, Mrs Rogers, Miss Christy is expecting you. She is in her small sitting room on the first floor.'

'Thank you, Mr Wilson. Elsie smiled as they passed through into the large hall and made for the staircase.

There was a faint smell of lavender, and as a shaft of sunlight from the high window at the turn of the stairway struck across their heads, Jane looked upwards. The walls were wood-panelled and there was the dull gleam of gilt picture frames. A huge chandelier was suspended by three chains, and there were many beautiful curtains, all tied back with heavy tasselled ropes.

In a voice that was little more than a whisper, Jane said, 'It's beautiful.'

She thought the house in which she had worked for Mrs Bonneford had been lovely, but now she saw how different Adelaide House was.

Its old-world beauty was timeless and majestic.

Mrs Rogers tugged at her arm and she followed obediently into a room whose French doors gave a view of never-ending gardens. The curtains and the covers for groups of chairs were made from a rich yellow brocade, but they had obviously had a lot of use, as had the big comfortable sofa. On small side tables there were tall crystal vases full of fresh flowers, the scent of which filled the air. The room as a whole had a feeling of old-world elegance and luxury from a bygone age.

Almost as if time stood still within these walls.

As she took all of this in, looking around her wide-eyed, Jane was scared. Yet she was filled with a curious kind of excitement, such as she had never felt before.

She really had no idea why she was here, except that Mrs Rogers had said there might be the possibility of a job. What kind of a job? What on earth was she capable of doing in such a beautiful place? She crossed her fingers behind her back, praying that she hadn't been misled and that whatever the job entailed she would get it.

And more to the point, be able to do it!

A lady who appeared to be in her late forties rose to her feet as they crossed the room, and Jane immediately thought that never before had she encountered anyone more elegant. Her thick fair hair was coiled up, she wore a dress and loose-fitting coat of palest-pink flimsy material, and her shoes were a soft grey leather worn with sheer grey silk stockings.

'Jane, this is my dear friend Christine Dennison.' Elsie Rogers made the introduction after she and the woman had kissed each other lightly on the cheek.

Mrs Dennison's hand, as Jane shook it, felt soft to the touch, and the smile she gave lit up her face and was enough to make Jane feel that not only was this person beautiful, but a true lady.

'Please come and sit by the window. Very soon now all

the green slopes will be covered in daffodils. Do you like gardens?' Mrs Dennison asked.

Jane stared at her, then, finding her voice, quickly said, 'Oh yes, very much.'

When they were all three seated, Mrs Dennison said, 'I'll ring for some refreshments and then I'll explain to Jane why I asked you to bring her here today.'

While they were waiting, Elsie and her friend spoke in low tones, catching up with each other's news, both business and personal. Jane didn't mind. She moved her chair nearer to the window. One part of the ground was covered in crocuses, and some trees were already leafy green while others were only now awakening from their winter rest. In the distance a lake could be seen, so large that Jane wondered how it came to be in someone's garden. It looked like a vast patch of silver as the water glistened in the sunshine.

There was a tap at the door and a maid entered, pushing a trolley. Behind her walked a man. The very sight of him had Jane catching her breath.

'Hello, Mother,' he said, putting his hands on Mrs Dennison's shoulders and kissing her on both cheeks. Then, turning, he did the same to Mrs Rogers.

Elsie looked a little flustered as he stood back and glanced at Jane.

'This is my ward that I have spoken of so often,' she told him, then, turning her head, added, 'Jane, this is Charles Dennison.'

Jane made to get to her feet, but he gently pushed her back down. Then, taking her hand in both of his, he said, 'I am really pleased to meet you and I truly hope things will work out well for both you and my mother.'

Jane couldn't understand what he was talking about, but decided to let events take their course rather than start asking questions. But her mind was racing. The moment she had stepped through the doorway of this house she had known it was a very special place. Even the people were different.

Charles Dennison was twenty-five years old but looked thirty, maybe because he had that worldly look about him. He certainly was a good-looking man with a great deal of personal style. He appeared self-confident and very composed.

There was no mistaking he was his mother's son. The same thick fair hair, eyes such a bright blue and a wide mouth that seemed to have a smile about it at all times.

He half smiled at everyone, turned on his heel and headed towards the door, saying, 'I'll see you tomorrow, Mother.'

'What? You're not staying for lunch, Charles?' Mrs Dennison sounded surprised.

'Sorry, Mother, things to do today.'

For a few minutes after he had left there was complete silence in the room. Then, very sadly, Christine Dennison lifted her head and, staring at Elsie, said, 'I think maybe Charles has met his Waterloo.'

Elsie leaned back against the soft cushions of the sofa. 'He hasn't had much luck with the ladies since Maureen died, has he?'

'No. I'm afraid you've never said a truer word, Elsie. Maureen was exactly right for him. Such an untimely death. I still feel for her parents. One doesn't expect one's children to go before oneself. To die at the age of twenty-one doesn't seem fair. There was no meaning in it. None at all.'

Jane felt uncomfortable. Should she be listening to this conversation?

'And now?' Elsie left the question up in the air.

Mrs Dennison turned to face Jane, who by now was

making a great pretence of sipping the cup of coffee the maid had poured for her. 'I'm so sorry, my dear, we did not intend to exclude you from our conversation. Charles's affairs are the reason you are here. So, very briefly, my son has left home. He has set up with a married lady and her teenaged daughter. Which rather restricts my way of living.' Christine paused, obviously upset.

Elsie got to her feet. 'Would you like me to outline the situation to Jane?'

'I'd be grateful,' Christine said.

'Jane, you probably haven't noticed, but Mrs Dennison cannot see very well. She is fine whilst she is in familiar surroundings, but at a loss when it comes to going out, and for her to read at the moment is an impossibility. That's where you come in. After I opened up my heart to her as to what a trying time you have experienced since leaving Winchelsea Lodge, she came up with the suggestion that you might like to come and live here with her and act as her companion.'

Jane's fingers flew to cover her mouth, otherwise she would have let out a few loud words in utter astonishment.

'You would of course receive a salary.' Christine Dennison spoke kindly.

If they dangle any more carrots I shall think I've died and gone to heaven! was what Jane was saying to herself. Come here to live! Even Winchelsea Lodge didn't bear any comparison. And it certainly was a different world to Tooting. Only yesterday Nancy had said that as soon as she got rid of her lodgers Jane could come and live with her in Selkirk Road. In fact, Nancy had gone to great lengths to point out that Jane would be doing her a big favour. 'I'd be right glad of yer company,' was how she'd put it.

Back in the street where Jane had been born, probably

with a job up the market or helping out on one or another of the street stalls.

Yesterday that kind offer had seemed like a lifeline.

Now this!

'Please don't look so alarmed,' Christine implored. 'You wouldn't have any rough work to do, nor anything really personal for me. I manage fairly well. Mainly I would love to have someone who wouldn't mind reading to me. Even the daily newspaper is denied me now, and a trip to a book-shop is a long-gone pleasure. Elsie has told me so much about you. Please, at least say you will think about it.'

Jane looked at this elegant lady in total disbelief.

'You want me . . . to come here . . . live in this lovely house . . . just to read to you?'

'Oh, I think we shall be able to find you a few more duties than that.'

Jane spread her hands out wide as if she were clutching at the chance, 'This can't be true, it can't be happening.'

When Elsie had first spoken about Jane and the desper-ate situation she was in, Christine had felt she wanted to help, though at the same time she'd been sceptical, wonder-ing what type of girl she'd be. But she'd taken an instant liking to Jane.

'It would be beneficial to both of us,' she assured her.

Elsie Rogers' hands were clenched tight in her lap. She had worried herself sick from the day that Jane had left Winchelsea Lodge. The girl was so young, so innocent to be out in the world entirely on her own. God knows she hadn't had much of a life so far. She deserved a break, and when Christine had suggested she came here as her compan-ion it had been an answer to Elsie's prayers. Looking across at Jane now, her pale cheeks flushed and her eyes sparkling, Elsie thought that she was growing into a lovely young lady, and she hoped and prayed that those looks would not be her downfall in life.

Finally, Jane pushed herself up out of her chair, glancing first at Mrs Rogers and then at Mrs Dennison. She saw again the flawless complexion of this attractive lady and just could not believe that her beautiful big blue eyes were almost sightless.

Very hesitantly she murmured, 'I would love to come here to live, but there still doesn't sound as if there would be very much for me to do.'

Both Elsie and Christine burst out laughing.

A few minutes ticked by before Mrs Dennison said, 'Well, Jane, if that is the only objection you wish to make, may I take it that my dear friend Elsie has solved my problems by finding me a charming companion?' She asked the question very slowly and very quietly, giving Jane even more time to realize that she truly wanted her to become her companion.

Jane turned to face Mrs Rogers. My God, she thought, you've done me some favours since I was eight years old, but this goes beyond all comprehension. Having got a nod and a wide smile from her benefactor, she walked slowly to stand in front of the lady she hoped would be her employer for a long time to come, and in a voice she hardly recognized herself said, 'I'd be more than happy to work for you.'

'And I,' Christine smiled, 'will be happy to have you as a companion. Now, I'm sure you would like to see over the house. There's just about enough time before we go down to lunch, I'll have Mary take you round.' She raised an arm, felt along the wall and tugged at a bell-rope. A different maid from the one that had brought in the refreshments appeared within minutes, and when she was asked to show Jane over the house, her rosy cheeks broke into a big grin and she said, ''Twill be my pleasure, Miss Christy.'

* * *

Jane followed Mary obediently through a long gallery, look-ing out at another view of the gardens beneath the windows. Another maid came out of a bedroom; it was the same girl who had brought the coffee, her arms now full of bed linen. She stopped and smiled, and Mary introduced her as Sarah. Jane looked at them both with interest, noticing their short hair and their calf-length skirts. She felt dowdy and plain. Her blonde hair had darkened to a rich golden colour and grown almost to shoulder length. It seemed such a long time ago that she had had it done at the hairdresser's in Rye, the one and only time it had been cut professionally. Her blue skirt reached almost to her ankles and was very faded. Her boots, for which she had been so grateful when it had been snowing, now looked worn and heavy as she glanced down at them. How she envied the pretty shoes the two maids wore. They were shiny black with little heels, rounded toes and a thin strap over the instep. They looked so light and so comfortable. She promised herself that one day she would walk into a shoe shop and buy herself a pair of shoes like that. It would be the first brand-new pair she had ever owned.

There were family rooms as well as formal ones. Mrs Dennison's bedroom was so feminine, with pretty curtains and a bedcover that matched. Her son Charles's room looked very orderly, with silver-backed brushes laid out on top of the tallboy. At the end of the corridor there was a nursery with a well-used rocking horse and shelves of children's books and games. Mary saw the curious look on Jane's face and explained, 'Mrs Dennison's sister comes to stay quite often, and she has five children. Or at least she used to; the children are like Master Charles, mostly grown up now.'

They wandered the rooms together, even the very top

floor, where the female staff shared rooms. Mary told Jane that the cook and the butler were a married couple, and they lived in the lodge which stood to one side of the house, near to where the stables were. Stables? That meant horses, and Jane wasn't too sure that she would want to come into close contact with those great creatures.

As Mary continued to talk about the house, her love for it and the family showed clearly and it went a long way to calming Jane's nerves.

They came back to the ground floor by the back stairs, and threaded their way through what seemed to Jane a warren of stone-flagged kitchens. Finally, they walked along a narrow and rather chilly corridor and then into a large cheerful kitchen. It smelt of roasting meat and savoury pies. There were two people there, a large, plump but happy-looking woman and a girl Jane judged to be a couple of years younger than herself.

Mary said, 'This is Jane Jeffrey.' Turning, she added, 'This is Mrs Wilson, our cook, and that young lass is Daisy, she's our tweeny, used to be our scullery maid but she was good and so she got promoted.'

Jane blushed as they stared at her.

Mrs Wilson got up from her chair. 'So, you may be coming to live here as eyes and ears for Mrs Dennison?'

'Oh, nothing is settled yet,' Jane hastened to assure her. Then she added, 'But hopefully.'

'Well, lass, you could travel much further and fare a whole lot worse than coming here to live.'

Jane was saved from having to answer by the ringing of a bell.

'That's to announce that lunch is ready,' Mrs Wilson smiled. 'Mary, take Jane to the dining room, for it's as sure as eggs are eggs she'll never find her own way there.'

When Jane was seated next to Mrs Rogers she felt nervous. There were only three places set but the table was so long and the room so grand.

Elsie leant nearer, patted her knee and gave her a re-assuring smile. At one end of the room there was a stone hearth with an open basket filled with burning logs. There were family photographs clustered together in silver frames, and many pictures of English landscapes. Books and maga-zines were scattered around on side tables and there was a pipe rack beside a big leather armchair.

As Jane ate her delicious chicken soup she was thinking that for all its size and grandeur, this room had a lived-in feeling. It felt as if there had been many a happy family meal served and eaten around this big table.

She still couldn't fathom out how or why she was being offered the chance to come and live here. So far every person she had met had treated her with respect, had been kind, had even smiled at her. Did they know that she had been brought up in an institution? That she had no proper family? Only her mother, as far as she knew, was still alive, and she had made it quite obvious that she wanted nothing more to do with her. Funny she should be thinking about her mother while sitting eating in this posh dining room with a lady who had said quite clearly that she wanted her as a companion.

Her mother had more than likely made a new life some-where with Wally Simmonds and it was more than possible that both of them would regard her as an embarrassment if she should ever turn up on their doorstep.

The meal was over. Elsie and Christine had moved to two armchairs by the fire and were lingering over their coffee. Jane had said she didn't want anything to drink and was filling the time by sitting staring out of the window.

She hadn't heard anyone move and jumped when Mrs Dennison came up behind her, lifted a hand and smoothed her hair. 'You're thinking that this will be a totally different life to what you have been used to. Does it frighten you?'

'Yes, it does,' Jane answered quickly, 'but on the other hand it is an unbelievably generous offer. I just can't understand. Why me?'

Christine stood very still. She moved her hand to rest on Jane's shoulder, a gesture that said they were already friends. 'I have never wanted for any material thing in my life. I do not know what it is to be unwanted or unloved. So, I count my many blessings. Now I need someone to be my eyes. What better person could I pick than a young lady who has so much love to give but no one to share it with? Tell me, Jane, what were you thinking as you gazed out of the window?'

Jane hesitated before answering.

'I was wondering what it would be like to live and work in a place as beautiful as this. To be able to see these lovely gardens every day. To be warm inside the house and when the sun shines to be able to be outside in the grounds. To be able to dig my hands into that rich earth, to plant my own bulbs. Oh, so many things. Most of all, Mrs Dennison, could I do what would be expected of me? Would I prove to be satisfactory?'

'Well,' Christine said, smiling her delight. 'Well. We'll have to see what we can do for each other. But first off, could you please get used to calling me Miss Christy, it sounds far less formal than Mrs Dennison.'

'If that's what you prefer, ma'am.'

Jane still couldn't believe her good fortune and suddenly blurted out, 'I'll do my very best, ma'am! I really will. I'll do anything you ask, fetch and carry, see to all your needs, you'll only have to ask.' By now she was on the verge of tears. She'd never expected anything like this. 'I just don't know how to thank you, ma'am.'

Christine smiled, and, doing her best to put Jane at ease, said, 'I expect you found the house to be a bit rambling. It will take some time to get used to it, but I'm quite sure we shall suit each other very well.'

Jane hoped and prayed that she was right.

Later, when the car was taking them back to Balham, Elsie took Jane's hand and squeezed it tight. Her eyes sparkled merrily. 'Oh, hasn't the day gone well? You and Christine took to each other, I could tell. Isn't the thought of the future now so exciting?'

Yes, it was, but it was also scary.

Chapter Thirteen

IT WAS BARELY eight o'clock the next morning when Nancy opened her front door to find Jane standing there.

'Gawd love us, where 'ave you sprung from?' she asked in surprise as she ushered Jane down the narrow passage. 'You ain't given the streets time enough t' get aired.'

Jane laughed as she took her coat off. 'I couldn't wait any longer to tell you what's happened. Honest, Nancy, you aren't gonna believe half of it! I still can't take it in myself.'

'Well, I've only just this minute washed an' dressed meself an' I can't be doing with surprises till I've 'ad at least three cups of tea. So, move yerself, fill the kettle and make a pot while I brush the tangles out of me 'air.'

Jane needed no second bidding. She hadn't bothered to get herself anything to eat before setting out to come to Tooting, knowing full well that she wouldn't be in Nancy's house for very long before the big black frying pan would be pulled to the centre of the hob and a smashing fry-up would be produced.

Half an hour later, Jane pushed her plate away declaring

that she couldn't eat another morsel, and as Nancy poured her third cup of tea she announced, 'I'm going to be a paid companion.'

Nancy's mouth dropped open and she spilled some of her tea over the tablecloth.

'Who in God's name is gonna give you a job like that?'

Jane began at the beginning, telling Nancy how Mrs Rogers had turned up, and the posh car that had taken them to Sussex for the day.

'So what's the name of the lady you're gonna work for?' Nancy asked.

'Mrs Christine Dennison. Her and Mrs Rogers have been friends for years but they said they became closer when they were both notified that their husbands had been killed in the war.'

'An' you're telling me this Mrs Dennison has a butler, a cook and three girls working in the 'ouse?'

'Yes, that's right, and two men, so I was told, to work in the grounds.'

'You said the poor woman was going blind. Surely if she'd that well off she could afford an operation to make her eyes better?'

'I don't know about that. I never asked no questions.'

'Shame.' Nancy tutted sympathetically. 'All I 'ope is that she treats yer better than that other mad woman did.'

'Oh, I hope so too. But I'm sure she will. All the staff speak ever so well of her.'

'Ain't she got no family?' Nancy wanted to know more.

Jane grinned. 'Only one son, and he's the reason I've been offered the live-in job?'

'What d'yer mean? Is he the skeleton in the cupboard? Got sent to prison, 'as he?'

Jane gave Nancy a playful push. 'Go on with you, they're

not that sort of family. It's just that Mr Charles, he's her son, has fell in love with a married lady. She's left her husband and they've set up home together. Which leaves his mother very much at a loss. Oh, and this lady has a teenage daughter who has gone with them.'

'Cor blimey, I don't like the sound of that. A married woman *and* 'er daughter! Two on the go, so t' speak.'

'Oh, Nancy! Trust you!' Jane couldn't help but laugh. She was so glad she had Nancy to come to. She was a real tonic and she couldn't be kinder if she were a true relative.

She said as much to Nancy, who straight off replied, 'Well, yer know what they say, gal. God gave us our relations, thank Christ we pick our friends.'

'Trust you to come up with a saying like that. But Nancy, will you tell me really honestly if you think I should go ahead and take this job? One minute I can't believe I should be so lucky, and then the next I keep asking myself, what if it all goes wrong again? There really didn't sound as if there were going to be much for me to do.'

'Huh,' Nancy scoffed. 'Wait till you get there before you believe that! I'll lay ten t' one the missus will keep you busy.' She took a sip of her tea and set the cup down again. Then she turned and stared hard at this young girl who had come to mean so much to her. She had felt so guilty for the years that she had lost touch. But even if she had known where Jane had been sent, what could she have done about it? Half the time she didn't have two pennies to rub together for herself, never mind trying to provide for a child. The authorities would never have allowed her to look after Jane. Then suddenly her face creased in a huge grin.

'Since you've asked my opinion, I'm going to tell yer, lass, t' grab this chance with both 'ands. Life's a gamble whichever way yer look at it. Whoever said life is what yer make it ain't never wanted like most of us 'as. 'Cos if that were true then we'd all be living in bloody palaces. No, my luv, life is what you make of the circumstances you find yourself in at any given point in time. As I said, you come to a crossroads and you gamble on which road t' take. An' if yer too yellow-livered to take a chance, then you stay put an' get nowhere.'

'My, my, quite a well of wisdom this morning, aren't we?' Jane teased.

'Yes, well, I ain't finished yet. If this job turns out t' be all that you're 'oping for, then that's fine, but just you remember you've always got a home with me, so no putting up with things that ain't right 'cos yer think you've nowhere t' go. You understand me?'

'Yes, Nancy,' Jane said, getting to her feet and putting her arms around Nancy's broad shoulders.

'Now, now, don't start slobbering all over me. And let's get one more thing straight. You might be gonna live in Sussex, but I expect a penny postcard once a week and a visit at least once a month. That's if you can tear yerself away from this life of luxury that you'll be living in.'

'I shall ask my new employer to have all your rules and regulations written into my contract. Will that satisfy you, madam?'

'You cheeky whelp!' Nancy went to box her ears but Jane was too quick for her. 'For that you can do the washing-up, and when it's dinner time you and me will toddle off t' the Selkirk pub where we will get ourselves a hot pie and drink to you moving into wealthy society.'

'Now who's taking the mickey?' Jane asked, but nodding her agreement she added, 'Maybe if we buy a drink and tell the landlord of my good fortune he'll give us each a pie for nothing.'

'And pigs might fly,' Nancy laughed as she began to clear away the remains of their breakfast.

While they were doing the washing-up Jane was feeling that perhaps her life really was taking a change for the better. Maybe she was going to work in a big house with servants, but it was this woman who had been there for her when life had seemed so bleak, and even offered her a home. It was true, Nancy was kinder than any relative. Jane wouldn't forget her; she'd visit just as often as it was possible and if she managed to save any money then she would help Nancy in any way she could.

Mrs Forrester's feelings were very similiar to those of Nancy as she listened to a very excited Jane tell her about the house and the offer of a job that Elsie Rogers had obtained for her. In one way she was thrilled for the girl, but on the other hand she was going to miss her terribly.

She admitted to herself that that feeling was full of irony!

The very first day that Jane had arrived at her house, she had been so determined to have as little to do with her as possible. After all, the girl came from an institution, and how was she supposed to know what her background was? Any help the landlady had given first off had been given grudgingly. It wasn't until Jane had been taken ill and she had been more or less forced into helping her that her attitude had changed.

Now, as she listened to a smiling Jane thanking her for her love and kindness, Mrs Forrester had to close her eyes to stop the tears from spilling out.

This young girl was something else!

Thick blonde hair, blue eyes, soft silky skin. Full of good humour and laughter, sprightly and energetic, she faced whatever life threw at her and was never heard to moan.

No wonder she had come to love her. Oh, please God, give her a break this time, she silently prayed. If anyone deserved it, this sixteen-year-old girl did.

Chapter Fourteen

CHRISTINE DENNISON TURNED her head towards where Jane was sitting and couldn't help thinking that the way this young girl had settled into her household was remarkable. Six months now she had been here, and to say that she had endeared herself to everyone she came into contact with would be no exaggeration.

Jane herself was far happier than she had ever thought possible. It was such a contented, orderly house that she couldn't feel otherwise. Both Mary and Sarah had become her friends, while Daisy, the tweeny, was at everyone's beck and call and did every job asked of her with a broad smile on her face. Jane's own tasks were varied, according to how Miss Christy was feeling. Sewing and darning took up a lot of her time, and Miss Christy was pleased to learn that she did her jobs well. The household linen went to a laundry but Jane washed Miss Christy's fine underwear and blouses by hand, and on the odd occasion that Mr Charles stayed in the house it was she who washed and ironed his shirts. She was mostly given an hour to herself after lunch but she was never idle. She would use the time to write letters to Mrs Rogers, Mrs Forrester and of course to dear Nancy.

She would read book reviews in the daily papers amd magazines which were delivered to the house, and then describe and suggest which books Miss Christy might find interesting. Her favourite task was reading them to her. At the moment they were reading Charles Dickens' *David Copperfield*, following the life of David through his many sufferings and misfortunes. Jane could hardly wait to read the next chapter. Though she had the distinct feeling that Miss Christy knew this story off by heart. One of her most enjoyable trips out was when they visited bookshops. Miss Christy never failed to make a purchase, which in turn opened up a whole new world to Jane.

She had wondered why the staff always referred to their employer as Miss Christy. Mrs Wilson explained that her husband had been in service to the family ever since he was a young lad, and that that was how Christine had always been referred to as a young lady growing up. The habit had never changed, even when she had become Mrs Dennison, and as each new member of the staff joined the household that was what they were instructed to call their mistress. Jane thought it was a nice idea. Not so stuffy as madam.

Today she had a tedious task but one that she hoped would be well worth all the trouble in the end. She was sewing seed pearls on to a velvet head-band for Miss Christy to wear on Saturday evening. She gave a small sigh which didn't go unnoticed by Christine.

'Is any thing troubling you, Jane?' she asked, showing concern.

Jane was sorry she had let that sigh escape and quickly said, 'No, it's just that I dropped a pearl and they are so hard to find if they sink into the carpet.'

Christine's instincts told her that wasn't the truth. 'The main topic of conversation in the kitchen is Saturday's party.' It wasn't a question, it was a statement. 'Tell me, Jane, what is being said?'

Jane had no option. 'Well, everyone is thrilled that Mr Charles will be home for his birthday, and Mrs Wilson is in her element, cooking enough for an army.'

'That was not what I asked you, Jane.'

'I know.' Jane hesitated before saying quietly, 'I think both Mr and Mrs Wilson are a bit uneasy because Mr Charles is bringing his lady friend.'

'They are not the only ones, and her name is Mrs Harman, Frieda Harman.' It was Christine's turn now to sigh, then very quietly she said, 'If we want to have my son to stay then we must accept that he and Frieda are . . . well, for want of a better word, an item.'

'Oh, miss, I didn't mean no disrespect, and neither do Mr and Mrs Wilson, it's just that, well . . . none of us are quite sure how to carry on.'

'I know, Jane, and it will be particularly hard for you, but I want you to treat Mrs Harman as if she were Charles's wife. I will speak to the rest of the staff myself. It's not that I approve of their relationship, but neither am I going to judge. Sarah will prepare a double bedroom and also the room next to Charles's own bedroom, then their sleeping arrangements will be up to them. However, Jane, I would appreciate it if you would see to the final touches, such as fresh flowers. I know I can count on you to use your discretion.'

Jane took a deep breath and let it out slowly. 'I'll certainly do as you ask.' She wouldn't dream of passing one iota of this conversation on downstairs, but she was afraid it would all come out over the weekend.

She continued with her sewing but half smiled as she thought of what Nancy would have to say if she were in her shoes.

Never trouble trouble till trouble troubles you!

Saturday had arrived.

Every member of staff was kept busy for the early part of the day. After Miss Christy had taken her nap and than bathed, it fell to Jane to help her dress. And it was such a pleasure. She stood back and gazed at her mistress. Elegant was the only word that Jane could think of. Her long evening dress, the palest shade of blue, was trimmed with silver, as were her high-heeled shoes and evening bag. The pearl headband had been woven into the high curls that the hairdresser had come to the house to do. Normally Jane did Miss Christy's hair, but not today.

Come evening, Sarah, Mary and Jane were all kept on the trot as the guests arrived, taking ladies' cloaks while Mr Wilson saw to the gentlemen's coats, hats and canes. It was taking Jane some time to get over her nervousness, for after all this was the first big party that she had ever been involved with. Suddenly she found she had a few minutes in which to breathe out, and she began to take more interest in what was being discussed and noted the different evening dresses all the ladies present wore.

She couldn't believe they owned so many jewels, and the various hairstyles must have taken their hairdressers hours to create.

She was quite shocked to see some of the young ladies smoking cigarettes in long tortoiseshell holders; there was even one using a gold holder. She had seen poor women in the streets of London roll their own cigarettes, but never anything like this.

There was no need to ask which lady was Frieda Harman. Jane looked across the room and could tell why Mr Charles had been captivated by her. She was truly beautiful. Small and dainty, even though she must be nearing forty, because she had a daughter who was seventeen years old. She looked so graceful in a deep-red velvet dress with a diamond choker sparkling in the light. Around her head was a band of the same velvet as the dress to which was attached two pale-pink feathers. That alone made her stand out from the others, Jane thought as she watched Charles lower his head and say something into her ear.

Then her heart thumped. He had looked up and seen her watching them. Now he was coming towards her and there was nothing she could do to escape without pushing her way through the throng of people, so she stood still, her eyes fixed on the tray of drinks she was holding.

'Jane, how are you?'

'I'm very well, thank you, Mr Charles.'

'Well, I'm glad to hear it, and I'll take this opportunity to thank you for all you do for my mother. She sings your praises. Says she has no idea of how she would cope without you.'

'It's very kind of her to say so, but it works both ways . . .'

Jane paused, startled, as she heard Miss Christy say from behind her, 'Is my son tormenting you, Jane?'

She blushed, unable to form an answer.

'She's still a little wary of us all,' Christine said kindly.

'Mr Charles was telling me that you were pleased with my work,' Jane finally managed to reply. Then she cast her eyes down and said, 'I'd better continue round with these drinks.'

All through the meal and the dancing which followed she felt jittery and on edge, often wondering how she came to

be here. This was not her world. These were not her kind
of people. She should feel privileged to be here. And she
did. But at the same time she felt afraid.

Of what?

She didn't know.

The four-course meal seemed to take for ever, but finally
everyone was moving into the drawing room. The room had
been stripped of the big furniture, and small tables and
chairs were set around the walls. The carpet had been taken
up and the floorboards polished. A group of four musicians,
all in black evening dress, sat in the window alcove.

Mr Wilson had been right in his prediction about late
nights, Jane thought. It was after one o'clock when the last
guests departed and the house fell silent.

Miss Christy came down to the kitchen on the arm of
her son. 'She looks as tired as we all are,' Mary whispered
to Jane.

'Mr and Mrs Wilson, I'd like to thank you both for all
your hard work that went to make this evening such a
success. Also, I am not forgetting all you girls, because each
and every one of you has worked terribly hard and must be
very tired. My thanks to all of you.' She smiled at them
before adding, 'My son has something he wants to say.'

'Yes.' Charles grinned. 'I certainly won't be wanting an
early-morning call, and since Mrs Harman is the only other
house guest, and I'm sure she will agree, we shan't require
breakfast before ten thirty, so please leave all the clearing-
up until tomorrow, or later on today, I should say. Get yourselves to bed. Good night and, once again, our thanks to
all of you.'

Christine nodded her head and took hold of Charles's
arm again.

'Will I come up with you now, miss?' Jane asked.

'Thank you, Jane, but no. For one night I'll manage. I will leave all my clothes on a chair for you to see to in the morning. You must be worn out.'

As mother and son left the kitchen, Mrs Wilson nodded her head approvingly.

Mr Wilson said, 'Now that's what I call a real lady and gentleman. Many employers would have insisted on us clearing up tonight.' Then, smiling broadly, he said to Daisy, 'Put the kettle on, lass, and tonight you can all have a choice, tea or cocoa.'

When they were all seated with a hot drink, Mary looked at Jane and asked, 'What did you think of Mrs Harman?'

'A very nice lady, I thought, and you only had to see the way Mr Charles looked at her to know that he thinks the world of her.'

'Really? I never got much chance to observe them except when they were dancing, and then I thought, like you, that they looked smashing together. Did you know they are staying on here for a week or ten days?'

'No, Miss Christy never said.'

'Well, I only know because I heard Mr Wilson tell Sarah not to strip off their beds but to put out clean towels when she does their rooms.'

'We'll all have our work cut out in the morning,' Jane said, nodding to the stack of dishes and glasses piled high on the the big wooden draining board.

'Yeah, an' you'll have your work cut out upstairs, Jane. Best we go up now and at least get a few hours' sleep. Really lovely do, though, wasn't it?'

Jane sighed happily. 'It truly was. All those lovely dresses, and that wonderful food.'

'Opens our eyes as t' how the other half live, though, don't it?' Mary said, sounding really envious.

Jane didn't answer. She still felt very privileged to be here in this house and at this party, even if it was only as an employee. It certainly beat working in a factory, or even on a market stall, and living in a bed-sitting room with no real family of your own.

At least in her book it did.

It was Wednesday morning and Jane was having breakfast in the kitchen with the other female staff. When the house was running normally she would take her meals in the dining room with Miss Christy. Since Saturday, the day of the party, nothing had been what one would describe as normal. Miss Christy had been out and about far more than was usual, and there had been no need for Jane to go with her. Charles and Mrs Harman had insisted that everywhere they went Christine was to accompany them.

The companionable silence around the breakfast table was broken by a loud knocking on the door of what was known as the tradesmen's entrance.

'Who in heaven's name can that be at seven o'clock in the morning?' A very disgruntled Mrs Wilson put down the heavy brown teapot from which she had been filling Sarah's cup, and, giving Daisy a push, said, 'Get yerself up an' go see who it is, an' if it's either of them gardeners tell them to buzz off and come back when Mr Wilson has finished his breakfast.'

Daisy was none too pleased to have to leave her hot porridge, but did as she was told. Having walked along the narrow passageway, she struggled with the heavy iron door. When she had it opened, she panicked as she saw two police-men standing there.

''Ere, there ain't been an accident, has there?' she said, because it was the first thing that occurred to her.

'Nothing for you to worry yer pretty little head about,' the taller of the two constables said kindly. 'But we do need to see your master, Mr Charles Dennison, isn't it?'

Daisy looked at him fearfully. 'Mr Charles don't live 'ere no more. Well, not all the time he don't, ain't done so for a long time now. But what I'd better do is tell Mr Wilson you're here and let him see what yer want.'

She didn't wait to hear what the policemen had to say about that, but turned on her heel and ran, yelling as she went, 'There's two coppers 'ere say they want t' see the master.'

'What the hell is all the noise about?' Mr Wilson demanded as he came out into the passageway.

Daisy just pointed, ran into the kitchen and sank down thankfully on to her chair.

By the time Mr Wilson returned with the constables, he was aware of most of the facts.

'Send the girls about their normal duties,' he advised his wife. 'I have to go upstairs and wake Mr Charles, that is, if he hasn't already heard all the commotion. I will also have to make Miss Christy aware of what is happening.'

Mrs Wilson looked bewildered but knew better than to ask questions, especially in front of the staff.

The two policemen stood against the wall, helmets held in their hands. They were having a job not to smile as they listened to the cook shoo the girls off and mutter to herself, 'Be a godsend if someone were to tell me what's 'appening, but then I only work 'ere.'

Forty minutes had passed before Mr Wilson was showing the constables out, this time through the front door.

Meanwhile his wife had washed her face and hands and tidied her hair, expecting at any minute to be called up to the drawing room.

'Put the kettle on again, love, an' I'll do me best t' tell you what's going on,' her husband said as he came into the kitchen and sat down thankfully. 'Miss Christy said she'll ring when they're ready for their trays to be sent up. Poor woman, she's beside herself. She'll live to rue the day her son got himself mixed up in all this.'

'Bert!' Mrs Wilson yelled at him. This was a most unusual way for her to address him; in this house, it was always Mr Wilson. 'Bert,' she repeated, 'will you please stop talking in riddles and tell me what on earth has happened that's bad enough to have brought two coppers round here at this time in the morning.'

He heaved a great sigh, put his elbows on the table and indicated that his wife should sit herself down opposite him. 'To begin with, Mrs Harman's daughter has been arrested.'

'Oh my God!' Mrs Wilson's fingers flew to cover her mouth.

'I know, love, an' she not yet seventeen. She's been formally charged on two counts, shop-lifting and drunk and disorderly. They are bringing her before the magistrate this morning.'

'But why have they come here? Where's her father? And now I come t' think about it, didn't someone say she was still at school? Some kind of finishing college?'

Mr Wilson looked at his wife. He loved her dearly, but he made a point of never telling her half of what he knew that went on or was said above stairs in this house. He had been in this job a good many more years than she had and had learned that women loved to gossip. They were well set up in this house. He had brought her here as his young bride, and to be given the lodge for their own living quarters had been an extra bonus. He knew when he was onto a good thing and guarded it jealously.

But now was different! If he told her the events as he had learned them it would save a lot of speculation, and so, taking a deep breath, he began: 'Mrs Harman's husband is very much older than her, so I've been led to believe, and was retired. But when his wife took up with Mr Charles he applied to the Government to be given another job and has actually gone back to his old post in India. And as far as I can tell you, his daughter is, or should be, at an expensive boarding school.'

'He must have plenty of money.' Mrs Wilson was thinking out loud. 'Don't they have that great big house out on the other side of the Romney Marshes, with loads of ground?'

'Yes, you've got that much right, but I'm fairly sure he leases off most of the land to sheep farmers. He wouldn't be hard-up. Although he was young to have retired I wouldn't mind betting his pension is colossal.'

'What about our Mr Charles? He's bought that lovely old cottage in Rye where he and Mrs Harman live now, or do you think Miss Christy paid for that?'

'We don't get paid to think, my dear, and remember, you have to keep your thoughts to yourself. I have been wondering, though, about Mr Charles's businesses. There's the offices he has here in the village, but his main earner I always thought was up in London. He himself is a fully fledged chartered accountant, but having inherited the firm which has been in this family for a few generations, I suppose it is a safe bet to say he can leave the daily running to his regular staff. There was a time when he travelled daily up to the City.'

The shrill clanging of the bell brought their conversation to an abrupt ending. At the same moment, Jane appeared. 'Miss Christy said to tell you that Mary is laying up the dining room and that I am to help you bring the tea, coffee and toast up; they won't be wanting anything cooked this morning.'

'How is she?' Mrs Wilson asked quietly.

Jane twisted her hands together before answering. 'I'd say she is very fearful. Mostly worried about the effects this will have on Mr Charles.' Then quickly she turned to face Mr Wilson and added, 'I can't help feeling sorry for Mrs Harman. You felt the same, I know you did. She's blaming herself for what her daughter has done and at the same time she is feeling utter despair. Mr Charles is going to the court with her. Poor Miss Christy doesn't know what to think.'

Mr Wilson looked into Jane's face and saw that it was filled with concern.

It wouldn't only be Mrs Harman and her daughter who would be affected by this.

No, not by a long chalk.

And the worst thing was that he knew damn well things were going to get a darn sight worse before they ever started to get better.

Chapter Fifteen

JANE STOOD IN the open doorway and gazed wonderingly at the change in the beautiful gardens. The fields beyond were empty of crops. All the harvest had been safely gathered in. Her mind wandered back over the lovely church service she had attended with Miss Christy to celebrate the Harvest Festival. The summer was over, she thought sadly. The hours of daylight were getting shorter. There was a nip in the air, and in the mornings, mist hung over the fields and hedgerows. The air was full of the earthy smell which came from falling and decaying leaves. Oh, but it was still nice to live in the country.

The past months had been so good for her, she mused. A time of new experiences. A time during which she had learned to adapt to a way of life so very different to that she had known. And now, with winter fast approaching, she would not have to dread the cold or wonder where her next meal was coming from.

The only thing that was worrying the whole household was this business about Glynis Harman. It would be a relief when Mrs Harman learned exactly what was going to happen to her daughter. And as for Mr Charles, he walked about looking as if he'd got the worries of the whole world on his shoulders.

Anyway, today was Jane's day off, and as soon as breakfast was over she was going to see Nancy. This would only be her second visit to Tooting in all the months she had been at Adelaide House, but she had kept her promise and written every week, even if sometimes it was only a postcard.

She felt light-hearted as she got off the train at Balham station and walked towards the tram stop. It would be such a change to have Nancy to talk to. Although they all tried to skirt around the subject of Glynis Harman, the coming court case seemed to have put a shadow over the whole household. And none more than Miss Christy.

Which, when you thought about it, was only natural. Charles was her son, her only child, and she had bent over backwards to understand and accept the fact that he was in love with another man's wife. The husband seemed to have washed his hands of the whole affair once his wife left him. The worst part was that he wasn't even in the country. He didn't have to deal with the shameful mess his daughter had got herself into.

When Nancy opened the door and flung her arms around her, Jane sighed happily. She loved living at Adelaide House: the rich furniture and curtains, the high ceilings, the marvellous wallpapers, and the paintwork such a pale cream which helped to make the rooms seem even larger than they really were. She especially loved the smaller sitting room which Miss Christy and herself used daily because it opened on to the gardens. Here in Selkirk Road, Nancy's living room window looked out on to a back yard and an outside toilet. Nevertheless, it was a joy to be here. She wasn't paid to come here; she came because she loved Nancy and Nancy loved her. This was her home should she ever have need of it, and Nancy was all the family she had. The only person in the world she could turn to should she ever lose her job.

'I knew there was something up by the tone of your letters,' Nancy said when they were settled with the inevitable cup of tea in front of them.

'Well, I wouldn't dream of writing the whole story, but it is a relief to be able to talk sensibly with someone.'

'Don't you talk to this Mary and Sarah that yer work with?'

'Well, yes, of course I do, but it's difficult. You see, Nancy, I'm upstairs most of the time and I hear Miss Christy talking to her son and even some of her friends when they call. I was there when Miss Christy discussed the case with her family solicitor. I do my best to keep my head down, not to deliberately listen but to get on with whatever it is that I am doing. Often I suggest to Miss Christy that I go into another room, but she won't even hear of it.'

'I see what yer mean. Privileged position is what you're in, although it does put you between the devil an' the deep blue sea. Must make life 'ard.'

'Not hard, Nancy, more awkward like. Even Mrs Wilson tries to question me. Anyway, I've got a bit of good news.'

'Well, let's be 'aving it,' Nancy urged.

'I'm to stay the night if you'll have me.'

'Oh, pet. That's real cracking, that is. Yer know God works in a mysterious way.' She nodded her head towards the ceiling. 'I got rid of my tenants only about a fortnight ago, and you know Hannah an' John Watkins who live opposite, well, they wanted to rent my two rooms for their married daughter but I told them I thought you might be wanting to come and stay with me quite soon but I'd let them know. The back bedroom is nice and clean and the bed all made up for you. Now what d'yer think of that?'

'That you are either a white witch or you've been practising a bit of telepathy.'

An answer to which Nancy merely nodded her head knowingly.

Happiness was flowing through Jane. She had been so grateful when Miss Christy had said that visiting for the day did not give her and her friend much time together and suggested that Brownlow, the chauffeur, drive her to the station and meet her from the train tomorrow evening.

They talked, going from one topic to another. And when Nancy related some of the things the neighbours had got up to since she'd last seen her, Jane found she was laughing fit to bust, something she hadn't done since the police had called about Mrs Harman's daughter.

'Tell you what, Nancy, I'm not letting you cook dinner for us. I'll go and fetch fish an' chips for us both, my treat.'

'Oh, Miss Money-Bags are you now?'

'Well, I do get paid twelve an' sixpence a week, or rather fifty shillings a month, and to be honest, there is nothing I need to spend it on. I mostly save it, since everything I need is provided for me. But if you pass me my bag I'll show you what I have brought.'

As Nancy handed the bag across, Jane stuck out her legs and added, 'Look, new shoes, brand new, and while I was in the shop I got these for you.'

Nancy was too choked to comment as she took the poshly wrapped parcel and gingerly tore at the wrapping paper. 'Good God!' she exclaimed, putting a hand inside a fur-lined slipper. 'I ain't never 'ad anything like these before.'

'I wasn't sure of your size so I got a seven. The lady assistant said better too big than too small and that you could always put an inner sole inside if they were too big. Go on, try them on, please.'

They were made of a bright-red plush material, designed to come up high around the ankles and fully lined. Nancy now had one slipper fitted over each hand.

Jane laughed, got down on her knees in front of Nancy, eased off her well-worn black shoes and slipped the new slippers on.

Nancy was choked. It was ten months since Jane had turned up on her doorstep after spending eight years in an institution because there wasn't a soul who was willing to take the responsibility for bringing her up. But it was a very different Jane who was sitting at her feet now. She would be seventeen this coming January, no longer a waif-like little girl, but a beautiful young woman whose features showed no trace of the suffering she had been put through.

She was kind and considerate, and it put joy in Nancy's heart to know that Jane continued to regard her as a close friend. She herself had no relatives left alive; she had good neighbours but it wasn't the same, and sometimes she felt lonely. Not now though; she was proud of Jane, in her heart regarding her as the daughter she had never had, and was thankful that she had been able to tell her that there was a home here with her if she should ever feel the need.

'Jane, luv, I don't know what t' say, they are lovely. They'll keep me feet as warm as toast.'

'Now don't go all soft on me,' Jane murmured, sensing that Nancy was near to tears. 'I've just had a better idea. I won't go and fetch us fish and chips; we'll go to Harrington's and we'll eat it there. That way you won't be able to make me do the washing-up.'

'As if I would,' Nancy protested. 'But it costs about a tanner each extra to eat in the café bit of the shop.'

'So what? Today I'm splashing out, so start getting yourself ready.'

'All right, no need to bully me.' Then as she crossed the room, Nancy turned, tilted her head and slyly said, 'I might even walk up the street in me new slippers.' The kitchen door had closed with a bang before Jane could think of an answer.

They had had a lovely day. Stayed up until turned midnight, both of them talking nineteen to the dozen. But now it was nearly time to go. Nancy was coming to Balham station to see Jane off on the train.

'You will let me know what 'appens to that young lass, won't you, Jane?' she asked as the tram rattled on through Tooting Bec.

The question had come out of the blue and Jane wasn't quite sure how to answer it, so she responded with a question of her own. 'Could they send her to prison, do you think?'

'Most certainly they could. But whether the magistrate will see fit t' do so is another matter,' Nancy replied knowingly.

'And what's that supposed to mean?' Jane was flabbergasted.

'Well, if it were the likes of you or me there would be no two ways about it. With no money for legal 'elp we'd be a dead loss. We'd get a sermon on the severity of our crime, probably get told that we lacked morals, the police wouldn't 'ave a good word to say on our behalf and before you know it we'd be locked away in 'Olloway.'

Jane stared at her in horror. 'I've heard about Holloway,

it's a women's prison, isn't it? Do you really believe they will send Glynis Harman there?'

Nancy grinned. 'Now I never said that! I said that's what would more than likely 'appen if it were you or me up in that dock. No, love, for one thing she ain't being tried in London, so I ain't got a clue as to where she would go if she were to be given a prison sentence. I'd take a bet, though, that she'll get off with a caution. Oh, the magistrate will add strings to it just to make it look as though he is un-biased, but you mark my words, money talks all languages. And breeding comes into it an' all.'

The tram had stopped again and Jane jumped to her feet, crying, 'Come on, you've nearly made us miss the station.'

It was only Jane's skilful shepherding that got Nancy's great bulk down from the high platform step from the tram to the road and then safely on to the pavement. It also took a bit of manoeuvring for the pair of them to cross to the other side of the main road. This was largely due to all the traffic, but the fact that Nancy decided to have an argument with the policeman on point duty because he had held them up so long before waving them across didn't help in the least!

Once Jane had shown her return half of the ticket, a porter pointed to which platform the train would arrive at and told them they had twenty-five minutes to wait.

Nancy fished in her bag, found two pennies and waddled off towards the sweet machine. Jane had to laugh as she watched her place one of the coins in the slot, thump the handle, then tug the drawer open and take out a bar of Nestlés milk chocolate, all neatly wrapped in its red and gold paper. Then she did exactly the same again.

''Ere yer are, me pet,' Nancy smiled, offering one of the bars to Jane. 'Let's sit down over there an' eat these while we wait.'

When Nancy was seated and munching happily at her chocolate, Jane said, 'Nancy, were you implying that money or breeding or even both would make a difference to whatever sentence a magistrate might decide was appropriate?'

'Course I was, luv. Like I said, no two ways about it.'

Seeing Jane staring at her in disbelief, Nancy put an arm across her chest and heaved her ample bosoms higher. 'Look at it like this, Jane. On the one hand you 'ave the father of this young girl living in Government 'Ouse in India as a representative of His Majesty our King. You 'ave 'er mother attending a glamorous party with 'er live-in lover who is young enough to be 'er son, while this poor lass who should be safely tucked up in some posh academy takes it in 'er 'ead to go for a late-night stroll an' maybe 'ave a drink or two. Which one of this group of people who should be looking after the girl do you think is going t' take the blame for her going off on 'er own?'

Jane was appalled!

It was almost as if Nancy had been at Adelaide House and heard everything that had been going on. She hadn't realized that she had given her so many details. In fact she was sure she hadn't. But Nancy was sharp. She had lived a long time and seen some goings-on. She'd certainly been shrewd when it came to putting the pieces in place as regards Mrs Harman's daughter.

Whistles were blowing, the train was approaching. Nancy took Jane's hand. 'Keep yer spirits up, pet. It's not your worry. It will get sorted and your Miss Christy will find out she's been worrying 'erself needlessly.'

They hugged each other tightly, and from the window Jane blew kisses as the train pulled away.

When she could no longer see her dear friend, Jane sank back into her corner seat. Her thoughts were going round in endless circles. She had never even met this Glynis Harman, and yet she and Nancy had spent hours talking about her. Funny, they both felt sorry for her. One thing she was very glad about, and that was that Miss Christy hadn't been around to hear Nancy describe Mr Charles as Mrs Harman's live-in lover, or the fact that he was young enough to be her son.

The first time the police had called at Adelaide House, Mrs Wilson had shown how very upset she was. 'A nice carry-on I must say, and for a respectable house such as this to be involved is just too much,' she had declared openly. Adding, 'Mr Charles should never have got himself tangled up with that Mrs Harman.'

Mr Wilson had grabbed her by the shoulders and told her to keep her thoughts to herself. Defiantly she had told him, 'Sometimes the truth hurts.'

Thinking back to that time, and now all of what Nancy had had to say, it was all too much for Jane to cope with. She shook her head, but was unable to clear her thoughts.

Had Nancy been right in her prediction? She hoped the part about Glynis Harman not having to go to jail would turn out to be true.

She also wished with all her heart that this affair hadn't affected Miss Christy so much. She was such a nice kind lady. Always thinking of others. She lived in a beautiful house and wanted for nothing, except for her eyesight to improve, though you never heard her complain about that. Now, instead of being happy, one only had to look at her to see that she was feeling despair.

As for Mr Charles, he seemed different, which was only to be expected. He had always been nice to Jane and she hoped for his sake that the court would be lenient towards Glynis Harman and that not too much scandal would rub off on him. The entire staff liked Mr Charles, and there wasn't one who didn't wish him the best of luck.

'God knows he'll need it,' Jane muttered aloud as the train took her nearer to Adelaide House.

Chapter Sixteen

THE ROOM BEGAN to spin sickeningly and Christine tried to grasp her son's hand, but there was a great rushing sound in her ears and everything was receding into darkness.

When she came to, she was lying on the floor, her head in Charles's lap and he was staring sadly down at her.

Mr Clarkson, the family solicitor, remained standing, looking down at her, unable to disguise the fact that he was worried. He had asked to speak to Charles in private, but Charles had insisted that there were no secrets between him and his mother.

'Don't worry, Mrs Dennison, I'll move heaven and earth to get this sorted,' he said softly, as he and Charles helped her up.

When Christine was seated he turned to face Charles. 'The young lady is clutching at straws, and not only that, she sees this as a way of paying you back for taking her mother away from her father.'

Charles sighed heavily. He was still holding his mother's hand, and she looked at him, her eyes brimming with tears, and asked, 'Why would she be so wicked?'

Charles shook his head. 'I know she has never liked me, and she was very rebellious the whole time she spent her half-term holiday with us. But this!'

Silently Mr Clarkson was thinking, who could blame the girl? Her mother had left the family home to live with a much younger man, and instead of the father doing his best to be there for her to make up for the loss of her mother, he'd upped sticks and taken himself back to India. A truly selfish reaction. It couldn't be counted as unnatural that the girl hated Charles and was out for revenge. But to name Charles as the father of her unborn baby was taking things to the extreme!

It had all been too much for Christine to take in. She shook her head dazedly before asking Mr Clarkson if he would outline the court's decision once again.

The solicitor looked to Charles, and, having received his nod of approval, once more took a sheaf of papers from his briefcase and began to explain.

'There was great weight set upon the fact that this was Glynis Harman's first offence. The extenuating family circumstances and the fact that the medical officer had found the young lady to be pregnant were also mentioned. A probation order of twelve months was made and conditions were set. In principal, Mrs Harman has agreed to return to the family home and to reside there and be responsible for the well-being of her daughter.'

Slowly Christine got to her feet and stared at her son. He looked ghastly. Her heart ached for him. She looked from him to Mr Clarkson, whom she had known and trusted for so many years. 'You will be able to prove that she is lying?' Her voice was a hoarse whisper.

'This terrible accusation will be sorted out in no time,' he assured her with as much conviction as he could muster.

'Folk will believe what she's saying. They will. They won't believe me.' Charles sounded scared.

'I think they will, Charles. You are a man of some standing.'

'Yes, and Glynis Harman is the daughter of a diplomat.'

'Charles,' Mr Clarkson quickly interrupted, 'we shall set the wheels in motion immediately. There are many ways to prove parentage; you are not to worry, leave it to me.'

'That's all very well, but mud sticks, and proving that Glynis is lying may take weeks, months even. In the mean time, what am I supposed to do? Hide myself away?'

'I'm sorry,' was all that Mr Clarkson could manage to say. Then he nodded sympathetically and shook hands with Charles. To Christine he said, 'Keep your spirits up, my dear. We'll sort it all out.'

Charles said he would walk with Mr Clarkson to his car.

When they'd gone, Christine sank back against the cushions and buried her face in her hands. Oh why on earth couldn't her son have found a decent young lady to fall in love with? It was tragic that Maureen, his first love, had died when only twenty-one, but to go from her to a married woman, causing the break-up of a whole family, was beyond her comprehension.

And now! To be accused of having made the woman's young daughter pregnant!

Poor Charles! What a state he had got himself into. And for what?

Where on earth was it all going to end?

God help us if the local press get hold of this story, thought Christine in despair. Or even, God forbid, the national newspapers.

'How are you feeling now?' Charles asked as he came back into the room.

Christine did her best to smile, but it didn't ease his

concern. 'Mother, I am so sorry to have brought all this trouble on you.'

'It can't be helped, not now.' She looked up into his handsome face, and her heart was heavy. She still felt dizzy but was determined to get the answers to a few questions. 'Let's hope this question of parentage will be over and done with before the birth. Meanwhile, what do you propose doing with yourself?'

'I'm going back to work full-time. If I travel up to the City every day, at least . . .' He didn't finish the sentence.

'I was asking more about your living arrangements now that Mrs Harman has returned to her own home.'

'Having bought the cottage in Rye, I shall live in it on my own,' he said with chilling finality.

His mother looked anxious. 'You could close it up for a while. Let the dust settle and give yourself time to think. You know you've always got a home here.' There was a moment of silence before Christine spoke again, and when she did it was a cry of anguish. 'Oh Charles, please come home. I shan't have a moment's peace thinking of you living in that cottage all on your own. Besides, you won't want to get back from the City each night and start cooking for yourself. Have you thought about that?'

Charles's face broke into a grin and for a moment his mother saw the old carefree, happy young man that her son used to be. 'I was going to call in here each evening to have dinner with you. You know, I really have missed Mrs Wilson's cooking,' he said, sounding almost cheeky.

'So, if we are to have the pleasure of your company, it won't be because you want to see me, but just to satisfy the inner man?'

When no reply was forthcoming, she teased, 'Have I got that right?'

'Of course not, Mother. All right, if it will please you I will move back in – come home, I should say – but I think I shall hang on to the cottage. I don't feel I want to sell it at this point in time.'

'Oh Charles, this is the first good bit of news you've given me in days. And I think you are right to keep the house in Rye. There will be times when you will want to be on your own, even do some of your office work down there.'

'Well, I'm glad we've got that settled,' Charles agreed, then added quietly, 'It upsets me, the thought that Frieda is having to cope with Glynis all on her own. I couldn't blame her if she believes what her daughter tells her, though I hope against hope that she knows me a darn sight better than that. I tried to explain that I never for a moment thought about Glynis in that way. In actual fact, I have never really spent any time alone with the girl. But instead of the two of us discussing it rationally, it turned into a really ugly scene.'

'Well, I suppose the poor woman is torn between the two of you. However, I can't feel too sorry for her. The daughter's the one who is in the wrong, not you.'

Christine was also thinking to herself that Frieda hadn't been much of a mother. Leaving home like that, her daughter away at boarding school, she had acted as if she were a free woman. Shaking her head, she dismissed the thought, because if her mind ran along those lines then she would have to admit that her own son didn't come out of all this exactly snow-white.

Aloud she asked, 'What kind of a young lady is this Glynis?'

'A rich, spoiled one. And a girl who is out for revenge,' Charles answered sadly.

Chapter Seventeen

JANE STARED AT the rain as it beat against the window pane, then impatiently threw down the needlework that she was doing. November was drawing to a close; it would soon be Christmas. It was supposed to be a happy time. The smells which daily came from Mrs Wilson's kitchen were enough to make anyone's mouth water. We should be thinking about getting the house decorated, getting the gardeners to select a tree and bringing in armfuls of holly, she reflected miserably. Instead a cloud still hung over the whole household.

It was two weeks since Mr Charles had learned that he was no longer being named as the man who had made Glynis Harman pregnant.

Not that the girl herself had finally told the truth.

It was a young man from a neighbouring college who had finally owned up and confessed that he and a couple of other students had made a habit of meeting girls in the woods after lights-out. The lad had been brave enough to offer to marry Glynis, even though his parents were dead set against the idea. When told that he was willing to under go tests to prove that he was telling the truth and in all probability was the father of her child, Glynis had no option but to admit that she had lied about Charles.

The air had seemed to clear for a while, and all the staff were pleased that Mr Charles was back home living with his mother. Still, Miss Christine was not herself.

Not by a long chalk she wasn't!

She's lived in a highly agitated state of nerves ever since this business with Glynis Harman had come to light. More so at weekends, when she needed no telling where Charles had taken himself off to.

Voicing her thoughts aloud to Jane, she would complain, 'Why does he go to her house? It's as if he is asking for more trouble, walking straight into the lion's den.' That was the question she'd asked Jane so many times. Always adding, 'Why doesn't he just cut the woman out of his life and be done with her?'

Of course Jane had no answers for her. If the truth be told, she herself was as impatient and frustrated as Miss Christy was. She thought Charles deserved so much better. His life had been almost ruined because of that spoilt young lady.

It had come as no surprise that both the local and the national press had run the story. Both Mrs Harman and Charles Dennison had some standing locally, and that kind of news sold newspapers. Charles's denial hadn't been given much coverage, and when the truth had been brought to light it was the young man who was made out to be a hero, while hardly a hint of an apology was forthcoming to Charles.

It was all so sad, for everyone concerned. There was no brightness about Charles any more. And now, when every-thing appeared to be sorted and the dust should finally be settling, there had been another turn-up for the books. This morning the police had arrived at Adelaide House for a second time and Charles had gone off with them, telling his mother not to worry.

Don't worry! He couldn't have said anything more daft if he had tried.

'Jane, will you please come and sit down. You pacing up and down isn't going to solve anything.' Christine smiled weakly.

'If you insist, Miss Christine.' Jane really wanted to fly downstairs to find out if Mrs Wilson was any wiser than they were as to why Charles had gone off with the police.

As Jane seated herself there was a tap at the door and Mr Wilson entered, his expression serious, his manner very formal. He was followed by an elderly grey-haired man in clerical garb.

'The Reverend Leonard Shepherd would like a few words with you, Miss Christy,' Mr Wilson announced in a deep and respectful tone.

Before Mr Wilson had closed the door, Jane watched as Christine rose to her feet, walked forward and held out her hand. 'Leonard, it is so good of you to call. I heard from your young replacement that you had not been well and I have missed you at morning service.'

'I am feeling a whole lot better, not quite ready to be pensioned off,' he laughed as he guided Christine back to her chair. 'I only wish I were the bearer of better news.'

Christine sighed, already anticipating that this visit was to do with Mrs Harman and her daughter. 'Come and sit beside me. Will you have a drink or a cup of tea?'

'I think a glass of your excellent sherry would be nice. It seems ages since I've been in this lovely old house.'

Jane stood up and went to fetch the decanter and glasses, while the Reverend took off his overcoat. She poured them a glass each, placing Miss Christine's to her right hand at three o'clock, as she had become used to doing, and then went to sit in the window alcove.

'I should be coming here full of congratulations that Charles has been cleared of that awful accusation which must have caused you so much unhappiness. Instead . . .' The Reverend paused, and Christine knew from the tone of his voice that something was wrong.

'Leonard, I guessed something had happened when the police came and asked Charles to go with them. Has Mrs Harman been involved in an accident?'

'Well, I suppose one could say that.' Again he seemed loath to come to the point. Eventually he said, 'I was visiting an old friend at the hospital when both Mrs Harman and her daughter were brought in by ambulance. I considered it my duty to stay long enough to see to which wards they were going to be admitted, and also if I could be of any help.' The silence hung heavily and Leonard Shepherd had no option but to continue. 'The daughter is probably going to lose her baby, but it is Mrs Harman who is causing the most worry.'

Christine gasped and dropped her head in her hands. A minute or two passed before she asked, 'What happened, do you know the details?'

'Well,' he sighed, 'only the bare outline. I have been told that mother and daughter were having an argument, that one or the other lashed out and in trying to avoid the blow they both fell. Unfortunately they were standing at the head of the stairs and they finished up in the hall, which as I know from having been in Ashford Manor is a very long way to fall.'

Jane had heard every word – it was impossible not to – but it was Miss Christine that she was worried about.

Christine had got to her feet. Now she walked towards the fireplace and stood with her back to it.

'Will this business with the Harmans never end? God knows, Charles won't walk away now. It is as if that woman has him tied to her with an invisible rope.' She stood for a few seconds, her almost sightless eyes staring across the room. She was shaking with temper, but her eyes were brimming with tears at the shock of it all.

The parson had been taken completely off his guard by her fury, but now he had gathered his wits about him and turned to Jane with raised eyebrows.

'Don't worry about her, she'll be all right. I'll keep my eye on her,' Jane promised.

Christine had sat down again, her anger quickly lessened, to be replaced by utter dismay, and she was quietly crying.

Jane came and put her arms around her. 'It won't help much, but I feel as if I want to cry with you.'

Christine dabbed at her eyes with her handkerchief and managed to give Jane a watery smile.

Jane had listened in a state of silent horror for most of the time, but now she looked at Mr Shepherd and asked, 'Do you know why the police fetched Mr Charles?'

'No mystery there, my child. Mrs Harman has no near relatives, and I'm sorry to say, but it's common knowledge that Charles Dennison and Mrs Harman have been more than just good friends.'

'You mean he'll have to be responsible for her *and* her daughter?' Now it was Jane who was showing signs of a temper.

'I think that will be a matter for Mr Charles to decide for himself when all the facts are out in the open. Till then . . . well, we can only wait and pray.'

Jane pulled a face.

The elderly parson got to his feet and placed a hand on Christine's head. 'Your son is a good man, he'll do the right thing. Now, before I leave you, shall we say a prayer together? For both the mother and the daughter, and for Charles, that the Lord may be with them and let his mercy and blessing shine upon them.'

'Oh, Holy Mary, Mother of our Lord Jesus Christ, look after my son,' Christine whispered quietly.

'God bless and keep us all,' the parson added.

Then, reluctantly, he took his leave, urging Christine to send for him if there was any way in which he could help.

The minute the door closed behind him, Christine gave vent to her true feelings.

'Just as Charles was getting his life organized, this has to happen! It's almost as if she's planned it. She'll have him tied to her good and true now, and knowing my son he'll stay linked to her like glue. And if I were to raise any objections I know exactly what his reply would be. What would you have me do, Mother? Desert a sinking ship?' She shook her head sadly. 'Oh Jane, what a mess.'

Jane gripped Christine's hand tightly. She knew what *she* would like to say to Mr Charles. Get on with your own life. He was such a lovely man. The whole house seemed brighter and happier when he was around. Mrs Harman and her blessed daughter had already sent him halfway to hell and back as a result of Glynis's malicious allegation, so why should he go running to help them now?

She knew the answer to her own question.

Because he was a decent man. Well, she wished that just this once he would think of himself and let that pair do what the hell they wanted without involving him.

Christine's senses told her what Jane was feeling and she

swiftly said, 'Come on, Jane, we'll have a cup of tea and some biscuits while we wait for more news from the hospital.'

'You stay here in the warm, I'll go downstairs and fetch us a tray,' Jane told her, patting Christine's hand, which rested on the arm of her chair.

Christine raised her head and smiled tiredly. 'What would I do without you, Jane? I dread to think.'

It was said so sadly that it prompted Jane to ask, 'Are you going to be all right?'

'Let's see. My son left home to live with Mrs Harman, a much older married woman. Her daughter accused him of having fathered her baby.' She heaved a sigh. 'The courts told the woman to come to her senses and take responsibility for her daughter, and Charles accepted that and came home to where he belonged. Now, at the first sign of trouble, the police come for my son. And if anyone should ask, Mr Harman has washed his hands of the whole affair and left my son to deal with it all as best he can. How does the saying go? If you have the sweets you have to put up with the sourers. Well, my poor Charles is certainly being made aware of that fact. Apart from that, everything is fine, wouldn't you say so, Jane?'

Jane had to smile. 'I'm glad you're not still in a temper and that you still have a sense of humour.'

'Only on the outside, Jane, believe me, only on the outside. Inside I am all churned up.'

Chapter Eighteen

MISS CHRISTY WAS in bed, and Jane was sitting in the garden room, as she had decided to call it. At the end of a long, tiring day it was real bliss to be able to sit in here with a cup of hot cocoa and relax a bit before she too went to bed. In her mind's eye she was making two lists. One consisted of good things, and the other of bad.

Forget the bad for the moment, she chided herself, and count your blessings. And she had to admit there were many. Only five days to go now till Christmas, and she was ready. Organized very well, really. She, Mary, Sarah and even Daisy had been given an afternoon off and had been driven into Hastings by Brownlow, the chauffeur, to do their Christmas shopping. They'd had a great time. They'd all bought Christmas cards and small presents for their relatives.

Buying gifts had brought a lump to Jane's throat. She had chosen well, though. Lavender-scented soap and talcum powder for Nancy and for Mrs Forrester. Prettily packed and finished with brown paper, those two parcels had already been posted. She had found the most exquisite lace handkerchiefs to give to Miss Christine and Mrs Rogers, because that was the biggest bonus of all: Elsie Rogers was coming as a house guest for two whole weeks! Oh, it was going to be such a wonderful time.

Jane had settled on small boxes of chocolates for her three workmates. The four of them had pooled their money and very extravagantly had bought half a bottle of whisky for Mr Wilson and a small bottle of port for Mrs Wilson. They had thought it would be presuming too much to buy a gift for Mr Charles.

Add all that excitement to the fact that the house was looking absolutely wonderful. Like a Christmas wonderland, had been Jane's thought as she wandered around the house after the gardeners had put the decorations in place.

Sighing softly, she turned to her not so happy thoughts. While out on her buying spree, she had been aware of how lucky she was to have money to spend on gifts for others, but oh, how wonderful it would have been were she able to buy something for her own mother.

Knowing that her brother Tommy was dead and that Mick Jeffrey had not been her father, she had, to her knowledge, only one real relative. She would give her eye teeth to be able to see her mother, or even to write to her, if it were true what Nancy had heard: that Alice and Wally Simmonds had left England together and had gone to live abroad.

She certainly did not want to appear ungrateful, but if she got a chance during the Christmas holidays she was going to broach the subject with Mrs Rogers. It was she who had said that there were ways and means of tracing missing relatives.

Living here in Adelaide House was like a dream come true. More than that! Because Jane had never known or even imagined that such an elegant way of life existed. Never would she take her job for granted. Nor the privilege of caring for Miss Christine. No, she'd never do that.

Every day was still a source of amazement. When she let her mind wander back to the time when she had had to leave Winchelsea Lodge, she would shudder. Sometimes she wondered how she had survived. She had felt so utterly alone, and there had been times when she'd been so cold, chilled right through to her bones, and even hungry. If it hadn't been for Mrs Rogers and Mrs Forrester, she probably wouldn't have made it. And there had been other caring people. She smiled as she remembered the café owner and his wife who had given her such heart-warming meals *and* provided her with a pair of boots to keep her feet dry.

Now her life was so very different and she was terrified of change. What if she should have to find another job, and go back to living all on her own in a bed-sitting room? It didn't bear thinking about!

The other thing on her bad list was the everlasting problem that Mr Charles had to face. Miss Christine did her best to hide the fact that still she worried over her son, but there were days when Jane knew her mistress was really sad.

Glynis Harman had suffered a miscarriage due to her fall down so many stairs. But she was young and fit and apparently had not sustained any lasting damage. According to the rumours that Mrs Wilson picked up from the delivery men who called at the house from the village shops, the girl could not wait for her probation order to be completed. Instead, her legal advisers had applied to the court for permission for her to leave the country to live with her father, on the grounds that her mother was now incapable of caring for herself, never mind her daughter. The court officials had agreed it was the best way out of a bad situation.

One had to feel sympathy for Frieda Harman. The fall had done her untold damage. If there were any truth in the stories floating around, she was practically paralysed from the waist down. Charles played his cards close to his chest. He never had a word to say on the subject. In fact he made no reference to Frieda Harman whatsoever.

Miss Christine had made it her business to find out as much as was possible. Especially when she'd learned that Mrs Harman was in a private nursing home. That, however, had only lasted for three weeks. Word was that she was an intolerable patient, and the main reason she had discharged herself was because she wasn't allowed to smoke cigarettes while lying in bed.

As far as was known now, Mrs Harman was at home. Attended during the day by a female nurse, while a male nurse took over for night-time duty. Charles spent the best part of every weekend up at Ashford Manor, and of course there must still be some staff employed in that house, but Jane had learned never to ask questions.

It had been exactly as Christine had predicted. Charles's only comments when urged to think of his own life had been, 'One does not desert a sinking ship.'

There had been one disastrous day when even Miss Christy had been moved to phone Charles at his office in London and urge him to come home.

Once again the police had been involved. The day nurse, for reasons of her own, had taken it into her head to walk to the village, apparently leaving her patient alone in that big rambling house. Burglars had broken in, even going so far as to ransack Frieda's bedroom while she lay helpless, watching them help themselves to most of her jewellery.

The men hadn't hurt her, only threatened her. But naturally the poor woman had been absolutely terrified. And it seemed that Charles was the only one who could calm her.

Much to his mother's annoyance, he had slept over at the Manor for three days after that incident. Jane grinned as she remembered how the whole household had breathed a sigh of relief when he had returned home. 'God forbid he should tie himself completely to that woman again,' had been Christine's anguished cry.

Jane had felt for her. How many times even she had asked herself, 'Oh why doesn't he break away from Mrs Harman for good?' She had never found an answer.

There wasn't one to find.

Just lately she had begun to question her own feelings where Mr Charles was concerned and she'd had to tell herself to keep her thoughts to herself.

Towards Miss Christine and of course Mrs Rogers she still felt so much gratitude and was never embarrassed when either one of them showed their affection for her. But lately with Mr Charles it was different. True, she felt sorry for him. But then so did every member of the staff. But it's me that comes into the closest contact with him, she was thinking. And she would have to deal with it.

Some time ago, she had been putting his freshly ironed shirts away in his tallboy when he had come back unexpectedly into his room. She had thought he had left the house. Suddenly she had felt self-conscious at the nearness of this handsome man with his thick blond hair and those blue eyes. He looked so manly. So well groomed, wearing his City clothes, a well-cut suit, crisp white shirt and dark-blue tie. And yet there were times when he looked and acted like a sad young boy. No wonder she had let silly girlish notions get the better of her.

Mary had started walking out with a lad from the village. He could be seen from the windows, waiting at the gate on

Mary's afternoon off. There had been a suggestion that Jane make up a foursome with another lad. The idea hadn't appealed to her. Her life was good. There probably would come the day when she might think about having a young man; even getting married might be on the cards, because a family of her own would be wonderful. But that day was a long way off.

She finished her cocoa and got slowly to her feet. It was time she was in her bed.

As she walked up the stairs, she sensed that life for Mr Charles had become very complicated. She had no idea why she should feel that somehow that fact was going to have a great effect on her own life.

If it were true, what was she supposed to do about it?

Her feelings were too mixed up for her to answer that.

Chapter Nineteen

JANE WOKE EARLY on Christmas morning and knew the whole holiday was going to be a great success. Mrs Wilson had been up half the night, and the smell of roasting turkey and pork filled the air. Beside Mrs Rogers, there were two other house guests: Dorothy and Richard Stuart, who, Jane knew, had been largely instrumental in securing a place for her at Winchelsea Lodge all those years ago.

Jane had been asked if she wanted to spend most of the time upstairs or below stairs with the other staff, Miss Christine not having quite so much need for her while Elsie Rogers was there. Jane was pleased to be given the choice and gladly said she would like to be with the three girls.

With breakfast over, they all trooped upstairs: Mr and Mrs Wilson, Mary, Sarah, Daisy and Jane.

Christine and Charles were standing in the main hall near to the huge Christmas tree, waiting for them. Elsie Rogers stood beside them looking very pleased with herself.

'We wish you all a very happy Christmas and we'd like

you each to have a gift. If you'd distribute these, please, Mr Wilson,' Charles said, smiling broadly.

Mr Wilson took his work very seriously and made a formal thank-you speech before giving everyone a small box with a name tag attached to it, and a festively wrapped parcel from Mrs Rogers.

No one opened their presents until they were back in the kitchen.

All four girls had each been given two half-sovereigns.

'Are they real gold?' Daisy asked, absolutely astounded at her employer's generosity.

'Course they are,' three voices assured her.

The girls' parcels were quickly unwrapped to reveal hand-knitted cardigans which Jane knew from experience Mrs Rogers would have bought at a church sale of work. They were all very nice. Jane really liked hers; it was a rich Oxford blue, with a pattern down each side in cable stitch and leather-covered buttons that did up to the neck. She held it up to her face, feeling the softness and the warmth of the wool.

A glance was exchanged between Mr and Mrs Wilson, who marvelled that the girl who had come to this house wearing a terrible dress and boots that were a couple of sizes too big for her, and looking as if she had been really ill, could have changed so much. About nine months ago, that was all it was. But what a change. Now she had blossomed, her cheeks had filled out, and yes, she was a poised and lovely young woman.

Mr and Mrs Wilson opened their parcels, and their faces showed they were more than pleased with what Mrs Rogers had bought for them. For him there was a sleeveless pullover, and for Cook a huge crocheted shawl. Their boxes containing money they put aside to open later in the privacy of their own house.

Mary, Sarah and Jane were allowed to accompany the five adults from upstairs to the special Christmas church service. Daisy remained behind to help Mrs Wilson. Once they were all back, it was time to serve lunch.

'I still think it should be called dinner,' Mary whispered to Jane as they followed Mr Wilson up to the dining room, each carrying a huge tureen.

Now it was late evening. Everyone had eaten their fill and Mrs Wilson had covered the kitchen table with a chenille cloth, placing a bowl of fruit in the centre and another bowl filled with brazils and walnuts to the side of it.

'Pull the curtains, one of you,' Cook called out. 'And you others sort out the board games and bring them to the table. With the cold buffet supper we've laid out in the dining room, I don't think they'll be wanting much more upstairs tonight if I'm any judge, so perhaps Mr Wilson will relax his rules for once and pour us all a drink.'

Mr Wilson nodded his head and gave his wife one of his rare smiles, saying, 'After all, it is Christmas.'

Jane went to the window and stood looking up into the garden. It was a bright starry night with signs that there was going to be a heavy frost. A few days ago there had been the mention of a white Christmas, but no snow had fallen yet.

She was about to pull the curtains when she saw Mr Charles. He must have fetched his car out from the garage earlier. She watched as he now stowed several parcels on the back seat, then got in behind the wheel, started the engine and put the car into gear. The wheels rolled forward across the gravel.

Even today he has to leave his family and go to her, was the first thought that came to her mind. Then she hastily told herself, not that it's got anything to do with you.

It had been a wonderful day. One Jane told herself she would remember for the rest of her life. Mr and Mrs Wilson couldn't have been nicer if they were the parents of the four girls.

They had all eaten exactly the same dinner as their employers: turkey with bacon rolls and sausages, leg of pork with crisp crackling, roast potatoes, buttered sprouts and baby parsnips, bread sauce and cranberry jelly, home-made, of course. And best of all, at least to Jane, had been the gravy! Dark and rich, made from all the juices from the bottom of the roasting pans, just as Mrs Wilson always did it, but today she had added wine. It had been gorgeous!

The pudding had been made weeks and weeks before, from candied peel, currants, sultanas, almonds and plump raisins. Daisy had moaned about having been given the job of stoning the fruit. It had also fallen to her to grate the huge lumps of suet that the butcher had delivered especially. Being the tweeny in a big house was hard at times.

Of course the pudding had to be eaten with brandy butter and clotted cream. And as if it were her consolation prize, Daisy had screamed with delight when she had discovered not one but two silver threepenny pieces in her portion.

'I shan't spend my silver joeys,' she had quietly stated. 'I shall take them home and give them to my mum, 'cos they're supposed to be lucky, aren't they?'

'They are indeed,' Mr Wilson assured her, thinking to himself how little it took to please this young lass.

Now they were playing games: snakes and ladders, ludo, housey-housey, draughts and shove-halfpenny. Jovial laughter and lots of teasing of each other was probably helped along by the fact that all four girls had been given a glass of port and lemon. It had certainly brought the roses to their cheeks.

'Time for a break,' Mr Wison declared as he got up to shovel more coal on to the fire, sending sparks flying up the chimney. And now there was more food being placed on the table, and what was this that was coming out of the larder? Funny hats, and a box of crackers for the girls to pull. Sausage rolls were going into the oven, and mince pies. It was like a real family children's party.

But finally Mr Wilson said it was time he took one last look upstairs to see if anything was needed, and that the girls should go to their beds.

They got up from the table, now littered with coloured paper from the crackers, jokes and riddles which had caused so much laughter as they had been read aloud, nutshells, and tangerine peel. Mary led the way. As they went, they each in turn paused to stoop and kiss Mrs Wilson's plump cheek and thank her and her husband for having given them such a happy Christmas Day.

There were only two days left of the old year. In the small sitting room, in front of a roaring log fire, Jane had been listening attentively to Elsie Rogers for the past half-hour. Now she said, in a low, thoughtful voice, 'So what you've found out is that both my mother and Wally Simmonds did apply for passports, and also made an application to be considered as emigrants to Australia.'

Elsie nodded. 'But as I have already told you, the trail went cold from there.'

'So what happened? Can we find out if they ever went or not?'

'I don't know.' Elsie gave a slight shrug of her shoulders. 'Despite all my efforts I truly don't have any idea.'

'But why would they apply and then do nothing about it?'

Elsie shook her head. 'I haven't a clue, Jane. I want to help you find your mother, you know I do, but I don't as yet know what my next step will be. They both went to Australia House, that much I have established, but from that point I can't find any trace of either of them. I'm baffled, truly I am.'

Jane sighed and took a sip from the cup of tea in front of her. Then she leaned back in the chair, and glancing round the room said quietly, 'Last night I couldn't sleep. I suppose I dozed off and on, but mostly my mind was wandering way back, trying to remember things.'

'And did you think of anything that would help?'

'Not about my mother leaving Mickey, though from what I do remember she would have had good cause. To my mind she was always terrified of him. No, the clearest pictures that came to mind were of me being in hospital. Whenever I woke up or cried because I was hurting, my mother always seemed to be there beside my bed. She would hold my hand, smooth my hair back from my face.'

There was a heavy silence between them. Eventually, Jane looked at Elsie earnestly, and said, 'She kept telling me how much she loved me.'

'We both know that is true, Jane. And I know full well that giving you up was the only thing she could do at that time. She had no other option.'

'I tell myself that over and over again, and I do my best to believe it. But if that was the way it was, why did she never keep in touch with me? Not even one birthday card in all these years! Why, Mrs Rogers? Why?'

All the feelings that Elsie had ever had towards Jane now rushed to the fore. She wanted to take her into her arms, tell her she would dearly love to be looked upon as her mother, but at the same time she knew it would be of no use.

It had been a privilege to be part of Jane's life, but the need to find her real mother was so great. Jane's big blue eyes were brimming with tears and her face was so bleak that Elsie's heart went out to her.

She swallowed hard. 'I don't know, Jane, she must have had her reasons. I'm sure it wasn't because she didn't want to.'

Jane's thoughts were rushing around in her head and she bit her lip before asking, 'Do you think she may be dead?'

'No, not for a moment do I think your mother is dead, but there's one sure way to find out. Somerset House is the next place I will check; it's where a register of births, marriages and deaths, for the whole of Great Britain is kept. It's a proper mine of information. And while I'm there I'll check if your mother obtained a divorce from Michael Jeffrey; that's if they keep records of divorces, I'm not sure about that.' She certainly would have had sufficient grounds, Elsie thought grimly. 'Can't think why I didn't think of going there before now,' she added out loud.

'Where is this Somerset House?' Jane asked eagerly.

'In London, between Victoria Embankment and the Strand. As soon as I can get up to town I shall spend some time there. We'll find your mother, Jane. Just be patient and bear in mind that it might take some time. But in the end we shall find her. You'll see.'

'I'd like to drink a toast to that,' Jane said, doing her best to smile as she raised her teacup.

'Me too,' Elsie agreed, 'even if it is only in tea, but come the day and we'll change it to champagne and that's a promise. Meanwhile, my dear, remember there are a great number of people who do love you, and I hope you know that I head the list.'

Jane leaned forward and took Elsie's hand between both of hers.

She was too full to speak.

Besides, words were not necessary.

There was a long-established bond between these two.

It was the second week in January before Elsie Rogers was able to get to London. She took a taxi from outside the railway station, and as she walked through the massive doors of Somerset House she found herself in the records office itself. Everywhere she looked there were stacks and stacks of ledgers lined up on shelves. What a daunting task if one had to search through that lot, she muttered to herself as she made her way to the main desk.

The officer in charge was a handsome man who wore his uniform well. He smiled as he said, 'Good morning, ma'am, sorry but I have to check the contents of your handbag.'

This didn't take long, and when he had finished Elsie said to him, 'Please can you tell me how I go about finding out if a person's death has been recorded.'

The officer directed her to an enquiry desk where two clerks were standing ready to be of assistance. Briefly, Elsie told one of them the reason for her being there.

'Have you any idea of the date when the death might have occurred?' this capable young woman asked.

'Well, yes.' Elsie hesitated. 'I know she was alive and well early in 1921.'

'Well, as we are only just into 1929, you only have to search through eight years, which shouldn't take you too long. Alternatively you may pay for a search fee and have the work done for you if time is of the essence.' Having said that, the young woman handed a pamphlet across the counter, saying, 'This tells you how to use the Public Search Room.'

'May I ask another question?' Elsie was feeling a bit bewildered by her surroundings.

'Yes, of course. I'm here to help in any way I can.'

Elsie nodded her thanks, then hesitantly said, 'If there is no record of this person's death, is it possible to discover if her marriage has been dissolved, and if so whether she has remarried?'

'Yes, though that would be in a different set of records, Marriages and Births. I'll get you another pamphlet.'

Elsie thanked her, but because she still looked so worried, the clerk said, 'To save time, why don't you go and have a cup of tea, read through both pamphlets and then decide if you are going to do the search yourself. It really is not too difficult. All ledgers are clearly dated, four books for the four quarters of each year, and they're alphabetical.'

Elsie acted on that good advice.

Whilst sipping her coffee she was talking to herself. Looking for a record of Jane's mother's death is just going to be a wild-goose chase. She is such a young woman, only about fifteen or sixteen years older than Jane. I'm quite sure she is not dead and I don't want to stay here all day, searching through endless ledgers. I so rarely get a whole day to myself and never up in London. So I know what I'm going to do, I'm going to pay the search fee, let someone else find the information for me, and I'm going sight-seeing.

When she came back to the enquiry desk, she bided her time, determined to see the young woman who had helped her earlier.

'I've decided to pay the search fee, please, but I do have one or two more questions. Is that all right?'

The young woman nodded her head. 'Yes, of course, fire away.'

'This lady I am trying to trace may have gone abroad to live. You wouldn't have her death recorded if it had taken place outside of England, would you?'

'Oh yes we would. Wherever a British subject dies, the death is eventually recorded here. The information comes through all of the British embassies around the world.'

'I see.'

'It's really quite straightforward,' the clerk went on. 'If your friend's name is not in one of the registers, then she is not dead. She is still alive.'

Elsie gaped at the clerk. 'Thank you very much for your help.' Still she hesitated.

'Was there another problem?' the clerk asked.

'Well, sort of . . . It's like this. If the lady I am looking for is not dead, she is probably living with an old friend. They would have liked to marry, I'm pretty sure of that, but the lady, when I last heard of her, was still married to another man.'

The clerk laughed. 'Don't sound so embarrassed, your problem is not unusual. We do have records of divorce actions. We could probably find the answers you're seeking, which from what you asked me earlier I presume will include whether or not the lady in question has remarried.'

Elsie breathed a sigh of relief before laughingly saying, 'You're a mind-reader. I would like you to make all three searches for me, please.'

'So . . .' The clerk drew a notepad towards her, picked up a pencil and said, 'First we have to affirm that the lady is still alive. Secondly whether she has been granted a divorce, and thirdly whether she has remarried.' Having written all that down, she raised her head and asked, 'Can you give me the lady's full name? And it would help if you can supply her last known address.'

This was no problem. Having reread Jane's case notes, Elsie knew the address in Tooting off by heart, and the exact date when she had last spoken to Jane's mother.

When all details were down on paper to the satisfaction of the lady clerk, Elsie took her purse from her handbag and with trembling fingers drew forth a note. 'How much will the search cost?' she enquired.

'It will be three separate searches and the fee will be seven and sixpence for each search, making a total of one pound two and sixpence.'

Laying the pound note down on the counter, Elsie searched in her purse for a half-crown to add to it.

'That's fine,' the young lady said, picking up the money, 'I'll just get you a receipt.'

A few moments only passed and the official receipt was in Elsie's hand.

'Will you be calling back for the information or would you like the search set out in detail and posted on to you?'

'Posted on would suit me better, please. Here's my address,' Elsie said, handing one of her business cards across the counter.

The clerk raised her eyebrows as she read the information on the card. 'You should have said you were involved in social work for the law courts. I'm sure one of my superiors would have gladly helped you at no cost.'

Elsie smiled softly. 'Please, don't worry, what I'm doing today is for my own personal reasons and I am truly grateful for your help.'

Feeling very relieved, the clerk held out her hand. 'I hope the search will bring forth all the information that you are seeking and that the outcome will be good.'

'So do I,' Elsie murmured as she turned away.

So do I.

Chapter Twenty

JANE HAD BEEN sitting sewing, only half listening to what Charles was saying to his mother. But when he raised his voice, sounding annoyed, she sat up and began to take notice.

'I never gave it another thought until I checked my diary last night,' he scowled. 'Bit of a nuisance but I'll have to ring the telephone exchange and ask them to put the engineers off.'

'I'm sorry,' Christine murmured without much enthusiasm. 'But my arrangements were made ages ago.'

'That's true,' Jane said beneath her breath. Mr and Mrs Stuart had offered some time since to travel up to Moorfields eye hospital with Christine. That fact had niggled Jane quite a lot. Not that she wasn't glad that Miss Christine was going to have a specialist examine her eyes once more and maybe, just maybe, hold out a little hope that some improvement could be made. It was more that she felt she wasn't needed.

And that fact worried her a great deal.

I should be going to London with Miss Christy. That's

what I get paid for! But she couldn't possibly put her thoughts into words. She just had to accept her mistress' decision.

She stood up. 'I don't mean to interfere, Mr Charles, but if it is only a case of someone being on the premises to let the telephone engineers in and stay there while they work, I'll willingly go there, if you'd like me to.'

Why had she made that offer? Pushing herself forward like that. She wasn't as shy as she used to be, but she wasn't normally forward either.

Charles was obviously taken back slightly by her offer. But he recovered quickly and with a serious look on his face said, 'If you are sure you wouldn't mind, I would appreciate it.' Then quickly he added, 'They don't give an exact time, so you might be there some time.'

Jane smiled. 'I'm sure I'll find a book to read.'

Christine said she thought it was a good idea. 'Be a change of scenery for you, Jane.'

'Well, if you're sure.' Charles turned to face her. 'If you could be ready by a quarter to eight on Wednesday morning, I'll drop you off at the cottage before I catch my train to town.'

By twenty minutes to eight on Wednesday morning, Jane was waiting in the main hall.

Charles parked his car at the foot of the steps, got out, came round to the passenger side and held open the door. He looked at her, just a quick glance, smiled slightly and said, 'All right, just push my briefcase down on to the floor.'

Before they were out of the drive, he leaned over and reached into the glove compartment, his forearm accidentally brushing across her knee. Jane felt the colour flood her cheeks. She had never been this close to him before. One eye on the road, he felt in the compartment and took out a Foyle's bookshop bag. 'I bought you a book yesterday just to make sure you won't be bored,' he said, dropping the bag into her lap.

'Oh, thank you.' Jane nodded, thinking how kind and thoughtful he was.

'I hope you like my choice.'

She withdrew the book and read the title: *Jane Eyre*. 'That's great,' she told him, smiling.

'Not a very nice day,' he remarked, glancing quickly up at the sky as he stopped the car at the end of a country lane. 'It's the last one. Far End is the name of the property. Bit isolated, one reason I've decided to have the telephone installed. You have brought something to eat?' he asked, nodding at the basket she had placed between her feet.

'Did you think Mrs Wilson would let me go hungry?'

'No,' he laughed. 'Plenty of tea and coffee in the kitchen. Did you remember to bring fresh milk?'

'Mr Charles! I'm only going to be here for a day at most. I shall be fine. You'd better get going or you'll miss your train.'

From his wallet he took out a business card and handed it to her. His office address was printed there, along with a telephone number. 'If they do manage to get me connected, give me a ring, and if I don't hear from you I shall pick you up this evening. With any luck I should be able to catch an early train. Be back five to five thirty, all right?'

'Yes,' she said. 'I've told you, I shall be fine.'

She stood by a hedge and watched him back up and drive off towards Rye railway station. Then a biting wind made her tug her hat down securely. It's really pretty here, she was thinking as she walked alongside a stream which ran on the opposite side of the lane. Further along she passed a row of six terraced houses. Then there were several yards of shrubs and trees with fields beyond on both sides of the lane before she came to the detached property known as Far End.

Her first impression was that it was just like an illustration from a child's story-book. Thatched roof, small leaded lattice windows, dark oak front door with heavy studded iron bars. A front garden with stepping stones. Shiny shrubs that were green and leafy despite the fact that it was still only early February.

She took a deep breath, swung open the garden gate and walked up the gravel path. She glanced around to see if anyone was about.

There was no one. She could have been in a world all of her own. It was so quiet. All she could see was sheep in a field, but as she put the key into the lock she noticed a blackbird sitting on a fence looking as if he were watching her. Then she heard the sound of pigeons cooing softly, although she couldn't spot them. She decided they were playing it safe and staying warm under the eaves.

The minute she stepped inside the cottage a smile settled on Jane's face. First glance said beautiful. Charming. There were silk-shaded wall lights and she switched them on. The hall was decorated in soft greyish blue and all the paintwork was gleaming white. She opened the door on the left, obviously a dining room. The table was an antique with brass claw feet and the chairs were covered in pearl-grey velvet, There was an open fireplace with an oak surround, and a basket of logs stood in the hearth.

Moving across the hall, she entered the front sitting room. Fascinated, she walked slowly round. If Mrs Harman had lived here, a fact of which Jane was aware, then all traces of her had been removed. This was a gentleman's retreat.

Certain things in the room were worn, even a little shabby, but the impression she got was one of leather and brass fittings. Two deep armchairs in a burgundy-coloured leather stood one each side of the fireplace. Peeping further she looked into a kind of alcove which made the room an L-shape. Oh yes, this was Mr Charles's retreat all right. One huge leather-topped desk and a swivel captain's chair, almost a replica of the one he used in his room at Adelaide House. There was a pipe rack on the wall and to her amazement a dog's basket in the far corner. A basket for a very large dog, by the look of it.

There were no dogs kept at Adelaide House, though Jane had often seen Charles set off across the fields with a labrador in tow, but that dog, Calum, belonged to one of the gardeners.

Strange! If she could summon up enough courage, she would like to ask him about that. After setting her packed lunch out in the small but very neat kitchen, Jane decided it was in order for her to look upstairs. Though as she trod the narrow carpeted stairs she smiled to herself and said aloud, 'Curiosity killed the cat!'

There were three bedrooms, although one was little more than a box room. Adequate, clean and tidy, but lacking a woman's touch was what she decided. The bathroom was tiny, and a big old-fashioned tub on feet took up most of the space. The washbasin was big, with heavy brass taps, and a wooden shelf above held everything a gentleman needed for shaving and grooming himself. Two white bath towels hung from a brass rail, not very tidily. Jane took them down, shook them, refolded them and placed them back over the rail. From a hook behind the door hung a gentleman's paisley dressing gown.

Halfway down the stairs she stopped on the landing and

perched herself on the wide windowsill. From this window she could see the outline of Rye's girls' school. The years she had spent there had not been unhappy and she smiled as memories came flooding back. When she had first gone there there had been no lighting at all in the school. If it got dark too early in the winter, the headmistress would pop her head round the door of each classroom and ask the teacher to allow the pupils to go home early. The excitement when electricity had been installed had been great, and that had only been a couple of years before she had left.

They had been taught that Rye was one of five ancient ports on the south coast of England lying opposite France. And the fact that it was so near to Winchelsea had been marvellous. Many a happy picnic the Matron of Winchelsea Lodge had prepared for the girls in her charge to eat on the beach there.

Jane sent up a silent prayer of thanks.

Her life to begin with had been rough. Very rough. She had lived in terror of Mick Jeffrey, knowing that no matter what she did, she could never please him. But since she had been taken away from him, life had not been so bad. The only blight had been the loss of her mother and Tommy. It had meant the loss of her whole family really, because as far as she knew she had no one else. Still, the years here in this area could have been a thousand times worse, and she had so much to be thankful for. Her time in the home had come to an end, as was inevitable, and again she had found that life on your own could be rough, even terrifying. Then look what had happened! She had met some bad people, but on the other hand she had meet some really good folk. And to have landed up as companion to Miss Christy was almost unbelievable when you compared the way she lived now to what her life might have been if she had stayed and found work in London.

The door bell ringing broke into Jane's thoughts, and she slipped off her seat and ran down the stairs to open the door to two energetic-looking young men.

One was dressed in blue overalls; the other had his hands stuck deep into the pockets of his short thick double-breasted jacket.

'Miss Dennison?' the younger of the two asked politely. 'All the outside work has been carried out; we only have to make the connection and install the apparatus.'

'No,' Jane stammered, 'I'm Miss Jeffrey, but I was expecting you, please come in.'

'We shan't bother you for long,' he said, stepping over the threshold and laying down his tool kit, while the other young man looked around before placing a shiny black telephone on its own stand on to the hall table. 'This is the model Mr Dennison ordered. He particularly stated he did not want a wall-mounted version.'

Jane smiled at him warmly, liking them both. 'It's a pretty horrible day out there. Would you men like a cup of tea?'

'Yes please,' they answered in unison.

By the time Jane returned to the hall carrying a tray, there was every sign that the work was well under way. A cardboard reel of white-covered cable was being slowly unwound and the second workman was fitting it to the wainscoting with funny-shaped little clips.

As she poured the tea, the older of the two men said, 'This is good of you. We appreciate it.'

Jane said nothing, but smiled softly and went back to sit in the kitchen. She could hear the low murmur of their voices but when, about half an hour later, the shrill ring of the telephone rang through the cottage, she almost dropped her book. The loud sound seemed an intrusion to the peace and quietness. It was obvious the engineer was talking to the main exchange. 'Yes, all right, we'll make the adjustment if you'll ring back in two minutes,' she heard him say.

She was ready for the second ringing and walked out into the hall as one of the men picked up the receiver. After a few short words he replaced the phone on its stand, picked up a clipboard and asked Jane if she would sign on the line that he was pointing to. 'Just to say that the work has been carried out and checked,' he grinned at her.

It was still early when they left, and Jane wondered what she should do now.

She didn't know anything about the buses, and anyway, with Miss Christine away in London, there was no urgent reason for her to return to Adelaide House. She unlocked and pushed open the back door that led out from the kitchen and went outside, across the gravelled footpath and on to the grass, which was bordered with shrubs. At the far end, almost hidden by trees, was a shed. She lifted the latch, had a good look round and found a pair of clippers lying on the bench. Within minutes she had cut a small bouquet of various evergreens. She looked towards the pastures that lay a few hundred yards away but decided the wind was too bitter for her to attempt a long walk. She turned around and headed back towards the house.

Rummaging in the cupboards beneath the sink, she found two yellow dusters and a tin of mansion polish. From a shelf in the pantry she took down a golden-coloured ceramic vase.

For more than an hour she hummed as she dusted and polished the front room. Her last task was the tidying of a magazine rack and the setting of the vase, which now held water and her glossy greenery, on to the centre of a side table. Was it her imagination, or did the vase of leafy branches bring an earthy garden smell into the room? They certainly looked good. Autumn colours, even though that season was long past, and Jane couldn't help but wonder how it would be to live in this lovely old cottage come the spring and then the summer.

The light was going, it would soon be dark. Back in the kitchen she washed the two dusters and hung them in the pantry to dry, put away the polish, filled the kettle and was just about to strike a match to light the gas when she heard a key being placed into the lock of the front door.

She stood in the doorway and watched Charles take off his overcoat. 'Would you like a cup of tea?' she asked quietly.

'Yes, I would, Jane, thank you.'

Her face coloured up. She could feel it. She hadn't done anything wrong, but she felt guilty. Turning quickly, she went and busied herself with the making of a pot of tea.

'Where would you like it, Mr Charles?' she called out when it was ready and a tray was laid.

'I'm in the den,' he called back, 'so we'll have it in here, shall we?'

The den was what she had been thinking of as the front room. She pushed open the door and set the tray down, and was about to go when Charles put out a hand to halt her.

'I can see you've been busy in here. I didn't expect you to clean up, but it is appreciated and the foliage looks great, alters the room, makes it looks lived in. Thank you, Jane.' Then he glanced at the tray. 'Oh, I say, come now, Jane, what must you think of me? Please, fetch another cup and join me.'

Again she felt the colour rise in her cheeks as she hurried back to the kitchen. She rinsed her hands, splashing cold water against her face, and only when she had dried herself and felt more composed did she do as he had asked.

He had lit the gas fire and the warm glow was welcoming. He had also set the two leather armchairs nearer to the fire, and the small table with the tea-tray on was standing between them. Jane had no option but to sit down and pour out the tea for each of them.

'Did you have a good day?' she asked, desperately wanting to break what was to her an awkward silence.

'Yes, I did. Clients were pretty reasonable today.'

'What is it you do exactly? I mean, I know it is office work.'

He laughed. 'I prepare the accounts for very large firms.'

Jane wasn't at all sure what that entailed.

'How about you? What did you do with yourself? I saw the telephone in the hall; were the men here for long?'

Jane hadn't expected him to be interested in her doings. She hesitated for a moment. 'Oh, first off I started reading my book, and then the workmen arrived. I made them tea, talked to them for a while and cleared up the hallway when they'd gone. Then I had a walk around your garden.'

'Why didn't you phone me when they had finished? They tested the line with the exchange, surely?'

'Yes, they did. But . . . if your secretary or someone else had answered, who would I have said was calling?'

He put his cup down on to the tray and turned his head until he was looking directly at her. 'Why, Miss Jeffrey, of course.'

She didn't attempt to answer him because suddenly she felt very sad. I'm not Miss Jeffrey, not really, she was saying to herself. Mickey Jeffrey was not my father. So who exactly am I? What name am I supposed to go by?

She noticed Charles's cup was almost empty. She got up,

tipped the dregs into a slop bowl and refilled the cup from the pot.

Charles said nothing for a moment. Then, 'It's almost a year since you came to my mother; have you been happy?'

'Oh yes.' She looked across the space to where Charles Dennison was sitting and stopped to consider how to put her feelings into words. Finally, with her voice very low, she told him, 'I could never have dreamed of a life such as I have now.'

'You were in a children's home for a number of years, weren't you?'

'Yes, for about half of my life. From the time when I was eight until I was sixteen.'

'However did you come to be sent away? Eight years in a home!' he remarked sadly. He had led such a sheltered life he couldn't imagine such a thing. It was beyond his comprehension. 'Were you taken away because your parents ill-treated you?'

'Not my mother. She was a saint. It was my . . . well, I now know he was not my father, but he was married to my mother and he resented the fact that he had to provide for me.'

'You mean he hit you?'

Jane hung her head. 'Whenever he felt like it. I hated the fact that my mother never stopped him, but now I am older I realize that there would have been severe consequences for her if she had. As it was, he didn't treat her very kindly. She did her best.'

Charles looked dismayed. 'To be turfed out like that! I can't begin to imagine a life without one's family.'

Jane smiled at him then. 'I was lucky. Largely due to Mrs Rogers. Everyone who lived in Winchelsea Lodge became my family.'

Charles studied Jane's face for a moment. There certainly was a vast difference in this young lady compared to the thin mite she had been when first she came to be his mother's companion. But he decided that the main difference was that Jane had learned to smile. Really smile. Such a lovely smile that it lit up her face.

Thoughtfully he said, 'Well, I'm glad you came to us. I've told you before, my mother rates you really highly.' He stood up and drank the last of his tea. 'We should be making a move. I've spoken to Wilson to let him know there will be only the two of us for dinner. I just have one call to make.'

Jane packed the cups and saucers on to the tray as she listened to him ask the operator for a number, using his new telephone for the first time. She felt bewildered. She had supposed that while Miss Christine was away she would eat her meals in the kitchen with the three other girls. Now he was taking it for granted that she'd eat with him in the dining room. She was used to having her evening meal with him, but only ever when his mother was there also.

During the short journey home scarely a word passed between them.

When Charles stopped the car she was out of it before he had time to come round and open the passenger door. Once inside the house, she went straight upstairs to her room, undressed and had a good wash. What should she wear? It wasn't as if she normally wore a uniform as Mary and Sarah did, but then she never dressed for dinner either, normally just freshening up by changing her skirt or her blouse.

It didn't seem proper, just her and Mr Charles eating together. Such familiarity couldn't be right. Should she object? And if so, how did she go about it?

Too late.

She desended the stairs to find that the table in the dining room was laid for two and Charles was waiting by the fire-place, one arm resting along the marble mantel-shelf.

'Come on in,' he called as she hovered in the doorway. 'I'll pour you a drink, you have certainly earned it.'

He walked to the centre of the room and handed her a glass of sherry. Then, returning to the hearth, he picked up his own glass and raised it. 'To better communications now that I have my own telephone,' he grinned.

Jane said nothing, but smiled and raised her glass a little before taking a small sip.

She was almost praying that Miss Christine wouldn't remain in London for too long. Her being alone with Mr Charles felt funny.

It was almost more than she knew how to cope with.

Chapter Twenty-One

As Jane picked up the letter that lay on her side plate, her heart was in her mouth. 'Who on earth would be writing to me?' she muttered.

Christine Dennison smiled to herself and said, 'There's only one way of finding out, Jane. Open it quickly before your breakfast gets cold.'

Jane pulled the single sheet of lined paper from the envelope. It looked as if it had been torn from an exercise book. She glanced quickly at the bottom and was perplexed to see the printed capital letters stating that it was from Hannah and John Watkins. She had to rack her brains, but as she read the note she realized that they were Nancy's neighbours, the ones who lived opposite her in Selkirk Road.

Their letter was short and to the point.

> Dear Jane,
>   Nancy Briggs is ill. We do our best but she needs someone to help her. She won't thank us for telling

you but we hope we are doing the right thing.

Yours respectfully,

Hannah and John Watkins

P.S. We found out where you work from one of the letters you wrote her.

Christine watched the colour drain from Jane's face. 'That letter has to contain bad news,' she commented. 'Is there anything that I can do to help?'

Jane handed her the letter.

Beside Christine's plate lay the silver-handled magnifying glass that she now used since an operation on her right eye had proved partially successful.

'Oh Jane, I am so sorry. If your dear friend Nancy needs you then there is no two ways about it, of course you must go today.'

Jane made a feeble attempt at protesting but in her heart she knew she had to get to Tooting very quickly.

'I'll have Brownlow fetch the car round and run you to the station as soon as you are ready,' Christine said kindly.

'But your post?' Jane nodded towards the pile of unopened letters that lay in front of Christine.

'Don't let it worry you. I'll read what I can, and anything to do with business that needs answering I shall pass on to Charles. Now eat your breakfast and then go and get yourself ready.'

Jane pondered on her position in this household. She had come here as companion to Miss Christine, but in the time that she had been here her role had changed considerably. Miss Christine was fond of saying that she was indispensable. Well, there had never been a job that she had refused to do, and she had learned so much. Sometimes she believed she must be the luckiest girl in the whole world. But she must never forget that when she had been lonely and very afraid it had been Nancy who had been there for her, even going so far as to offer her a home. Now it was her turn to repay some of Nancy's kindness.

Twenty minutes later, as Jane was leaving the dining room, Christine called after her, 'Don't forget to pack a case. You won't be able to sort Nancy out and come back tonight.'

It was that thought that was worrying Jane.

What if Nancy were desperately ill and she had to stay with her for a long time?

She couldn't bear to think along those lines. She just felt an urgent need to be there, as Nancy had always been there for her when she needed help.

Once settled in a corner seat of the train, Jane wished it would travel faster. Under different circumstances she would have been thrilled by the journey, for it was the second week in May and all the trees in the orchards that could be seen from the window of the train were covered in the most beautiful blossom. The sun was shining, the blue sky was cloudless and it would be easy to imagine that the whole world was wonderful.

Only it wasn't. Was it?

The last eighteen months had been good for Jane, just as the whole of the time she had been living with the Dennisons had been. But living with educated people, she had learned a lot. It was 1930 and the country seemed to be in a troubled state. Miss Christine always insisted that they listen to the BBC news on the wireless, and from what they had gathered, the United States of America was in a worse state than England was. If that were possible.

With so many men unemployed, things had gone from

bad to worse. On the first of this month there had been a great demonstration in Hyde Park in London. It wasn't only the fact that men had no jobs and so couldn't provide proper housing or clothing for their families; it had got to the stage when they couldn't even feed them. Hunger marches had been organized.

Last week, with the help of Mrs Wilson, Miss Christy had had Mary, Daisy and Jane down in the kitchen helping to pack food parcels, which were later collected and handed out to what Christine described as patient queues of unemployed men. So many men were out of work, tramping miles in a fruitless search for a job. Younger men were enlisting in the army as a way of helping to support their parents and themselves.

Sarah had left Adelaide House because her father had got a job up north and she had gone with her family. That had been nine months ago, and Jane often wondered whether it had been a good move. Sarah never wrote, so they had no means of knowing. Miss Christine had decided not to replace her.

Thinking about Sarah and her family made Jane feel a little envious. However her father's job had turned out, and whatever their circumstances, at least they were together as a family. Mrs Rogers' efforts to find my mother haven't been very successful, she thought sadly to herself.

In fact all the trouble that she had gone to had turned up nothing at all.

The only fact that the searches from Somerset House had proved was that Alice was still alive.

As to her having been divorced and remarried, there were no records to show that either event had taken place. It was as if Mrs Rogers had come up against a brick wall.

She had been so kind when telling Jane that awful news,

going to great lengths to explain how difficult it would have been for Alice. As the law stood, for a woman to petition for a divorce was barely an option. It seemed, in the main, that only men were allowed that right. Unless of course if the woman in question should be wealthy. That altered the situation considerably, Elsie Rogers had said wryly; it made all the difference because money talked all languages.

Mrs Rogers had promised not to give up searching, but Jane thought it was useless to pursue the matter any further. At least they had tried, though.

It seemed as if Alice had just wanted to disappear, and if that were the truth then she had certainly covered her tracks well. Jane sighed sadly and told herself to stop going over old ground. Today Nancy had to be her number one concern, and she was dreading what she was going to find when she stepped into Nancy's house.

The journey seemed to have taken for ever. But at last she was in Tooting.

Women were bustling along carrying shopping bags over their arms and dragging children with them. The rag-and-bone man came trundling his barrow round the corner as Jane turned into Selkirk Road, and the ice men were delivering great blocks of ice to the pie and eel shop. Nothing much had altered.

Hannah Watkins was standing on her doorstep, and when she saw Jane she quickly crossed the road and stood outside Nancy's house, waiting for her.

''Allo, luv,' she greeted Jane. 'I 'ope we didn't get you in no trouble, writing t' yer like that.'

'No, it's all right, I am very grateful that you let me know. How is Nancy?'

This kind woman sighed as she stared at Jane. Everyone

in the area was struggling to get by, and there wasn't a soul in the whole street who wasn't saddened by the fact that Nancy Briggs was not getting any better. But there was only so much that any of them could do. Hannah herself was was finding it a great strain caring for her husband and five children, more so since Christmas, when her John had been thrown out of work.

'She seems t' be a bit better this morning,' she lied. 'She's such a nice woman, it must be a terrible worry for 'er lying there not knowing if 'er rent's going t' get paid.'

Fear clutched at Jane's heart and she felt terrible. She knew Nancy had never been well off. She took in washing and did a couple of mornings' work in the big houses up near Wandsworth Common, but as to a regular income, Jane had never asked.

Christ almighty! How could I have been so selfish. She had to swallow hard before saying, 'Well, I'd best get inside and let Nancy know that I'm here now.'

'All right, luv, We've tied her key t' a bit of string since she's bin taken ill so's the neighbours can get in, like. Just put yer 'and in and pull it through the letter box.'

'Thank you very much, Mrs Watkins, I'll see you again.'

'Yeah, I'll pop in later,' she said.

Jane let herself in, walked down the passage and into the kitchen cum living room. She took off her jacket and hung it behind the door, then turned to survey the room.

My God! What a difference to when she was last here. In spite of the bright spring sunshine outside, this room felt cold and damp. The grey ashes in the grate looked as if they hadn't been raked over for days. There was crumpled clothes on two chairs, and looking through to the scullery she saw dirty dishes lined up on the wooden draining board.

Guilt was nagging away at her as she took herself upstairs.

With a hand that was shaking she turned the handle and went into Nancy's front bedroom. Here she was surprised. The room was neat and tidy; in fact it looked quite homely. There were even a few flowers in a jar at the side of the bed. Nancy lay propped up in the big double bed, her arms folded across what had once been an ample bosom. It would have been hard to say who looked the more surprised.

With tears stinging the backs of her eyes, Nancy struggled to sit up. 'My, but you're a sight for sore eyes,' she said. 'You're the last person I expected.'

Jane flew to the side of the bed and, leaning forward, wrapped her arms around her dear friend. She could feel Nancy's shoulder blades sticking through her skin; she must have lost an awful lot of weight. 'Why on earth didn't you let me know you weren't well?' she muttered, unable to stop her own tears.

'Why would I be worrying you? An' I'll 'ave t' be finding out who let on. I bet it was Hannah. Still, I suppose she means well. Anyway, now you are 'ere will yer stop yer blabbering, you're making me nightdress all wet, and please, Jane, make me a decent cup of tea.'

That speech had been an effort. Nancy flopped back against her pillows, and it was then that Jane noticed the blue tinge to her face.

Straighting herself up, she made an effort to smile and said, 'I'll be as quick as I can.'

'Oh pet, you don't know how pleased I am t' see you, an' as for being quick, I ain't going nowhere, so take yer time.'

Downstairs Jane got two clean cups and saucers out from the bottom of the dresser, and laid a tin tray with a milk jug and sugar basin while she waited for the kettle to boil. It would seem that the neighbours had done their best in making sure that Nancy's bedroom was kept clean and tidy, but she wrinkled her nose as she looked around downstairs. Still, these women had their own affairs to take care of. She fell to wondering if Nancy had any family, and if so whether any of them were still living. She knew Nancy had been married because she was Mrs Briggs, but whether or not she had had any children she didn't know. It had never seemed that it was her right to pry.

Jane went back upstairs with the tea and Nancy drank hers slowly but gratefully. When she had finished, Jane wiped her face and hands for her, using the cold water that stood in the jug on the marble-topped washstand. 'When you've had a nice sleep I'll bring up some hot water and give you a good wash. Is there anything particular that you fancy for your dinner?'

'Not really.' Nancy shook her head and it tore at Jane's heartstrings to see that her hair was all grey and so very thin that in places she was almost bald. 'A drop of soup might be nice. Can't seem to manage solids, they won't stay down.'

'Right. And I'll do you some really creamy mashed potato to go with the soup,' Jane told her, wishing with all her heart that she was nearer to Mrs Wilson and her plentiful kitchen. At the thought of the motherly cook, Jane felt a moment of longing, wondering whether she would be able to cope on her own.

'That'll be smashing,' Nancy said, smiling gratefully. 'But don't you go doing too much and making yourself late getting back. We don't want you losing that lovely job of yours, do we?'

'I'm on a week's holiday,' Jane lied. 'Miss Christine said it was about time I took one.'

'That's nice.' Nancy's eyelids were drooping as Jane crept from the room.

The front door was opening as Jane came down the stairs, and Hannah Watkins followed her through into the kitchen.

'It can't 'ave been nice for yer seeing Nancy in such a bad way, an' we guessed yer would want to stay a while, so t' save yer the trouble of going shopping straight off we've gathered together a few bits and pieces.'

'Oh, Mrs Watkins, that is very kind of you,' Jane replied as Hannah opened the brown paper bag she was carrying and tipped the contents out on to the table.

'It's not much, but we're all in the same boat really. That tin of corned beef came from Jenny at the corner shop, an' she put in a pint of fresh milk. Mavis next door put in that packet of Edwards desiccated tomato soup powder. I bought yer some potatoes and a few carrots, an' Stan, whose garden backs on this one, gave two fresh eggs, 'cos he keeps chickens.' Having explained all that, Hannah dived into her pocket and pulled out a handful of pennies, smiling as she said, 'An' the men had a whip-round. It's only coppers but they said it would make sure that you'd got some pennies for the gas meter.'

God! That flung Jane's memory back into the past and that first awful week she had spent on her own in that top room of Mrs Forrester's house.

For a moment she was unable to speak. She was full of gratitude that her own life was now so good, and at the same time overwhelmed and even ashamed that these good folk who were scraping along as best as they could to keep body and soul together were still more than willing to help each other.

Taking a deep breath she said, 'Thank you, Hannah, and please thank all the neighbours. But truly there is no need to worry any longer. I'll stay with Nancy for as long as she needs me.'

When Mrs Watkins had gone, the truth of what she had just said struck Jane full force. Of course she had meant it. She would stay. But would it mean that she would lose her job? She shook her head hard.

There was no choice. None whatsoever.

Some time later, having watched Nancy struggle with a few spoons of soup and potato and then fall back heavily against the pillows and close her eyes, she decided she would let her be. Come back later and wash her and remake the bed.

She closed the door quietly.

With a terrible feeling of fear and dread, she tidied the living room, raked out the cold ashes from the grate and laid a fire ready to be lit later. Then she put dirty clothes out to be washed, did the washing-up and scrubbed the scullery floor. Outside, she cleaned the lavatory pan with Vim and scrubbed the wooden seat, then swept the yard. From time to time she went upstairs to listen outside Nancy's bedroom door. As she worked she couldn't help making comparisons.

Her own way of life was so different to what these poor folk had to deal with. She thought about the delicate clothes that she washed and ironed for Miss Christine. The car that was there whenever they needed it. The wonderful meals that Mrs Wilson prepared day in day out. Even afternoon tea served on white lace-edged cloths and bone china.

All were expressions of wealth and by and large taken for granted. But now she was really seeing how the other half lived and how her own life could so easily have been spent in this part of London. 'I have so much to be grateful for,' she said aloud as she poured yet another kettle of hot water into the enamel bowl and began rubbing a nightdress of Nancy's with a bar of yellow Sunlight soap.

It was almost dusk by the time she had finished. Taking a box of matches with her, Jane climbed the stairs, but before she could put match to the gas mantle she stood by the side of the bed staring down at her dear friend. She felt so utterly useless. And she blamed herself for not having known that Nancy was so ill. Tears burnt the backs of her eyes and the lump in her throat threatened to choke her.

Nancy's head was slumped on her chest, and terrible sobbing sounds came from her mouth. She was crying in her sleep.

Kneeling at the side of the bed, Jane touched her arm lightly.

'Nancy, I'm here, shall I make some tea and we'll have it together?'

Nancy's eyes opened and she stared at Jane, bewildered, frightened. 'Jane . . . ?'

'Yes, I'm here. You must have been dreaming.'

'Yeah . . .' She shuddered.

'Nancy, it's all right. I *am* here and I shall stay for as long as you need me. Truly I will.' She held her friend's face between her palms, covering the weatherbeaten cheeks with kisses. 'You're going to be all right. You'll soon be feeling better.'

'You're staying the night?' Nancy asked, disbelief sounding in her voice.

'For as many days and nights as you need me.' Jane patted her shoulders and back, soothing her as if she were a terrified child.

'Never felt so rough that I've 'ad t' stay in bed before,' Nancy muttered. 'Me legs are so bad it don't feel as if I'll ever be able to walk again.'

'You will,' Jane told her, rubbing the space between her bony shoulder blades. 'You will.'

'Jane, I'd give anything t' be able t' get up an' cook you a nice tea. Never wanted you t' see me like this.' Her words slurred drowsily.

'Ssh,' Jane murmured. 'I'm going down now to make us that cuppa.' She straightened up to go, but suddenly Nancy put out her arms. Jane went into them and they hugged, each comforting the other.

'I've not 'ad a bad life an' you're not to upset yerself over me.'

'Oh, Nancy,' were the only words Jane could bring herelf to say.

As she walked to the door she tossed her head as if to throw off the doubts and insecurities that were filling her mind.

She paused and looked back, and Nancy raised her head and smiled.

Jane spent a restless night in the single bedroom, remembering how much happier she and Nancy had been when she last stayed here for the night. Three times she got up when she heard Nancy coughing. The doctor had left some brown pills and a bottle of what looked like red syrup. Nancy said he wasn't due to come again and Jane at once sensed that it was because she could not afford his fee. Well, we'll see about that! she declared to herself. Probably it would be around five shillings, or with any luck only half a crown. Thank God she'd had the sense to bring her post office savings book with her. She had saved up three pounds, eight shillings and ninepence, and first thing in the morning she was going to withdraw two pounds of it. Then before she went shopping she was going to call in at the surgery in Garrett Lane and she wouldn't leave until she'd had a good talk with that doctor. Somebody had to tell her what was wrong with Nancy and why nothing was being done about it. Surely if she was that ill she should be in hospital.

At last it began to get light.

Jane peeped round the door and sighed with relief that Nancy appeared to be sleeping peacefully. Treading softly, she made her way downstairs. In the scullery she filled the tin kettle, and when it boiled she poured half of the water over a teaspoon of tealeaves in the brown pot. Having drunk two cups of tea, she poured what water remained in the kettle into an enamel bowl, and stood naked at the stone sink and washed herself from head to foot.

Later, Nancy did her best to act as her usual cheerful self as Jane carefully washed and dried her, gently combed her hair and finally, with difficulty, got her to sit on a chair at the side of the bed.

She had found a pair of clean sheets and two white pillowcases in the cupboard on the landing. As she furled the first sheet open there was a strong smell of lavender, and Jane smiled, thinking to herself that Nancy must have bought the lavender from the gypsies who regularly called at the houses in all the back streets. Lucky lavender, the gypsies always insisted it was. Well, it hadn't brought Nancy much luck.

'Come on, you old lazy-bones, let's get you back in bed,' Jane said as she lifted Nancy's legs and then straighted the pillows behind her head. 'Now, how about a nice boiled egg and soldiers? I'll bring it up and we'll have breakfast together, but then I have to go out for a little while. Will you be all right or shall I ask Hannah to come and sit with you?'

'Jane, luv, I'll be fine, but I don't really want an egg.'

'What you want an' what you're going to get is two entirely different things,' Jane told her, doing her best to laugh.

Over breakfast they discussed, in a rambling kind of way,

what they were going to do over the next few days. From her handbag Jane brought out a notepad and pencil and began to make her shopping list. Post office first. Doctor second. Try and catch a milkman and ask him to leave a pint each morning because all Nancy seemed to use was tinned condensed milk. Thank God the lady at the corner shop had sent a pint yesterday, but Jane had used a lot of that for the mashed potatoes. Loaf of bread and half a pound of butter. What about dinner? Wait until I see what's in the shops, she decided. Fish might be good for Nancy, a nice fillet of plaice done in the oven in milk and butter the way Mrs Wilson often cooks them. Oh, and I must get a letter-card while I'm in the post office because I have to write to Miss Christine. I'll get two or maybe three, then I can keep her posted as to what is happening.

Friday morning in Tooting Broadway seemed busier than Rye on a market day. People crowded the pavements with baskets, prams and pushchairs, stood in groups chatting, took their turn at market stalls, in the fishmonger's and the grocer's, all the while exchanging snippets of gossip and family news. Jane listened and laughed to herself as women lowered their voices to tell of the goings-on in certain families. This was an entirely different world to the one in which she lived.

She had been out a lot longer than she had intended and it was a quarter to eleven when, burdened with a bulging shopping bag and a brown paper carrier, she made her way to Hannah Watkins' house and knocked on the door.

'Jane! Come in, luv, I've just made a cup of tea.'

'No, I won't stop, I've left Nancy on her own too long as it is.'

'I've been over and Mavis from next door has popped in. Nancy's all right an' we see you've washed 'er an' seen to 'er bed. So come on in, you look as if you could do with a cuppa.'

In the narrow hallway, Jane dumped her shopping and took off her short coat. She had barely time to ease herself on to a chair before Hannah was standing in front of her holding out a mug of tea. 'There you are. Yer'll feel better after this.'

Jane sipped the strong tea, afraid to speak, because tears were not far away.

'There's something yer want to tell me, isn't there, Jane?'

When no reply was forthcoming, Hannah again urged, 'Come on, spit it out. You didn't knock on my door for nothing.'

Jane couldn't help herself. The words came out in a rush. 'The doctor said they can't send Nancy to hospital because there is nothing anyone can do for her. He said her kidneys are failing and it is only a question of time. He didn't try to offer any hope,' she said bitterly.

Hannah took the mug of tea out of Jane's hand and placed it on the table. Then she turned and folded Jane into her arms. 'We all know that, Jane,' she said, her voice ringing with sympathy. 'And we've all done our best. Jenny from up the corner shop even bought two officers from the Salvation Army down here to see Nancy and they offered 'er a place in one of their 'omes. Nancy would 'ave none of it. I'll die in me own bed, is what she told them. In a way I'm sorry we let you know. She never wanted us to.'

Jane sniffed away her tears. 'I'm grateful that you did. I couldn't have lived with myself if she'd gone and I'd never lifted a finger to help.'

'Well, that's as may be. You're 'ere now and you just remember you're not alone. Call on anyone in the whole street, day or night, and fer Nancy Briggs there's not a soul that wouldn't come running. Now drink yer tea and I'll come over the road with yer.'

And after that there didn't seem the need to say any more.

Chapter Twenty-Two

IT WAS TEN o'clock in the morning of the first of June when Nancy Briggs died.

She died, as she had wanted to, in her own bed in the house in which she had been born.

Three days previously she had seemed free of pain and had asked Jane to stop reading to her and to listen to what she had to say.

Slowly she had told Jane things that had amazed her.

Her affairs were all in order, and in a tin box in the cupboard under the stairs were all the papers that would be necessary for her to be given a decent burial.

She also painfully related the story of her early life.

She had only been married six months when her husband left her for another woman. Jane's heart had ached as Nancy had said, 'I was pregnant at the time. I had a son, a perfect little boy, born in this very room, only he was stillborn.'

Jane's head was lowered, cupped in her hands, her elbows resting on the edge of the bed as she listened.

Nancy placed her hand on Jane's thick golden hair and there had been a long silence, only broken when Nancy said, 'I took your mother under my wing when that bugger Mickey Jeffrey brought her to live in this street. Then you were born and you brought me more joy than I can tell you. I could 'ave done murder for what that man did t' yer mum, an' as fer what he did to you . . .' She struggled to sit up. 'If there's any justice at all in this world, that sod will be made to pay.'

The effort of the telling had proved too much. Nancy had slept for most of the rest of the day, and somehow Jane had known that the end was not going to be long after that.

The morning had started off wonderfully.

Jane had come into the bedroom and laid down the tin tray on the bedside table, and then gone to draw back the curtains and let the early sunshine in.

'Lovely morning, Nancy,' she had called. 'And it's the first day of June.'

They had each drunk a cup of tea. Nancy said she did not want anything to eat, and so Jane set about making her clean and comfortable.

Finally Nancy lay quietly, her head on the raised pillows, and just as Jane thought she was going to go to sleep she suddenly opened her eyes and smiled.

'Be 'appy, luv,' she said quietly, then gave what sounded like a long-drawn-out sigh.

'I'm happy to be with you. You know that, Nancy, don't you? Don't you?' Jane repeated, but she knew even as she raised her voice that Nancy wasn't going to say anything else.

Nancy lay quietly, looking for all the world as if she'd

gone to sleep. Her eyes were closed and she looked oh so peaceful.

Jane leant across the bed, kissed Nancy's forehead and let her tears drop on to the cheeks of her dearest friend.

Then she pulled the curtains shut and slowly went downstairs.

For the next hour Jane cried softly to herself until she had no tears left.

The sound of the front door being opened startled her and she hastily got to her feet, went out into the scullery and washed her face and hands beneath the running cold-water tap.

'It's only me, Hannah,' the call came from the kitchen.

Jane buried her face in the rough hand towel and took several deep breaths before saying, 'It's all over, Hannah. Nancy died about an hour ago.'

Hannah frowned. 'You're quite sure, are you?'

Jane swallowed painfully and nodded. 'I'm sure. Quite certain. You can go up, she looks very peaceful,' she said, her voice a hoarse whisper.

Hannah did not take up the offer. She said gruffly, 'We ought to notify the undertakers. They'll see to everything. Would you like me t' go an' fetch my John? It's only weeks since he buried his mother, he'll know exactly what t' do.'

'Yes please,' Jane managed to say.

The local undertaker took everything in his stride. Nancy's death was no surprise to him. 'Mrs Briggs came in to see us about three months ago,' he told Jane. 'Soon after Christmas it was. Told us she had an insurance policy that would cover everything. Very precise, she was. Even chose what hymns were to be sung. God rest her soul.'

Jane looked at Hannah Watkins and they both had to smile. They were imagining Nancy placing the order for her own funeral and thinking to themselves, God help the man if he gets it wrong!

Later that day Jane screwed up courage and went to use the public phone box that stood in the post office. She heaved a sigh of relief when she heard Mr Wilson's familiar voice. She pressed the button, heard her two pennies fall and began to talk. Not very clearly but in short sentences, she managed to convey that Nancy had died. Now she had the funeral to see to and was it all right for her to stay on here in Tooting until it was all over?

'Jane, slow down.' She almost dropped the receiver. The voice speaking now was that of Miss Christine. 'Jane, are you there? I am on the other line.'

'Yes, Miss Christine. I'm here.'

'Dear Jane. We are all thinking about you. Of course you must stay until after the funeral, and if there is anything that you need or that we can do, you have only to ask us. Do you hear me?'

'Yes, Miss Christine. Thank you. But Nancy left everything in order. Though I . . .'

'Jane, what is it?'

'I was wondering . . .' Again she couldn't get the words out. 'If it is all right . . . do I still have a job?'

'Oh Jane,' Christine murmured sadly. Then, as if talking to herself, she said quietly, 'We've let you down badly. Left you to cope. Now as soon as you are ready to come home you ring again and Brownlow will come and fetch you.'

'Oh miss, there isn't any need for that!'

'Just listen, Jane, and do as I tell you. We've all missed you. Me especially. And whereas I wouldn't have dreamed of encroaching all the time your friend needed you, now that you've done all that you can do you *must* come home. Promise me you will ring again soon.'

'Yes,' Jane replied, 'I will.' But she stood holding the tele-phone receiver against her cheek for a while before replacing it.

Miss Christine had twice referred to Adelaide House as 'home'. Oh, that was music to her ears. At last she had a place where she belonged!

Jane had asked that both Mr and Mrs Watkins be present when she unearthed the tin box from under the stairs.

The three of them sat around Nancy's table, over which Jane had laid a gingham tablecloth, and watched as, at her request, John Watkins tipped the contents out.

There wasn't a great deal. A birth certificate which showed that Nancy had been born in the year 1869. God, she was only sixty-one years old! Jane had thought of her as being much older. There was no marriage certificate. Jane made no comment on that fact. More than likely Nancy had burned it, wanting only to erase all memory of that painful time.

There were two assurance policies. One with the Prudential, taken out by Nancy's father and changed to Nancy's name on his death. It had been fourpence per week from the week she was born. Sum insured, fifty pounds, plus bonuses payable on death. The other policy was with the Royal Britannia Assurance company, the proposer being Nancy herself. It had been taken out at the turn of the century, 1900, the premium being one shilling a week. Sum assured, three hundred and fifty pounds.

John Watkins gasped. So did Jane. Hannah, feet ever firmly on the ground, muttered, 'How in hell's name did she manage to pay a shilling a week?'

The only other thing was a flat jeweller's box which sadly looked very much the worse for wear. 'It must have been in the water at some time,' John said, turning the box over in his hands. 'These are water marks.'

'Open it up,' his wife urged.

A sheet of notepaper lay inside the lid, and John passed this to Jane. The box contained only two things: a very ornate cameo brooch and a gold locket and chain.

'I'd better read the letter,' John suggested, quickly adding, 'It looks more like a will.' He cleared his throat and began.

'"To whom it may concern. I have no wordly goods other than what is in this tin box. The two policies should see me buried. Any cash left over is to be given to the Salvation Army, please."'

Jane smiled to herself at the 'please'.

'"The two pieces of jewellery are for Jane Jeffrey, and I state now that had I been able I would have adopted her right from when she was a baby. The rest of my wordly goods I leave to Jane to do with as she thinks fit."'

It was signed 'Nancy Louise Briggs', and two more signatures showed that she had got two people to witness this written will.

Jane's face coloured up. She needed no telling what she would find if and when she opened the locket. She had no intention of doing this until she was safely on her own.

It was a perfect June morning. Nancy lay peacefully in her coffin, which rested on trestles in her front parlour. Friends and close neighbours popped in to see her for the last time. Every window in every house in the street had its curtains closed tight.

Outside on the pavement lay a wreath that had been bought with subscriptions from local shopkeepers. There were small bunches of wild flowers picked by schoolchildren who Nancy had many a time fussed over. There was a sheaf of white lilies intertwined with green fern sent by Christine and Charles Dennison, and by the kerbstone stood a basket of summer blooms embedded in moss. This was from Jane. She had stood in the shop at the Broadway and watched the young lady florist skilfully make it.

Now the men were taking their caps off. The hearse had arrived. Two men dressed in black removed their top hats as they came into the house, closing the door of the front room behind them.

'They're screwing the lid down now,' Mavis from next door whispered to Hannah.

On the shoulders of six strong men, Nancy was borne from her home and out into Selkirk Road. The black-plumed horses stood stock still as her coffin was lowered to rest inside the carriage, which had glass windows on each side. Flowers and wreaths were arranged.

Jane, Mr and Mrs Watkins and Mavis got into the only car that had been provided. Men and women slowly fell in behind to walk the short distance to the church.

The wooden pews were filled with all sorts of people, some of whom had known Nancy for the whole of her life. Jane and the main mourners took their places at the front of the church, and everyone stood as the coffin was carried in.

The young vicar stood silent as folk blew their noses and some cried into their handkerchiefs.

'"I am the resurrection and the life, saith the Lord, he that believeth in me, though he were dead, yet shall he live . . ."'

'Please turn to hymn number twenty-four.'

And they sang 'The Old Rugged Cross'.

Then Nancy's doctor read a few verses from the twenty-third psalm. Then there were prayers and a minute or two of silence, during which Jane did her best not to cry. She was thinking of the moment she had opened the locket. It contained a faded photograph of a new-born baby, and a few strands of dark hair. Poor dear Nancy.

Finally they sang 'Abide With me'.

Then Nancy was being carried to her final resting place.

By the graveside, an elderly woman dressed entirely in black touched Jane's arm. 'It makes it all so final, doesn't it?'

Jane looked bewildered.

'Death, I mean.'

'Oh yes. It's final all right,' Jane quietly agreed.

Afterwards, back at the house, neighbours crowded in. Jane, with a lot of help, had done her best. Out in the kitchen all had been previously prepared. The big table had been laid with a white cloth and the local bakery had provided almost everything. Their fee was to be added to the cost of the funeral, so Jane had been informed by the undertaker.

There were sandwiches of cheese and pickle, fish paste and tomato; bridge rolls topped with boiled ham; spring onions and celery in tall glass vases. To finish off there were Victoria sponge cakes filled with raspberry jam, and two large fruit cakes; or for the not so sweet-toothed there was cheese and biscuits. For the children of the street there was jelly and blancmange. To many the sight of so much food had their eyes popping.

They drank to Nancy. Not much choice there! Tea or brown ale.

By the time the table was almost cleared, one and all agreed that Nancy had had a good send-off and that she had done her friends and neighbours right proud.

Jane drew Hannah to one side.

'I shall be leaving here first thing in the morning.'

'Oh pet, I shall be right sorry to see yer go.'

'Well, I shall miss you too, Hannah. I couldn't have got through all of this without your help, and indeed everyone else's too.'

'What's 'appening about the 'ouse, d'yer know?'

'Yes,' Jane smiled. 'The rent will all be paid up and I have arranged for the Salvation Army to collect most of Nancy's belongings. But I have told them that if there are any clothes of Nancy's or any pieces of furniture that you, or any of Nancy's friends, could make good use of, then you are to have them.'

'Really?' Hannah queried in disbelief.

'Yes, really. And when I go in the morning I will take the key off of the string and bring it over to you. The rent is paid for another week and the Salvation Army ladies won't be coming until after that. So you have plenty of time to sort through, and if you would pack up the things you don't want ready to be collected, I would be grateful.'

'Oh Jane. You suddenly sound so old and so organized. Come here and let me give you a hug.'

Tears were still never far away, and Jane went into Hannah's arms and rested her head on her shoulder thankfully.

It was true. She not only sounded older; she was older. This past month had certainly aged her. Still, she had learned a lot. The main thing being that you didn't need money to have good friends.

This part of London where she had been born certainly didn't have many advantages at the moment. Men with no jobs, children bare-footed, their mothers going hungry themselves in order to put food into their bellies.

Life could be so cruel, thought Jane. But to have friends

around you such as Nancy had had must serve to make it a little easier.

She knew now from her own experience that these Londoners were worth their weight in gold.

Chapter Twenty-Three

FOUR MONTHS HAD passed since Jane had returned to Adelaide House. It was a Thursday morning, the first week in October. Miss Christine was getting herself changed because in an hour's time Brownlow was going to drive them into Hastings. Jane was in the garden, gathering flowers for the sitting room. There were still a few roses and the first Michaelmas daisies, as well as some beautiful bright chrysanthemums. The bunch grew in her hands and the scent of the blossoms was gorgeous.

She heard the telephone ring in the house and paused a moment. Mr Wilson would more than likely answer it. But it went on ringing, so she hurried across the grass and through the side door into the hall.

'Adelaide House,' she said into the mouthpiece.

'This is Mr Thomas, the butcher. That's you, isn't it, Jane? I think I'd be better off having a word with Mr Wilson. Is he about?'

'Yes, I'll fetch him for you if you hold the line.' Jane laid the bunch of flowers carefully down on the hall table and turned to see Mr Wilson coming down the stairs. 'Mr Thomas wants a word with you.' She smiled as she handed over the telephone.

She had never really got over the relief of being back in this beautiful house. The autumn sun was pouring through the landing windows as she walked slowly across the hall, and for the umpteenth time she thought what a wonderful place this was.

'Oh, what a bloody mess!' she heard Mr Wilson roar.

He never, ever swore. What on earth could have gone wrong? She stood rooted to the spot.

'Yes, yes.' Mr Wilson was nodding his head. 'Yes, you're right, she should have been looked after better. Never had much time for the lady myself, but now's not the time to air one's views. Yes, I'll let Miss Christy know and she'll have someone notify Mr Charles as soon as possible. No, no, you did right. Absolutely. Thank you. I'm sure Miss Christy or her son will be in touch with you.'

He replaced the telephone and stood tapping his foot. It wasn't like Mr Wilson to let anything upset his serene manner. But that conversation had! The expression on his face was hard to fathom, but Jane was thinking that it was one of deep regret.

Jane didn't need any telling. Something was wrong. Very wrong. She walked to the door, taking deep breaths. The day was crisp and clear, autumn was in the air and she smelt smoke from the gardener's mound of burning leaves.

Jane shuddered. Whatever Mr Thomas had said to Mr Wilson, it had shaken him really badly. And she'd be willing to guess that it had something to do with Mrs Harman. Suddenly she didn't like her own thoughts. Ten to one it will be more trouble, she said softly to herself.

Over the weekend, Mr Charles had taken the last of the

soft fruits down to Mrs Harman. He had also taken a blackberry and apple pie that Mrs Wilson had made especially. Time had eased everyone's feelings, and if asked they would all agree that sympathy was uppermost in their minds where Frieda Harman was concerned. Money was no problem, that was one thing to be thankful for. Right from the start she had been looked after by a trained nurse, several in fact, because none of them seemed to stay very long.

The fact was that she wasn't an easy person to live with. A troublesome patient, was how the nurses put it. Poor Miss Christine worried over her. It wasn't her problem, but as she said, who else's was it? Who was there to care for the poor woman except Charles? And the burden on him was growing greater by the day. The way things were going, it seemed inevitable that Mrs Harman would have to spend the rest of her life in a home. There just didn't seem to be any other alternative.

Jane had turned, ready to set about arranging her flowers, when she saw Christine coming through the hall, looking, as always, immaculate, but frowning heavily. 'There you are, Jane, I feel we shouldn't be involved in what has happened, but . . .'

'It's Mrs Harman, isn't it?'

For a moment Christine closed her eyes and swayed a little. 'Burglars have got into the house again and this time it sounds as if Frieda has been badly hurt.' She paused and then whispered, 'God help us.' It was a plea, a prayer from the heart, but whether that prayer would be answered remained to be seen.

'Oh . . .' Jane's hands covered her mouth. Who would have thought that burglars would go back a second time? Poor Mrs Harman! With her being unable to move she must have been terrified. For it to happen once was bad enough, but twice!

'Jane, I feel I should go to her, what do you think? I'll ring Charles first, see what he has to say.'

Jane knew, and so did his mother, what he would say.

Brownlow pulled the car to a halt in front of Ashford Manor. As Jane helped Christine to get out of the car, she could feel her trembling. It was the shock of seeing two police-men on the steps. With them was a young woman dressed in a navy-blue suit with a crisp white blouse beneath. The young lady came towards them and introduced herself as PC Howard.

'If you are a police constable, surely you should be in uniform?' Jane had never heard Christine speak so sharply.

'On these kind of cases, ma'am, we try to be as informal as possible. It is only recently that the force has asked for volunteers to work in plain clothes so that invalids and disabled people such as Mrs Harman can feel more at ease.'

'That's good,' Christine murmured. 'Shall we go in? I understand Mrs Harman has been hurt. Is she very bad?'

'Yes, I'm afraid she is. The doctor and a police officer are with her now. The night nurse is badly shaken and I was just about to go and talk to her.' Then, as an afterthought, she added, 'She may prefer it if you were to be present.'

As they walked up the front steps, Christine began to talk, more to herself, certainly not to anyone in particular.

'Years ago this was a fine old house. Mr Harman employed more than twice as many servants as my father did. There was a cook, two kitchen maids and a tweeny, a butler, a footman, two grooms and an endless number of stable lads. Mr Harman had a valet of his own, the mistress had her lady's maid and a housekeeper was in overall charge. How

times change! And they were such good times. All gone so
horribly wrong.'

Jane made no comment, nor did the constable, who had
walked on ahead.

The moment they stepped across the threshold on to the
deep-pile carpet of the huge sitting room, Jane could feel
the tension.

Two females and one male sat in a group near the spacious
bay window. All three wore nurse's uniform. The man, tall
and thin, stood up and came towards them.

'I am Keith Johnson. All this happened before Miss
Russell and myself arrived. We can't tell you anything. If
Mrs Harman needs us then we should be allowed to go and
attend to her, and if not, is it possible for us to leave?'

PC Howard cast a disapproving glance over Nurse
Johnson, who held his head high and returned the look.
'Mrs Harman is receiving medical attention, and no, you
may not leave. I would like to talk to all three of you infor-
mally, just for the moment, and then my colleagues will take
your formal statements later on, if that is all right.'

Keith Johnson nodded his head and sat down.

PC Howard lowered her voice and spoke kindly. 'Nurse
Ryan, this is Mrs Dennison and Miss Jeffrey. They are well
known to Mrs Harman.' Then, turning to Christine, the
constable explained, 'This is Martha Ryan, she was the nurse
on night duty. She had the misfortune to open the door to
the intruders.'

Both Christine and Jane made sympathetic noises.

'Miss Ryan, do you feel well enough to tell us exactly
what happened?'

'I have already told the two policemen. I did so as soon
as they arrived,' Martha Ryan said quietly as she stood up.

This night nurse was a tall, stately and overbearing figure

with steel-grey hair wound up into a bun at the back of her head. It was not so neat-looking at the moment. Great wisps of hair had been torn loose from the bun, and there was a deep cut above her right eye which had already been attended to by the application of iodine, causing a nasty-looking yellow stain on her forehead. The bib of her starched apron was badly torn and there was a streak of dried blood running from her elbow to her hand.

'Where do you want me to begin?' she asked in a gruff voice.

PC Howard smiled gently. 'Let's all sit down and get comfortable. The doctor will be coming down soon, I hope, and he'll let us know how Mrs Harman is. Meanwhile, as I said, it's all very informal.'

'Well,' Martha Ryan began, 'the door bell rang and I was pleased because I thought that for once my colleagues had arrived early. Though I did think it was a bit strange because the time was only twenty minutes to eight. I had lifted Mrs Harman out of her bed and got her sitting in a chair. That's no problem because she weighs barely seven stone. I went to the doorway, then I looked back and asked her if she'd be all right. She nodded her head, even smiled at me, and I told her I would only be a few minutes and that I'd give her her medication when I came back.

'As I was running down the stairs I heard the bell ring again, and this time they must have kept their finger on it. "All right, all right, I'm coming," I shouted. No sooner had I got the door open than a heavy fist poked me hard in the chest, and a big, broad-shouldered man shouted at me, "Why's it take so long to open a bloody door?" He was wearing a woollen mask that covered the whole of his head, with slits cut out for the eyes, nose and mouth. He was yelling loudly all the time, pushing me backwards into the hall. I couldn't understand a word, he was incoherent with rage. There were two other men, though not as big as the first man, each wearing the same kind of woolly face mask. "Calm down, Tony," one of them urged, because he was still shouting and poking at me. He'd formed his hard, bony fingers into a fist and believe you me, every poke hurt like hell. I must be black and blue.' She shuddered and crossed her arms over her chest as if to protect herself.

'I asked him what it was he wanted, though I guessed it was money and any valuables that they could lay their hands on. All he said was . . .' and she made a brave attempt to grin, '"Not you, luv, that's fer sure. Just tell us, is the missus still bed-bound in the front bedroom?" That's when I knew they had been here before. But this time I knew they meant business. They weren't going away empty-handed.

'I knew it would be useless to lie, so I just said yes. Then he asked where the safe was, and when I didn't answer he said, "An' don't try saying there ain't one, 'cos we know damn well there is." I suppose it was stupid of me, but I retorted that if he already knew then he didn't need to ask me.

'That's when the smallest, skinny man found his voice. "Yer saucy bitch," he shouted at the same time as he lashed out at me. His arm might have been thin but it felt like a rod of iron, and the blow knocked me down. As I went to get up, I slipped on the parquet flooring and lay stretched out. That's when this skinny one started to kick me.

'Up until now the third man had taken no part in all of this and I got the feeling that he was much older than the others. Suddenly, though, as I was struggling to get up on to my knees, it was he that dealt me a terrible blow which caught the side of my head. Then he had a fistful of my hair and he was dragging me across the hall.

'The big man turned his back, yanked off his woolly mask and without turning round passed it to his mate, who let go of my hair and tugged the mask over my head, back to front, so that I couldn't see anything at all. My hands were tied behind my back and my ankles were roped together. Then I was practically thrown into the hall cupboard, the door was closed and I heard the key being turned in the lock. Some time passed before I heard their footsteps going up the stairs.'

The silence that followed was unbearable. At least it was to Jane. She leaned towards her employer and whispered, 'Aren't there any full-time staff employed here now?'

'I don't think so. Only a daily cleaner, as far as I know.' Christine sounded puzzled by the question.

Jane felt it was time for her to be bold. 'I think everyone could do with a cup of tea or coffee, don't you, Miss Christine? If someone would point me in the direction of the kitchen, I will make myself useful.'

Christine, who was feeling that the situation in this house today was more than she knew how to cope with, smiled to herself. Her young Jane had certainly come out of her shell since having had to cope with the death of her dear friend Nancy.

'Jane, I think that would be an excellent idea, if the police officer has no objections.'

'None whatsoever,' PC Howard quickly replied. 'I think everyone will be glad of a drink.'

It was more than an hour later before a kindly police sergeant came to talk to Christine and finally tell her that it was all right for her to go upstairs and see Mrs Harman.

Jane opened the bedroom door and stood back to allow Christine to enter first.

The sight of Frieda Harman, head laid back against a pile of snowy-white pillows, her face a mass of bruises, one eye badly swollen, and dried blood around her nose, was enough to make even a grown man cry. Keith Johnson stepped away from the bed and motioned for the two ladies to come forward.

'I'll bring a chair for each of you,' he said, keeping his voice low. Dr Haines said it will do Mrs Harman good to talk, so if it's all right I'll leave you alone with her for a while and go and see how my colleagues are faring.'

'Nurse Russell is preparing some lunch, but Nurse Ryan has been seen by the doctor and is now on her way home. PC Howard has gone in the police car with her,' Jane told him.

'I'm glad to hear that. The poor woman bore the brunt of those men's cruelty,' Christine said in a voice that trembled.

Keith Johnson nodded his head. 'Can't think what we'll do about the night shift. Martha certainly won't be up to it. Dr Haines is insisting that Mrs Harman be taken into hospital, or failing that a private nursing home, but not one of us has been able to convince her that it would be for the best.'

'Please don't talk about me as if I weren't here.' Frieda Harman was struggling to sit up, then her gaze rested on Christine and she looked amazed. 'Oh, you are the last person I expected to come to my aid, Christine. It is so good of you,' she said, but managing to sound as if she didn't want to be beholden to anyone.

'Now, Frieda, don't let's have any of that silly talk.' Christine was doing her best to speak firmly and show that she was in control of the situation. 'We can't believe what you have been put through, but I'm here now and Jane is with me, and we won't leave until you are feeling heaps better.'

'Then you'll be here for a very long time,' Frieda answered obstinately.

Nurse Johnson looked at Christine and raised his eyebrows, but Christine smiled and said, 'You go downstairs and have a little break. We'll be fine here, and if we should need you we'll ring the bell.'

'Hmm,' Frieda sniffed. 'You can ring the bell until your arm aches, but they'll only come when it suits them.'

Christine pulled her chair close to the side of the bed while Jane looked around for something to do. She decided that the flowers and plants which stood on the windowsill could do with a bit of attention.

'Would you like me to sit here quietly, or would it help to tell me what happened?' Christine asked Frieda, her voice full of sympathy.

'Please keep me company. I just can't fathom why those men came back for a second time. Would you be a dear and not tell Charles that I was so frightened?'

'Why ever not? I would have been terrified. Your poor face, it takes some believing that men will stoop so low.'

Frieda had begun to cry softly, and the tears were trickling slowly down her cheeks. Christine took a clean handkerchief from her pocket and gently wiped them away.

'I don't deserve for you to be so good to me. Don't you blame me for messing up Charles's life?' Frieda's voice held a plea.

'Shh, shh, that's water under the bridge. It's cost you dearly.'

Frieda sighed. 'You don't know how true that is. When Nurse Ryan was washing me this morning I was looking out over the garden wishing that the bottom half of my body still worked. I thought how I'd love to be out there today, feeling the frosty autumn air on my face, seeing the trees turning a golden russet colour, knowing the ground would soon be covered with fallen leaves. I haven't been out of this house since the accident, apart from a short stay in a nursing home, which mostly certainly was not for me! I know it's my own fault. Charles always offers. And the do-gooders would be only too willing to push me out in a basket bed-chair. Show me off as a freak. Let folk look and say, quite rightly, that I deserved what has happened to me. No thanks. I prefer to stay here in the safety of my own home.' Her hand went up to touch her face and she winced. 'Only it's not very safe now, is it?' she said sadly.

Christine took her hand between both of hers and soothed her as best she could.

It was a while before Mrs Harman spoke again.

'You know, Christine, when that bedroom door burst open and those three darkly clad men burst into the room, all I could think was, not again! I was so frightened I wanted to die. Yes, I did. There and then I wanted to end it all. Then I realized that I wasn't entirely helpless. Nurse Ryan had got me out of bed, I was sitting in a chair and I could reach the telephone which was standing on the bedside table. And that's exactly what I did. Or more precisely what I tried to do.

'Wham! The biggest of the men moved like lightning. He had my arm in a vice-like grip and dragged it up and behind my back. How it wasn't broken I'll never know. That's when I started to scream, and the skinny man grabbed a linen hand towel, rolled it into a ball and did his best to stuff it into my mouth. I wasn't going to let him off scot-free, so I raked the back of his hands with my fingernails, and I'm not sorry to say I drew blood. Didn't do me much good, though. He said I was a right bitch, slapped me around the face and head and didn't stop until blood spurted from my nose.'

'Oh Frieda! You have been so brave. You really have. Now soon you are going to have some lunch and then you must sleep. You must be worn to a frazzle.'

'Sleep is all I seem to do these days, Christine.' And having said that, she smiled.

'What are you smiling at?' Christine felt the need to ask.

'It was something the police sergeant said to his mate when he didn't think I was listening.'

'Oh, and what was it he said?'

'He murmured that I could so easily have been murdered, and then he added, "But we'll have a hard job proving it".'

Christine looked so shocked that Frieda quickly said, 'Don't worry, it didn't happen.'

Jane who had heard everything, looked across at Mrs Harman's badly bruised face and thought what a plucky little thing she was. Aloud she said, 'Why don't I go down and see if your lunch is ready, and I'm sure Miss Christy could do with another cup of tea. I know I could.'

She was glad to get out of the room. Going down the grand staircase, she couldn't help thinking to herself that the matter of Mrs Harman's safety from now on was going to take a month of Sundays to sort out.

With a note of wisdom she muttered, 'And I don't envy Mr Charles his part in all of this. Not one jot I don't!'

Chapter Twenty-Four

CHRISTINE DENNISON SIGHED heavily as she replaced the telephone receiver. Charles had been on the line again asking her advice. She had no idea what to say to him.

It was a fortnight since the burglars had broken into Ashford Manor for the second time, and in the whole of those two weeks Charles's life had been put on hold. He hadn't been to the office and he had not been home.

His plea, over and over again, was that he could not leave Frieda.

As a woman Christine appreciated that. She herself felt nothing but admiration for Mrs Harman and the way she had tried to stand up to those bully boys. But as a mother, well, that was an entirely different story. How could her son be expected to be in constant attendance on a severely disabled woman? He had his business to consider and his own life to lead. Though never in a million years would she voice these thoughts out loud.

Frieda was adamant that she couldn't be left alone. And that was understandable. On the other hand, there was not a nurse who was willing to undertake the night duty in Ashford Manor. Even the day nurses had stated that they would not attend Mrs Harman unless there was another person in the house who could take responsibility for the patient.

Friends, well-meaning ones at that, had tried to persuade Frieda that she must consider long-term nursing in a residential care home. She would have none of it.

The clergyman had tried, as had her own doctor and a specialist he had brought down from London to examine her. All to no avail. She'd thrown her heavy silver-backed hairbrush at Charles when he had tried to reason with her.

Now Charles was begging Christine to tell him what to do.

He didn't ask my opinion when he first took up with her, and she not that much younger than I am, was what Christine was thinking, and her thoughts were full of regret.

Regret that Frieda Harman had seen fit to leave her husband and in the process had ruined the life of her own daughter and Christine's son.

Not that Charles was blameless. Far from it. He had bought a house and set up home with her. Infatuated by the fact that an older woman had found him attractive, he hadn't stopped to think of what the consequences would be. Now he was paying the price.

And now I'm thinking spiteful thoughts, and that won't help anyone, she chided herself. 'I've almost forgotten what peace of mind is,' she said out loud. 'What do they say? No peace for the wicked, eh? Though what I've done to deserve this load of trouble, I just don't know.'

The day that Charles did come home to fetch a change of clothing, Jane thought her heart would break. He came upon her so suddenly, so quietly, that she didn't hear him approach. She had been brushing the shoulders of Miss Christine's coat and was reaching up to hang it in the wardrobe.

She looked round to see him standing there, so tall and splendid, and as always when she set eyes on him she felt a jolt of genuine pleasure.

'Have you come back home to stay?' she asked.

He was looking at her and smiling gently. 'Afraid not. At the moment it is not possible.' His face looked sad for a moment, then he said, 'I think you, of all people, understand why I have to stay at Ashford Manor, don't you, Jane?'

She nodded. 'Yes.' Her voice was no more than a whisper. 'Yes, I do understand. But . . . your mother worries so . . .' She couldn't bring herself to tell him how she felt he was wasting his life.

He forced a cheerful laugh. 'Oh Jane, there is no need for either of you to worry about me. I haven't thanked you for going to the Manor with my mother. That day must have been pretty awful for both of you. I did appreciate it and I still do, the way you care so well for her.'

Jane felt a lump in her throat so big that she couldn't answer.

'I have to stay at the Manor all the time Mrs Harman needs me,' he said softly, coming further into the room to stand very close to her and take her hands in his.

'Do your best to stop Mother worrying, won't you?'

'Yes, yes, I will.' There was a tremor in her voice and she found she had to blink away tears.

'Jane?' He put his arms around her, lowered his head and leaned his cheek against her hair.

Her heart was pounding against her ribs. Surely he could hear it?

'Oh Jane,' he murmured, over and over again.

She was overwhelmed with love for him!

The full realization shot through her.

It shouldn't be happening. She worked in this household. She might be treated as one of the family, but for all that she was a paid employee. Yet she couldn't help it, no matter what. She knew that she loved this man deeply. Maybe she had done so from the moment when she first set eyes on him. The first sort of love she'd felt was because he was kind to her. It had grown because he noticed her. Made time for her. Let her feel she belonged. This was real love.

Nothing could ever come of it. She was well aware of that. She wasn't in the same class as he was. No matter. Whatever turns her life took, what she felt for this man at this moment in time would never, ever change.

It was as if he read her thoughts, for against her hair he whispered softly, 'Oh Jane, why was I ever so foolish? Why did I rush in head first? I am so weak compared to you. You're so young. You've had a hard life and yet you have come through it all because you're so strong, so positive, so sensible about everything.'

Jane pressed her lips together to stop them from trembling. Against his shoulder, she shook her head, not trusting herself to speak. If she were to say one word, just one word, then she was so afraid that her feelings would come pouring out.

Charles's feelings were much the same.

His infatuation with an older woman had trapped him. At the moment he felt that he would be shackled to Frieda for life.

Only now, as he put Jane from him and walked from the room, did he realize where his true feelings lay. He wanted to tell Jane of the fierceness of his love for her, but that wouldn't be fair on her.

Week after week Charles continued to live at Ashford Manor, indulging Frieda's every whim.

'He's resigned himself to the fact that he has no get-out,' Christine told Jane after he had come to lunch one day. 'It's as if he is taking all the blame on his shoulders, as if . . . he's trying to make amends for the fact that her husband and her daughter have washed their hands of her. He regards taking care of Mrs Harman as his duty.' She sighed heavily before adding, 'Which I suppose is true, really. I just don't want to admit it, even to myself.'

'I think you're right,' Jane said quietly. 'We haven't seen much of him since that second burglary, but he seems changed. Very subdued. Not at all the same Mr Charles as when I first came here.'

'I agree wholeheartedly with you, Jane, and yet . . . he's softer. That's a funny word, but I can't think of another way to put it. He cares so much for me, and for you too, Jane, You know that, don't you?'

'Oh Miss Christy, he's always been kind to me.' She felt her face reddening. She wished she could read Christine's thoughts. Would she approve of her son liking me? she wondered. Or of me loving her son? Never. It just wasn't possible. There would always be that great difference between master and servant.

She realized that her love for Charles had been there for a long time, but it was a true, unselfish love, and because of who he was, she would never, ever tell Charles how very much she loved him.

Chapter Twenty-Five

'NINETEEN TOMORROW, EH, Jane?' Elsie Rogers smiled across the breakfast table, then sat back and studied Jane's face. You've done well, she thought, but what she said was, 'I was more than pleased to receive Christine's invitation to spend New Year's Eve here, because I have a special birthday present for you this year.'

'Really?' Jane sounded excited

'Yes, really, though it isn't a present as such, more of an outing.'

Jane looked at Christine, and with a laugh in her voice asked, 'Did you know about this? And are you coming too?'

Christine grinned. 'The answer to the first part of your question is yes, and to the second part no.'

Jane swivelled round in her chair.

'Jane, be still and listen to me,' Elsie ordered. 'Some very old friends of mine, Betty and Bert Smith, run the café in Tooting Market. I have come to know them well over the years, and whenever I am in south London I usually drop in on them, have a cup of tea and a chat.

About a month ago that is exactly what I did.

'They have six children, only one of them a girl, and she works in the Royal London Hospital in Whitechapel. She's not a nurse; a ward-maid I think is how they described her. When I saw Betty and Bert they had just returned from a weekend break. Their daughter had treated them to tickets for a West End show and on the Sunday morning they decided to pay a visit to Petticoat Lane. And here's the coincidence. They overheard a stall-holder asking for the market manager, and the reply was that Wally Simmonds was attending to a bit of business over in Middlesex Street. Bert made himself known and established that it was the same Wally Simmonds they had known so well when he too lived in Tooting and was market manager there.'

Jane's eyes were wide and her mouth had dropped open. 'Did they know if my mother was with him?' she asked timidly.

'Whoa, hold your horses, Jane,' Elsie cried. 'I didn't want to appear too eager. However, Bert did tell me that he'd learned that Wally was living in one of the little streets near Spitalfields and that he'd now got a wife and a little boy.'

Jane looked perplexed. 'But you said there was no record of them having got married.'

'My thoughts exactly. But at present we have no way of knowing if the lady referred to as his wife *is* your mother. Then it came to me. Just because it is being said that Wally Simmonds has a wife doesn't necessarily mean it's the truth. They could be living together. Your mother might even have changed her name to Simmonds by deed poll.'

Jane put her elbows on the table and rested her head on her hands. Thoughts were whirling round and round in her head. Had her mother been living in the East End of London all this time? Was she with Wally Simmonds? Someone had said he had a wife and small son. Did that mean her mother had had another baby?

Elsie and Christine had discreetly left the room, leaving her on her own with her thoughts. Memories. She was dragging them up.

Her dear little brother Tommy. He'd died and she had never even known that he was ill. Her father had never picked on him. Only on her.

Since Nancy had enlightened her, she knew the reason for that.

Another man had fathered her. Mickey Jeffrey had never been her father and he had looked on her as being nothing but a burden.

But her mother had loved her. She knew that much without a doubt. And her mum had been so beautiful. Nancy had often told her that she had her mother's colouring. Fair clear skin. Big sparkling blue eyes and thick straight dark-golden hair that was so long when she took the pins out at night that it hung well past her shoulders.

That was how she remembered her mother.

But there still was, and always had been, that one question: if her Mother had loved her so much, why had she not kept in touch?

Why?

Jane had never found an answer to that question. Only her mother could give her that answer. If and when she and Mrs Rogers ever found her.

Was the fact that Elsie had stumbled on the whereabouts of Wally Simmonds going to make any difference? Would it bring her face to face with her mother?

Her thoughts were interrupted.

'Bit cold outside, but as it's the last day of the old year, Christine and I thought we'd go for a short walk. How about wrapping up well and coming with us?' Elsie Rogers urged. And when no reply was forthcoming from Jane, she asked softly, 'Are you all right?'

Unable to speak, Jane still didn't answer. She took her time, sat up straighter and wiped her eyes with her handkerchief.

'I wish I knew why she didn't contact me,' she mumbled. 'Up until today I thought we would never find her, but now I feel we might. And Mrs Rogers, I just want to ask her why.'

Elsie came closer and put her arm around Jane's shoulders. 'I think this is the break we've been waiting for. We thought your mother might have gone abroad, but maybe all this time she and Wally Simmonds haven't been too far away. They say plant a tree in a forest and you'll never find it. Perhaps that's the way Wally was thinking. Move from south London into the East End. Who would ever think of looking there? And after all, markets are what he knew about, and he had to earn a living. Oh, and by the way, Jane, I think now you're all grown up that it is time you stopped calling me Mrs Rogers and made it Elsie'

Jane managed a smile. 'Got it all worked out, haven't you . . . Elsie?'

They both laughed, and Elsie said, 'Yes. I think this is what we've been waiting for. We're going to find your mother now, you'll see.'

Jane couldn't bring herself to sound that confident, so she just nodded her head.

'Right then, my birthday present to you, Jane, is a trip up to London on Sunday and a visit to Petticoat Lane. How does that sound? Or, if you want to be a real cockney, you just call it "the Lane".'

'Oh, I do. I've discovered that Londoners have hearts of gold.' Jane smiled properly for the first time since the beginning of this conversation.

It was a real smile that lit up her whole face and made those blue eyes of hers twinkle.

'Put your hand through my arm and hold on tight.' Elsie grinned at Jane, who was standing stock still, gazing at the sea of people and the great mass of stalls that stretched away as far as the eye could see.

'It's only on Sunday mornings that it's like this,' Elsie said, laughing. 'It's when the Lane comes alive and offers what must be one of the most colourful scenes in London. Just listen to the spiel the stall-holders are shouting to gather the crowds around them. It's almost as good as going to the music hall. It's the atmosphere, hard to explain, but I don't think you'd find it anywhere else in the world.'

Jane agreed with every word, her eyes popping out of her head. Surely there wasn't a mortal thing that you couldn't buy in this market, and according to the stall-holders most of them were giving the merchandise away, or at least selling it at a loss! Suddenly they were facing a row of stalls that sold food, and folk were standing on the pavement, even in the middle of the road, eating strange delicacies off small china dishes.

'Stay there.' Elsie pushed Jane up against a lamp-post. 'And don't move. Here, hold on to my bag. I've got my purse and I'm going to get you a real treat.'

It was some minutes before Elsie came back holding a cardboard tray in front of her which held four of these china dishes. 'Come on now, which d'you fancy trying first?'

Having said that Elsie burst out laughing, for to see the look on Jane's face was something else. It was a cross between horror and utter disbelief.

'What on earth are they?' Jane managed to ask.

'Well, the ones that look like snails are whelks. Gorgeous,

but need a lot of chewing. Those in jelly are absolutely delicious. They're known as jellied eels. You have to spit the bones out, though, mind. The small ones are cockles, another kind of shellfish. I've put plenty of pepper and vinegar on them. And the last ones are hot grilled sprats, tiny fish dipped in batter. Tuck in,' Elsie urged.

To Jane's amazement she found she actually liked the food – at least the three that she tried, she did, and especially the jellied eels. The whelks she just could not bring herself to place in her mouth. Though she laughed fit to bust as she watched Elsie chewing away at what she was convinced was a snail.

It seemed that Londoners never stopped eating on a Sunday morning. Loaded down with parcels and bags, men, women and loads of small children munched away at saveloys, hot faggots and even pigs' trotters. There was steaming pea soup being sold by the mugful. Elsie said they couldn't go home without taking something for Christine and the staff, and so she bought gingerbread, muffins and crumpets, and for Mr Wilson there had to be hot chestnuts and salted peanuts.

'But they'll be cold by the time we get back,' Jane protested.

'Oh, never fear, Mrs Wilson will pop them straight on to her hot range, and her husband won't be getting them all to himself, never fear. Now choose yourself a present for your birthday, anything that takes your fancy, and then you and I are going to make a beeline for the market manager's office.'

Wally Simmonds was in his office, and rose to his feet as Mrs Rogers ushered Jane through the door. He looked what he was: a self-assured, thick-set, good-looking man in his early thirties with a weatherbeaten face, dark-brown eyes and a cheerful smile.

Jane had no recollection of ever having seen him before. But it was eleven years since she had, and she'd only been a little girl at the time.

'What can I do for you ladies?'

Jane jumped in feet first. 'I'd like to talk to you about my mother,' she said quietly.

Wally Simmonds looked startled. 'Hang on a minute. I didn't get your names.'

'I'm Elsie Rogers,' said the older woman, extending her hand to him. 'And this is Jane Jeffrey. I suppose you could say she is my ward, since I've been partly responsible for her since she was eight years old.'

Wally glanced from Mrs Rogers to Jane and, having heaved a great sigh, addressed the girl. 'When did you last see your mother? Can you remember that?'

'Vividly,' Jane answered without hesitating. 'It was the last time she came to the hospital, and it was eleven years ago.'

'And since?'

Jane didn't know how to answer that, and Mrs Rogers took over, briefly telling Wally how the Guardians of the Poor had found Jane a place at Winchelsea Lodge, where she had remained until her sixteenth birthday.

'I see.' Wally sat back in his chair, his face showing just how troubled he was. Slowly he stood up and came round from behind his desk. He pulled two metal chairs from a stack that stood in the corner and urged them both to sit down. 'Because this is going to take some time,' he said, shaking his head as if to clear it before he really started to talk. 'I'm not sure how much you know, Jane? About Tommy, for instance?'

Jane raised her head and looked straight at him before

saying quietly, 'When I first went back to Tooting and found Nancy again, she told me everything that had gone on since I'd been taken away. She said that Tommy had died and that . . .' Jane hesitated and swallowed hard. 'Mickey Jeffrey was not my father.' She couldn't go on. Her eyes filled with tears.

Wally took over. 'I found your mother lying on the floor in her kitchen. I thought at first that he had killed her. She was white, white as a sheet, with blood oozing from a great gash in the side of her head. I called an ambulance, but it took twenty minutes to get there. She was taken to Wandsworth Infirmary and two days later they transferred her to Belmont. Said she had suffered brain damage. She was there a long time, and to put it bluntly, the doctors said she had gone out of her mind.'

Jane gave a gasp of horror, but eventually managed to ask, 'How long before she got better?'

'Several months,' he answered quietly.

Jane's eyes were riveted on Wally Simmonds. 'What happened to my little brother, Tommy? And to my . . . father?'

'I don't rightly know. At least not all the details. The police were after Mickey but he'd scarpered, and as far as I know it were neighbours that took Tommy in.'

'So what happened when my mum did come out of hospital?'

'Oh, she came back to Selkirk Road but she was very frail, and trying to look after Tommy on her own wasn't easy. Then Tommy dying was the last straw. It hit her so hard. Set her back no end. I did what I could for her.' He looked away into the distance as if remembering was killing him, and it was in barely a whisper that he murmured, 'For a while Alice believed she had buried not only Tommy but her little girl as well.'

Jane's eyes were brimming with tears. 'Mr Simmonds, are you saying my mother became ill again?'

He nodded his head. 'Yes, very ill. To be fair, Mickey felt the death of young Tommy. It was a great blow to him. He was calm enough at the funeral and indeed during the church service, but back at the house he really let his temper get the better of him and that's when he laid into your mother. She was in Belmont a second time.' He hesitated and turned to look at Elsie Rogers. Almost apologetically he added, 'For a while she lost her mind completely.'

The heavy silence was unbearable. And when Wally spoke again it was to Jane.

'Your mother's illness started because Mickey Jeffrey practically bashed her brains in,' he said bitterly. 'Then the fact that she had lost you and then Tommy unhinged her. She convinced herself she had nothing left to live for.'

'Didn't she even bother to find out where I'd been taken?'

'Yes, she did when she first came home from Belmont, but she hadn't much stamina and all the London associations swore they had no knowledge of your whereabouts. After the second bout in Belmont, she didn't know where she was or what she was doing half the time.'

Suddenly he stood up and spoke with a marked determination. 'Jane, I am so pleased to see you, truly I am, but you couldn't have picked a worse day. Sundays are a nightmare for me.' He looked at his watch. 'I've stacks of paperwork to get through, and in another hour or so I have to be out there in the Lane. By-laws and regulations as to how the clean-up proceeds are all down to me. Can we meet up later? I'll try and give you more information.'

'I want to see my mother,' Jane cut in aggressively.

'I know you do, and of course you shall, but I have to prepare her. We can't just spring you on her. Believe me,

Jane, it's been her life's ambition to find you. She'll be over the moon, I promise you, but you have to give me time.'

Elsie felt sorry for the man. He was all at sixes and sevens.

'We could go to a hotel, have some tea, if you could meet us before we catch our train. Would that be all right?' Elsie asked.

He gave a sigh of relief. 'That's a jolly good idea. I'll call you a cab and you wait at the Great Western Hotel. I'll delegate most of my jobs and be with you as soon as I can.'

It was early evening when Wally Simmonds shook hands with Elsie Rogers and very cautiously put his arms around Jane to give her a gentle hug. 'It will be fine,' he whispered. 'Your mother will be reborn. Mind you, I am going to have to break it to her gently, so be patient, Jane. I promise you and she will meet up soon.'

'Well, Mr Simmonds was really nice and very helpful,' Elsie said as she and Jane settled back in opposite window seats in the train. 'But you don't remember him, do you?'

'Not really. I wish I did.' Jane sighed. 'I suppose it was all a long time ago.'

'Does it matter? Think about it, Jane. It came across to me that that man has stuck to your mother through thick and thin. It's obvious that he really loves her. Try and do as he asked, be patient. I'm sure he'll tell us a whole lot more when he's had time to get over the shock of you turning up.'

Jane felt she had no option.

Was she pleased with the way the meeting had gone? In some ways, yes. On the other hand, she was heartbroken to learn that her mother had been so very ill.

I just can't wait to meet her, she cried inwardly as she closed her eyes and listened to the steady drumming of the train wheels on the railway tracks.

Chapter Twenty-Six

THE TELEPHONE CALL came ten days later.

Christine and Jane were sitting in the garden room having coffee and going over their notes on the upcoming events which were held regularly in the church hall when Mr Wilson came calmly into the room.

'Excuse me, you have a phone call, Jane. It's Mrs Rogers.'

Christine and Jane exchanged smiling glances, and Jane got up quickly.

A few seconds later she was saying, 'Hello, Elsie, have you had news?'

'Yes, I have. I had to be in London so I took a chance and telephoned Mr Simmonds. We met for lunch. You don't mind, do you, Jane?'

'No, no, of course not, but please go on. When am I going to meet my mother?'

'As soon as you like now. Mr Simmonds has prepared her.'

'Elsie, we didn't ask if he was married to my mother.'

'Well, no. Not at that first meeting we didn't. I told him

how we searched the records at Somerset House, and he apologized. They learned Mr Jeffrey was in prison and Mr Simmonds paid him a visit but was unable to persuade him to divorce Alice. Apparently they tried very hard, but it all got a bit messy, so they decided to take the quiet course and move away. Mainly because of your mother's illness. Least said soonest mended kind of thing. They did change her name by deed poll and they never mention the fact to anyone. Alice is, and has been for a long time, to all intents and purposes Mrs Simmonds.'

'Oh Elsie, thank you, thank you so much. May I ask you one question?'

'Of course, fire away.'

'Have they got a little boy?'

'Jane, I'm going to leave some things for your mother to tell you herself. I think that's best.'

There was a lengthy silence until Jane said, 'Now that I know my mother is only a few miles away, I feel strange.'

'Do you mean about meeting her?' Elsie asked, sounding worried.

'Yes.'

'Are you frightened?'

'Yes, a bit.'

'You'll be fine, I promise you. You'll see.'

Jane only hoped that she was right.

It was with her heart in her mouth that Jane walked up the pathway of a small house in a dull street. So many similar streets, surrounded by ugly, grimy buildings. Homes where folk struggled against the dirt and poverty to keep their families close-knit. But since having to cope with Nancy's death, she knew that nothing altered the warmth and good humour of these Londoners.

The house was not as big as Nancy's had been. It was, though, still in the kind of terrace where neighbours would help each other. This particular row were well kept, with clean white lace curtains at the windows and the doorsteps regularly hearthstoned.

Now Jane was facing the brown-painted front door, her hand on the black knocker, and her nerve almost failed her. Taking a deep breath, she banged it once and then stood back to wait.

The door was opened almost instantly by a lovely-looking woman with deep-golden hair, who was dressed in a tweed skirt and a pale-blue jumper covered by a wide white apron. Jane stared into the blue eyes that were gazing into hers, and a warmth such as she had never felt before surged through her body. She had no doubt whatsoever that this was her mother.

They continued to stare at each other for what seemed ages, both at a loss for words, until finally Jane gave a great sigh. It was a sigh of relief, as if she were thankful to have come to the end of a long, long journey.

And indeed that was exactly what it was. It was suddenly all Jane could do not to burst into tears. The relief of suddenly finding her mother again was fantastic, marvellous! It might be that now, at last, she would feel wanted again.

Finally it was Alice who opened her arms wide and said, 'Oh Janey come here,' and when she held Jane tight she started to softly murmur, 'Oh thank you, God, thank you. My beloved little girl. How I've longed for this moment. You'll never know. You'll never know.'

It was a long time before they separated. Neither could find the words they so badly wanted to say.

Then Jane brushed away her tears and said, 'Oh Mum. You really are my mother.'

And Alice was saying, 'Is it really you, luv? At long last. Is it true?'

Tears were trickling down their faces as once again they came together and held on to each other tightly.

They broke apart again and Alice began to sob as though her heart were breaking.

'I've waited eleven years for this day. There have been times when I've given up hope of ever seeing you again. Times when I was convinced you had died.'

Mother and daughter stood for a long time in the narrow passageway, holding on to each other as they shed their tears of sorrow and joy. Sorrow for all the years they'd spent apart, for all the heartaches they'd suffered, for all the things they'd missed doing together. And joy that at last they were reunited.

They sat together on a small sofa in the front room, a tray of tea and biscuits on the table in front of them. Neither of them had touched the biscuits. They held hands. Couldn't take their eyes off each other. Their faces sometimes showed wonderment, even astonishment. Alice shook her head, did her best to swallow the lump in her throat that was choking her, and in little more than a whisper began to talk.

'I never came to terms with losing you, but I had to let you go. Mickey was so cruel and there were times I feared he might kill you. Yet I felt so guilty. I *was* guilty. It was my fault, I should have stood up to him more. Wally said Nancy told you he wasn't your father.'

Jane nodded. 'Dear Nancy, she was such a good friend to me.'

'To me too. Always,' Alice said. 'I was so sorry when Wally came home and told me that she'd died. I ought to have kept in touch, but there were times when I . . . when I wasn't exactly with it.'

'Oh Mum, stop blaming yourself. Nancy told me what a terrible life Mickey led you from the very beginning.'

'Not only me, you too, luv. I thought he was being so kind when he offered to marry me. I convinced myself he would take care of me and my baby. The only other option was to have you put up for adoption, and I didn't want that. He turned out to be a nasty man. A cruel one at that. When he'd put you in the hospital and I agreed to let you go into a home I felt it was for the best. I truly believed that if you stayed with me, one day he would end up killing you. I thought about you every day, Janey. Wondered if you hated me. The times I've wished I could put the clock back.'

Jane rubbed her thumb over and over the back of her mother's hand, all the while staring into those beautiful blue eyes. 'I know, Mum, I know. You did what you thought was the best for me.'

'And you never felt hatred for me?'

'No. I never hated you. But I have to admit there were times when I yearned for some answers. I was always wondering about you, wondering why you didn't write to me, why you didn't want me. Wondering if you did love me.'

'Oh darling, don't say that,' Alice pleaded. 'I went mad with worry and that is the truth. Being in Belmont was no picnic. It was a terrible place. A place for lost souls.'

Jane bent over and fished around in her handbag until she found a clean handkerchief, and then she blew her nose hard.

'Mum, I am so sorry you suffered such nightmares. More so because the place I went to was very nice really. I should have left there when I was fourteen but they let me stay on for another two years, and I learnt such a lot. All that was because Mrs Rogers took me under her wing. Have you heard about her?'

'Yes. Wally told me he had lunch with her. And since my memory has become clearer, I do remember her being some sort of a social worker when you were in the hospital.'

'She's a bit more than that, Mum. She lost her husband in the war and devoted her life to helping children. She has a great influence within the law courts. You'll like her, Mum.'

'I think I shall. I got a long letter from her after she'd had that meeting with Wally, and she seemed nice.'

'Oh Mum, she is. From the day I left the hospital she's been my friend. She's gone to such lengths to find you for me. She even went to Somerset House to see if you were still alive and if you and Mickey had been divorced.'

'I know. Wally told me all about that. I'm glad you had someone you could turn to. I need to tell you, Jane, Wally and I aren't married.'

'I know, Mum, it makes no difference. Wally explained the details to Elsie.'

'Oh.' Alice sounded so sad. 'Divorce for someone like me, with no money, was an impossibility. Changing my name was the next best thing. Wally is a good man, an honourable man. He did it legally to make sure his surname was on your little brother's birth certificate.'

'Really, Mum? I still have a brother?'

'Yes, luv, you do. Sadly not Tommy, as you know. But he's a little beaut. Andrew we've called him. Wally's taken him out so as to give us some time together. They should be back soon.'

'I can't believe it! I have a family again,' Jane exclaimed, her face lighting up.

Alice wiped her eyes and smiled broadly. 'The one thing you haven't told me is how you've fared since you left the children's home. What kind of a job have you got? Where are you living?'

'That's a tall order, Mum, and if I started at the beginning it would be a very long story. But it will keep. All you need to know for now is that I've fallen on my feet.' She paused, leaned across and gently kissed her mother's soft cheek. 'After all, we'll have loads of time together from now on.'

There was the sound of the front door being opened and running footsteps in the hall. Jane swung her head round as the door burst open. She saw an adorable, chubby, dark-eyed little boy wearing a red and white woolly hat on the back of his head. He pulled his hat off to reveal a mop of unruly dark curls.

Jane stared at him in amazement. She couldn't take her eyes off him. The boy hesitated for a moment, then flung himself at Alice, who wrapped her arms around him and covered his face with kisses.

'We've bin playing football with a load of kids an' Daddy fell over,' he gleefully told his mother. Alice whispered something in his ear and he turned around to stare at Jane.

'Hallo, Andrew,' she said. 'My name's Jane.'

The small boy giggled, but said nothing.

Wally Simmonds put his head around the door then came further into the room, a look of immense relief spreading across his face.

'You two getting along all right, then?'

'Like a house on fire,' Alice told him, beaming. 'Like a house on fire.'

Having nodded his head in approval, Wally turned and without any warning pulled Jane to her feet and into his arms, and hugged her tightly.

Seconds passed before he said quietly, 'Now at last my

Alice can really start to live again. She'll have two children and peace of mind from now on.'

When he let her go, Jane found herself really liking this big man. He had one of the kindest and nicest faces she had ever seen, and his smile was warm as he studied her. With her voice full of emotion Jane managed to say to him, 'Thank you for taking such good care of my mum.'

Then she felt a tug at her skirt. A chubby face with enormous brown eyes was staring up at her. Suddenly the little boy grinned, showing a deep dimple, and asked, 'Don't yer want t' hug me? Mummy said you would.'

'Oh you little darling,' Jane cried, sweeping him up into her arms. 'You've no idea how much I want to.'

And in her mind she was saying, no idea at all. I can't believe this is happening. At last!

Chapter Twenty-Seven

'GOOD MORNING, MR WILSON. Is my mother up and about yet?'

Jane heard Charles's voice in the hall, and her heart began to pound. She finished addressing the envelope for the letter she had just written to the League of Friends on behalf of Miss Christine, and then made her way out into the hall.

Charles was speaking on the telephone. She watched him in silence, wondering why she felt something was terribly wrong. It was more than just a premonition, and she shuddered at the thought of what had brought Charles to the house so early in the morning.

Charles replaced the receiver and stood looking at it for a moment or two. After a bit he turned to Mr Wilson and said quietly, 'Mrs Harman is dead.' Then he walked across the hall and made his way slowly upstairs.

He found his mother in her bedroom. He tapped at the half-open door, and when she called, 'Come in,' he took a deep breath and entered the room. Seated at her dressing table, Christine wore an elegant swans-down-trimmed silk dressing gown over a lacy nightgown, and fur-trimmed mules on her feet. She had brushed her hair until it shone and she sat with it hanging loosely over her shoulders.

His eyes met his mother's in the looking-glass.

'What brings you here so early in the day?' Christine smiled as she asked the question, but at the same time there was a note of apprehension in her voice.

Charles was reluctant to answer, but it had to be done.

'I'm sorry, Mother, disturbing you so early. Frieda is dead. Last night in her sleep. I found her this morning when I took her her early-morning cup of tea. I telephoned the doctor straight away but I knew she was dead.'

He paused, and on his face was an expression of such sadness, anguish and regret that Christine felt her heart would break. What could she do? There ought to be something at a time like this. But there wasn't anything.

For a while a silence lay between them, and Christine could think of no suitable words to break it.

Then Charles shook his head. 'Oh God, it's difficult to tell you the rest.'

Christine felt fear clutch at her heart, and Charles sensed it. He placed a hand on her shoulder and said, 'Mother, you are sure to find out sooner or later, and better you hear it from me. The doctor fears that Frieda might have taken an overdose of her tablets.'

Christine was stunned. 'How sad,' she managed to say at last. 'Is he certain?'

'No. Not exactly.'

'Well, how would she have got hold of the tablets? I thought there was a nurse always in charge of her medication.'

'There is. Or rather there was. I didn't detect anything wrong. I sat with her until very late last night, and when I did go to bed she was fast asleep. Peacefully. She hadn't complained of any pain or of feeling ill. It doesn't feel right. Maybe I just don't want to believe it.'

Christine sighed and pulled her dressing gown more tightly around her body. 'I still can't fathom out how she could have had enough tablets to kill herself. Where the hell would she have got them from?'

'Oh Mother! That's exactly what I asked the doctor. He thinks she must have saved them up, one or two at a time. Hid them, probably. We won't know until after the inquest. But I don't believe it.'

'I am so sorry, Charles.'

'I know you are, Mother. Oh God, it's so difficult to take in.'

'Charles, go downstairs and have some hot coffee. I'll be down in about a quarter of an hour.'

'Yes, all right.'

She wanted to tell her son not to worry, but realized that would be a daft thing to say. Her innermost thoughts were best kept to herself as well, because if the truth be known, she was thinking that at least now the poor woman was out of her misery. No more suffering.

Hopefully Frieda had found peace at last.

It took two whole weeks before the verdict was given as natural causes.

'She went to sleep and didn't wake up. You must try your hardest to be grateful for that much, Charles,' his mother urged. 'I know it feels as if your world has collapsed around you, and you must be devastated, but Frieda had suffered so much. Now she is at peace.'

Charles, who had been moved by his mother's words,

exclaimed, 'I know you're right, but it doesn't make me feel any better.'

The day after the verdict, Charles sought Christine out again and attempted to explain the situation.

'I've been staying at my own cottage since the day Frieda died,' he began. 'I thought it better. With her gone, legally I was trespassing.'

Oh dear God, Christine thought wildly. If it's not one thing it's another. Aloud she said, 'Why on earth haven't you come home?'

'Mother I'm a grown man, I must take the consequences for my own actions, not keep running home to you. What I do have to tell you . . . it's hard . . .'

She waited, not saying a word.

Charles took a deep breath before saying, 'I'm not allowed to attend the funeral, and neither are you.'

Christine hung her head. This was not entirely a surprise, but nevertheless it hurt. Mr Harman and his daughter had flown home, which was entirely the right thing to happen. All arrangements for the funeral were in his hands. And who could blame him for not wanting any member of the Dennison family anywhere near him. After all, Ashford Manor was still his property.

'You wanted to go?' she timidly suggested.

'Yes, yes, I did.'

'You sound uncertain.'

'Oh Mother, didn't you intend to be there?'

'I don't know. If I did attend I would only have sat at the back of the church. On the other hand, I'd probably have made some excuse.'

When her son made no reply, she said, 'Darling, you have

to put all of this behind you now. You didn't desert Frieda, you did your best. You can't go on punishing yourself for the rest of your life. You must get back to work. See all your friends.'

'As always, I know you are right, Mother, and I will make the effort, I promise.'

But Christine remained doubtful. To all outward appearances, her son was coping. But as his mother she knew that Frieda Harman's death had hit him badly. He was still blaming himself for so much, and if he didn't set about pulling himself together he might never come to terms with all that had happened.

'Why don't you go away for a while?' she pressed him. 'There's really no reason why you shouldn't. I don't want you to go, of course I don't, but I do feel it would be for the best.'

'What about you, Mother? I feel I should be around for you.'

She did her best to laugh. 'A few weeks without you around won't kill me. Besides, I have Jane, and since my last operation I am able to see fairly well with that eye. I try to be independent.'

'Mother you do remarkably well. And regarding Jane . . .' He hesitated. 'You don't think she will want to leave you now that she has found her mother?'

Christine sighed softly. 'The thought has entered my head, I won't say it hasn't. I know she's very excited. Really happy, I can tell, and that's only natural. But as for leaving me, I don't think so. I hope not. In any case, she would give me plenty of warning, never fear. Do you want to know something? I can't imagine my life without Jane, can you?'

Charles felt his cheeks flush up. How badly he wanted to say, no, I can't, and I hope I never have to.

But now was not the time.

'A few weeks away will give you breathing space. You would feel altogether better for it,' and this time Christine's words were said with some force behind them.

And so Charles was persuaded. 'All right, I'll go somewhere,' he said, and smiled, relieved that the decision had been made for him.

When he came home he would come back to Adelaide House, to comfort and warmth, where love abounded freely and he could revel in the sensation of having shed his worries and paid for his folly. He would be able to begin to live again, as his mother had so rightly put it.

He had one great hope: that when he did return, Jane would still be here taking care of his mother.

If she was, then he knew his heart would be filled with gratitude and he would have high hopes for the future.

Chapter Twenty-Eight

THREE MONTHS PASSED before Charles returned home. It was, the first week in July. The sun was shining, the gardens were a blaze of colour and the grass was like green velvet as it stretched away in the distance to the lake.

The house was quiet, not a soul about, but there were flowers on the hall table which stood near to the main staircase, and the usual pile of letters waiting to be taken to the post.

Charles picked up the top one, instantly recognizing Jane's small neat handwriting. He smiled, paused for a moment, and then, when nobody appeared, started across the hall and on towards the door of the garden room. This stood open, and across the room, near the open French doors, he saw Jane, sitting sewing. It was without a doubt the most lovely sight he could have wished for.

There she was, no longer the young, timid girl she had been when she first came to be his mother's companion, but transformed into a beautiful young lady, dressed in a long, full-skirted blue-printed cotton dress which was set off by a plain blue short-sleeved linen jacket. Her dark-golden hair was her crowning glory.

She *was* beautiful.

Charles whispered her name. Jane turned her head, and for a moment her lovely clear blue eyes stared at him in disbelief. Then she put her sewing aside and stood up murmuring, 'Mr Charles.'

At that moment Christine appeared, perfectly groomed as always, wearing a sage-green linen dress with a matching soft silk scarf tucked into the neck and a contrasting cardigan draped around her shoulders. Her make-up was slight but perfect, her perfume flowery.

'Charles,' she exclaimed in delight. 'We've missed you. I thought you were never coming home.'

'Oh Mother, I've missed you too.' He crossed the space between them quickly, stooped, took her into his arms and kissed her on both cheeks.

'You've never written, not one letter,' she rebuked him.

'I know. I had a lot of thinking to do.'

Jane felt that she had to leave the room because she so badly wanted to show Charles how glad she was to see him, and she knew that was not possible. The truth was, she no longer thought of Charles as her employer's son. To her now he was a lovely man. A man she had lost her heart to. Although recently she had accepted the fact that while she truly did love Charles, there was nothing she could do about it.

'Shall I fetch coffee for you both?' she asked.

'That would be nice, Jane,' Charles said softly.

'You make that for the three of us,' Christine said firmly. 'I don't want you asking me endless questions as to where Charles has been or what he's been up to.' She smiled directly at Jane and added quietly, 'Fetch the coffee by all means, but then come and sit down with us and hear Charles's news first-hand.'

Jane felt gratitude flood through her. She so badly wanted to be included yet did not feel she should intrude on his homecoming. Miss Christy was so kind and thoughtful.

Seeing Jane hesitate, Christine added, 'Charles wants you here, I know he does, and we all want our mid-morning coffee, so . . .'

Jane smiled her thanks, not daring to let her gaze rest on Charles.

When she came back with the coffee tray, Charles was breaking the seal on a bottle of brandy. There were three glasses on the table. While Jane poured the coffee, he opened the bottle and poured a measure into each glass.

'To Charles's homecoming and future happiness,' Christine said as she touched her glass to her son's and then to Jane's.

For some reason those words made Jane's heart leap, because Christine was smiling at her in a knowing way as she said them.

They drank their coffee, at ease with each other. Charles was not looking at Jane, but she knew he was aware of her nearness even though he was gazing down the garden.

Christine began asking questions. Where had he been? Whom had he seen? Was he going back to the office? Would he prefer another bedroom for a change or was he content to use his old room?

Their glasses were empty, the coffee drunk.

'I'd better have a word with Mrs Wilson about there being one extra for lunch,' Christine said, rising to her feet.

Jane knew it was an excuse. Mrs Wilson was well aware that Charles was home. Was Christine deliberately leaving the pair of them on their own? Did she know about their feelings? She wasn't at all sure how her employer would react if she did. There had been times and a few words said that had encouraged her to believe that Christine might approve. But what if she was wrong?

When Christine had left the room, the silence lay unbroken. Jane almost wished the floor would open up and swallow her. Had she presumed too much? What had given her the right to think that Charles could ever care for her as she did for him?

He was staring at her so intently she didn't know what to do. It was as if he wanted to stamp an impression of her into his mind.

Was it a vain hope that he did care for her? Jane asked herself. And the only answer she could come up with was that she would have to be patient and let things run a natural course.

Jane had Andrew on her lap and was reading him a story. She heard the knock at the door but took no notice, giving her full attention to her half-brother, who had taken his thumb out of his mouth and was asking, 'Just how big is a giant, Jane?'

'Oh, ever so ever so big,' she told him.

'Even bigger than my Daddy?' he badly wanted to know.

Jane held her head up. It couldn't be! She had heard his voice in the passageway but could not bring herself to believe it.

Then, 'Mister Charles,' she gasped, feeling her face flush a bright red as her mother ushered him into the kitchen. She set Andrew down and rubbed her hands down the sides of her dress. They stood staring at each other while Alice picked Andrew up and quietly left the room, closing the door behind her.

What on earth was Charles Dennison doing in her mother's East End house? She had to swallow a couple of times before she eventually managed to string some words together. 'Mr Charles, won't you . . . sit down,' she murmured, dragging an upright wooden chair forward.

But he continued to stand, just looking at her. 'Oh Jane,' he said at last. 'When my mother told me it was your day off I wormed this address out of her. She said she was sure you'd be here with your family.' He went quiet for a moment and then almost shyly added, 'And I wanted to be with you as well. I knew I had the right house as soon as your mother opened the door. You two are so very much alike. I hope you aren't cross that I've turned up.'

She looked down at the floor, feeling awkward and unsure, only able to murmur, 'Oh Mr Charles.'

The kitchen was so small that he was able to cover the space between them in two strides. Then he put his hands gently on her shoulders, sighed and said, 'Jane, don't you think it is about time we talked? Perhaps we should start off by telling each other exactly how we feel. And please let's drop the Mister, eh?'

She looked around the room and felt the lack of space. The whole house was so very different to what he was used to. She loved this little house, loved coming here. The black-leaded grate, each side of which hung brasses, gleamed bright. The faded cretonne curtains, the wooden dresser with its mismatched sets of china, the threadbare rugs, none of it mattered. Here she was part of a family. Her very own family. She loved and was loved in return. But Charles Dennison would never fit in here. He shouldn't have come.

Charles sensed her embarrassment. There was no need for it. He had to find a way to tell her how he felt.

From the moment he had stepped over the doorstep, the

house had appealed to him. He thought back over the extra-ordinary chain of events that had brought him here. The harsh early years that Jane had suffered. His mother's dear friend Elsie Rogers had taken her under her wing, secured a place for her in a decent children's home. But in all the eight years she'd remained there she had had no link with anyone she could claim as her own relation. She had been turned out into what she had found to be a cruel world at the age of sixteen. Left to fend entirely for herself. Until, thank God, Elsie had brought her to be his mother's right hand. For that was what she had turned out to be.

And then, what a wonderful climax. With a great deal of help from Elsie Rogers, Jane had found her mother. And that had led to so much more: a stepfather who loved her, and a little boy who she could call her brother. She was no longer alone. She had a family of her own.

Would that make any difference to what he was intending to ask her?

He rued the day that he had let his heart rule his head, because his disastrous affair with Frieda had caused heartache for so many people. He had known for certain soon after he had met Jane that what he had felt for the older woman was not love. The day he had had the telephone installed in his cottage had marked the first stirring of his feelings for Jane, even though she had been like a frightened newly born colt whenever he held out a hand to her.

After that evening there had been no going back, although he had not allowed his feelings to show. He had a duty to Frieda and he hoped he had not transgressed in any way while she was alive. After her death, just to be near Jane had been impossible. He hadn't been able to think straight. At that point in time the last thing he needed was another emotional involvement. He had had to get away. Sort out his priorities. But always at the back of his mind had been the strong hope that Jane would still be there when he got back. He had isolated himself from everything and everybody that was familiar. Now he was home, and there were no doubts left in his mind.

He had come here today with his heart in his mouth. In the taxi which he had taken from the station, he had passed dirty, bleak buildings covered in bird droppings. Several pubs, and grey-roofed factories, and the endless rows of terraced houses with not a sign of a tree or a bush. In the main these houses seemed to open directly on to the pavement.

He knew his life had been a privileged one, but he had to convince Jane that nothing that had gone before really mattered.

'Jane,' he began, his voice sounding very serious, 'I want you to listen to me.' And when she turned to look at him he added, 'Just listen.'

'All right, I'm listening,' she told him.

'This shouldn't come as a surprise to you. I love you. I think I always have, from the very first time I saw you, because even then I wanted to protect you. Never let anyone hurt you ever again. I want us to be together. For the moment, how about you just agree that we can have a real commitment? But that would only be the beginning, because when we have spent time together and you can form a true opinion of me . . . well, I will know the time has come for us to be married.'

Jane realized that her eyes were filling with tears. She began to search in her pocket for her handkerchief. 'But . . . Charles, your world is so very different from mine. You can't be sure . . .'

'I *am* sure. Never more so. Because one thing is really certain, and that is that you mean the world to me. While I was away I went through a dark and painful time, only bearable when I was at last able to forgive myself for all the heartaches I had caused others. I can't turn the clock back, no more than you or even your mother can, but we can look to the future. Life for both of us might never be the same as it was, but it can be different, and I know that as long as we are together it could be good. I have given so much thought to this, and I honestly cannot imagine an existence without you.'

Jane, having at last found her handkerchief, now blew her nose.

Suddenly she felt very humble. 'Oh Charles, if only you knew just how long I have loved you, but whatever would your mother and your friends say?'

'Hush, my love . . .' Then his lips touched hers in a kiss so tender she could not believe it.

After a while he released her and she shrugged helplessly. 'I really don't think anything could possibly come of this, Charles. We couldn't . . . it wouldn't be right.'

'Why ever not, Jane?' His tone was gentle but she could see the hurt in his eyes. 'I promise I would take care of you, do my utmost to make you happy. You've just said you have loved me for a very long time. Did you mean it? Really mean it?'

Suddenly she was overcome with shyness and stammered, 'Of course I meant it, that's what's so awful. Ever since I first came to Adelaide House and you were so kind to me, I used to long for you to come home.'

'Oh Jane, whatever can I do to convince you that we shall have a future together?' he said, touching her face with the tips of his fingers.

Jane took a step backwards. 'Have you thought what your friends, your business partners, not to mention your mother, might say if you were to tell them that you were thinking of marrying me?'

Slowly and deliberately he placed his hands on her shoulders and looked into her eyes. 'Do you really think I care about what people might say? Whatever happens, you are the one person I want to spend the rest of my life with. I don't want you to answer me today. I want us to spend time together. Enjoy each other's company, really get to know each other's likes and dislikes. And then one day soon I shall do the whole thing properly. I shall get down on one knee, produce a diamond ring from my waistcoat pocket and ask, Jane, will you marry me. Please?'

She couldn't resist the look on his face. She burst out laughing, stretched out a hand and ruffled his hair.

He seized the opportunity and pulled her tightly into his arms. They overbalanced and, arms and legs entwined, fell to the floor, the pair of them laughing fit to bust.

Alice Simmonds, shelling peas in the scullery, heard their laughter, and from her heart she sent up a prayer of thanks that fortune was at last smiling on her daughter.

Chapter Twenty-Nine

'WILL I DO?' Jane asked, sweeping into the big lounge with an uncharacteristic flourish and giving Charles and Christine a twirl, the cream chiffon folds of her very first long evening dress swirling around her ankles.

'Beautiful, really beautiful,' Charles murmured. He too was looking very smart, in a dinner jacket with a crisp white dress shirt, his fair hair sleeked back, giving him a distinguished air.

'You look mighty fine yourself,' Jane smiled, her face specially made up for the occasion, hair piled high in a sophisticated style that had taken her ages to get right. She turned her gaze to Christine. 'Perfection,' she murmured. 'The only other word I can think of is sleek.'

'That describes you exactly, Mother, it really does,' Charles added.

Christine did look as if she had been poured into the tight-fitting golden dress. Around her shoulders she wore a fine stole that looked like a floating spider's web.

'I feel very honoured to have two such beautiful ladies for my companions tonight,' Charles said.

They were going to a hotel in Folkestone to a charity dinner in aid of an association for the disabled of which Charles was a member of the committee. It was a first for Jane and it had taken a lot of persuasion from both Charles and his mother to get her to agree to attend the function with them.

Life was like that lately!

There had been so many firsts. It was as if she had gained entry to an entirely different world. From the day that Charles had first put in an appearance at her mother's house, he had been as good as his word. They had spent hours together, walking across the Romney Marshes, lunching at the weekends in quaint country pubs. Some Saturdays, when Charles hadn't to go up to town, they spent the day in Folkestone, mixing with families on the beach, watching children build sandcastles and run in and out of the shallow waves, the boys dressed only in shorts, their chests bare, the girls with their dresses tucked safely into the waistbands of their knickers, children and adults alike licking their ice creams and running with balloons or kites on the end of long strings. It was an easy, happy companionship.

At other times, Charles took Jane and Christine to race meetings. Oh the excitement! Placing bets with the funny-looking man who wore a bowler hat and had a cigar sticking out from the side of his mouth even when he was talking. He was known as Honest Jack, the bookie.

Wonder of wonders, Jane, on Charles's advice, had laid out half a crown each way on a horse called Nice and Easy. It had come home first at ten to one and she had collected one pound eleven shillings and threepence plus her own stake money back.

They also spent quiet times. Times when Charles encouraged Jane to talk, always proving himself to be a good listener. He astutely made a mental note of everything she told him. Later, alone in his room, he would transfer his own thoughts down on to paper, the written word often making his heart ache just as it had done when listening to the telling from Jane.

Not all their outings or walks were in the south of England.

They had become regular visitors to the East End of London. Some Saturday afternoons Alice particularly loved. She had her Janey all to herself, while Wally, Charles and Andrew went off to watch a football match. When Arsenal, known locally as the Gunners, were playing a home match at Highbury, nothing would have kept them away. Even though Charles's business partners teased him that football was played with the wrong-shaped ball, the fever of being amongst the crowds that gathered at Highbury soon captured Charles as a fan.

When Charles Dennison had made his first appearance on her doorstep, Alice hadn't known what to do. It had taken her ages to really feel at ease in his company. Not his fault, bless him, she would say, just her leftover fearfulness from having spent time in a mental institution. Now she would watch them set off with tears of joy running down her cheeks. Her big burly husband, Wally; Charles, who, against all the odds, seemed to fit in with her family with such ease; and Andrew, with his beautiful happy little face with its high forehead, plump cheeks and dimpled chin, so unmistakably like Wally. The two men would swing Andrew along, his feet barely touching the ground, and Alice would turn and go inside the small house that was her pride and joy, to spend several hours alone with her lovely daughter. God had been good!

There had been times when she had felt she had been

entirely forsaken, not only by people but by God himself.

Not now, Alice Simmonds would say to herself on many occasions; now my cup is so full it runneth over.

Jane couldn't believe that the only doubts about the two of them getting married had come from her mother and Wally Simmonds rather than from Charles's family.

It would be like mixing oil and water, according to Alice. And as much as she wanted her lovely Janey to have the top brick off the chimney stack, she felt she had to voice her fears. They were together in the scullery, washing up the coffee cups, when Alice felt she had to voice her fears. She dug her fingers into the palm of her hand, then, heaving a great sigh, pulled the plug from the sink. As the soapy water drained away, she wished her fears could disappear just as easily.

Alice's face wore a serious expression as she squarely faced her daughter.

'Jane, no one wants you to be happy more than I do. But think about it. You both come from different worlds. Charles has always been treated as someone special. He's been waited on, given opportunities, never actually wanted for anything. In fact you could say he has been spoilt from birth.'

'Oh Mum,' Janey cried out in anguish. 'Keep that up and you'll have me convinced that I should run a mile from him, that it could never work between us.'

'Now I never said that,' Alice protested. 'I'm just pointing out what problems may crop up. I know from what you tell me how good Charles's mother has been to you, but . . . marrying her son? I don't know. Still, answer me one thing before we put our coats on and go for a walk: do you really love Charles?'

Jane felt her cheeks flush and again she cried, 'Oh Mum!

I thought it showed. From my first days at Adelaide House I was happy, but never more so than when Charles was at home. He was kindness itself right from the start and I truly believed that I was grateful to him, nothing more. But I missed him more each time he went away. My heart ached for him during the awful troubled times he went through, and I longed to comfort him. Until one day the realization dawned on me that I was in love with him. I kept it to myself. My love for him was precious and no one could take it away from me. I was fully aware at the time that nothing could come of it: as you so rightly say, I came from an entirely different background, but that didn't stop me from loving him, even though in my wildest dreams I never thought his feelings for me would ever amount to more than friendliness.'

Jane paused and took a deep breath before saying, 'So, Mother, to answer your question, yes, I do love Charles, with all my heart.'

'That's all I wanted to know.' Alice smiled broadly. 'They say love conquers all.'

It was days later, when out walking across the fields, that Jane again screwed up courage to broach the subject with Charles.

'You really mean,' she asked him for the umpteenth time, 'that it was your mother who urged you to propose to me?'

'Yes, yes, yes,' Charles said, hugging her. 'She approves wholeheartedly of you. Ask her yourself. She will tell you that she has looked upon you as a daughter for a long time.'

'Yes, but I didn't think . . .'

'Well,' he said modestly, 'anything that makes me happy is all right by my mother. I may have lapsed for a while, but by and large I've always been her golden boy. Truly,' he added seriously, 'if Mother had chosen you herself she couldn't be more happy. She loves you dearly. She never treated you as a servant even at the beginning, did she?'

'No, she never did,' Jane quietly admitted, on the verge of tears. She put her arms around his neck and kissed his cheek, trying to imagine how her life would be from now on. The most lovely thing of all was that she wouldn't have to stifle her feelings for Charles. She could let the whole world see how much she loved him if she wanted to. And she did want to!

'Charles, oh Charles,' she whispered against his cheek, 'I do love you so.'

On the first Saturday of the new year they were married quietly in the old church in Rye. It was to have been only their immediate families present. However, Jane could not believe how many folk were seated in the pews as she walked down the aisle on Wally Simmonds' arm. It was a testament to Jane's popularity.

The bride's family were in the front row on the left, her mother and her brother Andrew, together with Elsie Rogers and the Matron from Winchelsea Lodge, while Christine and her distant relatives plus many friends were seated on the right-hand side. With her heart so full she thought it would burst, Alice watched her daughter become a married woman. She had been completely overwhelmed as she'd watched her Janey being escorted through the church on Wally's arm. She was sure there had never been a more beautiful bride.

Jane wore a simple high-necked, full-skirted, long-sleeved white silk bridal gown, but because of the bitterly cold weather and a threat of snow, a red velvet cloak was draped around her shoulders. On her deep-golden hair, which had been professionally dressed that morning, she wore a triple crown of snowdrops intertwined with seed pearls.

The sight of Jane taking her place next to Charles at the altar, and the loving look he gave her, had been almost too much for Alice, and the tears spilled down her cheeks. She blew her nose and managed to control her emotions until she heard Jane's voice, soft but firm, saying, 'I will.'

After that Alice saw everything through a haze, and only pulled herself together when they were outside the church once again, being formed into small groups for the photographer.

Christine Dennison held a generous reception at Adelaide House, where everyone seemed entirely at ease. Wally Simmonds saw Alice and Christine deep in conversation, and he was grateful that two women from entirely different walks of life should be at ease with each other so quickly.

His glance went across the room to where Mrs Wilson was smiling as she helped her husband to carry in more food. Earlier in the week she had spoken to him freely, told him not to worry and assured him that the wedding would go off without a hitch. But it was the words that this homely, kind and wise woman had added that had set his mind as rest: 'If ever I saw a man in love with a girl, then that's Charles Dennison. Take my word, this time he's got it right, and he's a lucky beggar, 'cos there aren't many like our Jane about.' When he had repeated the words to Alice, her heart had swelled with pride.

The time went too quickly. 'We should go upstairs to change,' Charles said, tucking Jane's hand through his arm, and added, 'I can't wait to take my wife off on our honeymoon.' They wandered through the guests saying their thank-yous until they came to Christine, Alice and Elsie Rogers.

Jane had a job to find the words, but eventually she murmured, 'I owe it all to you three.'

The look of love on the faces of these three ladies as they each gazed at the newly married couple was enough to pull at anyone's heartstrings.

It had been an absolutely wonderful happy day.

But Charles was determined that it was not to be the end of the celebrations.

He had planned for weeks now. Studied for hours the notes he had made after the lengthy talks he'd had with Jane. It might still take him some time to pull it off, but he was determined that the minute they got back from their honeymoon he was going to do his damnedest to put his plan into action.

Chapter Thirty

'WHATEVER MADE YOU think of doing this?' Jane stared at her husband, her face showing a whole range of emotions.

It was the last Monday in February and the invitations Charles had sent out had stated that it was to be 'A buffet luncheon, and a time to meet and mingle with old friends.' He had arranged everything down to the last detail, Monday being the rest day for most of the London market traders.

Jane stood beside Charles, her eyes wide with amazement, as her stepfather proudly introduced his workmates and their wives to the newly-weds. Their voices were loud and rough but their pleasure at being here was evident. It took quite some time for all the introductions to be made, and Jane wasn't sorry when Wally suggested that he and Charles should fetch drinks from the bar. To say that she felt bewildered would be putting it mildly.

'You all right, love? You look pale.' Alice looked at her daughter with concern.

Jane shrugged. 'I'm fine, Mum, just a little overwhelmed.

Can't believe that Charles thought of putting this do on all
by himself.'

'Well, I know for a fact that he did. Even his mother
wasn't in on it until the last moment. He said he wanted a
do in London so that all our neighbours and friends could
be invited. After all, we didn't invite many friends to your
wedding.'

Jane looked across the huge hall and watched her mother-
in-law throw back her head and laugh heartily. The woman
Christine was talking to was large and heavy-breasted with
bleached hair and quite a lot of make-up. But when Wally
had introduced her, he had also told Jane that she was one
of the hardest workers for unprivileged children in the whole
of the city.

Christine, as usual, was perfectly groomed, looking better
than a lot of woman half her age. She seemed entirely at
ease with these Londoners.

Charles came back with a tray of drinks, but Jane felt at
odds with him. She really couldn't fathom the reason he
had set up this luncheon. There was an undercurrent of
tension between her and her mother, and Christine was staying well away from her. Something was going on and no
one seemed prepared to tell her what it was

They sipped their drinks in silence, watching a good
number of children running round the hall. Jane spotted
Andrew in a line of kiddies. Each had their arms around
the waist of the one in front and they were singing at the
top of their voices. Andrew broke free, crossed to her side
of the hall and stopped in front of his big sister.

'Good 'ere, ain't it, Jane?'

'Yes, it is. Are you having a good time?'

'Not 'alf,' said Andrew. 'You see the girl that was in front
of me, well, 'er name is Bessie an' 'er dad works in a circus

an' Uncle Charlie an' me Dad said they're gonna take all
of us t' see the show. That'll be great, won't it? See yer.'

Andrew was laughing as he sped off, and his laughter was
infectious. Jane shook her head but she was smiling! All that
had been said without Andrew pausing once for breath, and
suddenly Charles had become Uncle Charlie. Oh well, she
grinned to herself, this certainly was a different world, but
it had to be a case of when in Rome . . .

It came to her mind that there was nothing of their mother
in Andrew; he was the spitting image of his dad, he even
had a dimple in his chin like Wally. Well, she decided, if he
grew up to be as good-looking as Wally, with the same kind
and generous nature, he wouldn't want for friends.

Charles left the group of men to whom he had been talking and moved to be beside Jane. He kissed her cheek and
said, 'I'll only be a few minutes.' Then, turning, he called
to Wally, 'Would you like to give me a hand? I think the
cars have just drawn up.'

'Cars? What cars?'

Moving quickly to where her mother stood, Jane asked,
'Mum, do you know something I don't?'

Alice didn't answer. Instead she changed the subject.
'Charles really did do his homework. He's a good man, you
know, so stop worrying and enjoy the day.'

A hush settled and a group of people that Jane could not
place came across the floor and stood rather awkwardly in
a sort of line-up.

'Ladies and gentlemen,' Charles shouted, and as the hall
grew silent he spoke. 'Today I want to say thank you to
many people who were kind to my wife when she most
needed friends. I wanted Jane to be able to meet them again
in order to be able to say her own thank-yous. But I also
wanted those kind folk who befriended her when she was

alone in London to see how well she has coped over the years. I needed to let them know that their kind-hearted gestures were appreciated.'

The first couple to stand in front of Jane were Mr and Mrs Forrester. Jane's arms were flung wide; she needed no reminding that her first landlady and her husband had nursed her when she had been so ill. 'Friends for ever,' she murmured as they hugged her.

Elsie Rogers had joined the group and was now saying, 'You won't remember, Jane, but this is Sister Walker from the hospital where I first met you.' She lowered her voice and added, 'She and her nurses clubbed together and bought you a winter coat.'

'Oh, what can I say . . .'

'Nothing, my dear, you were a delightful child, badly in need of some loving care. My Christian name is Glenis, and I am really pleased to have been invited here today. It isn't often one gets the chance to meet up with old patients.'

It was Jane's mother who took hold of Glenis's arm and led her towards the buffet, saying as they went, 'I remember you well. It was me who suggested Charles should invite you. You were kindness itself when I needed it most. To agree to have my small daughter taken into care was the hardest decision I ever had to make, and God knows I paid dearly for it.'

Glenis squeezed Alice's arm. 'You had no option at the time and you were very brave. Besides, us being here today to celebrate just goes to prove that the ends have certainly justified the means.'

'Thank you,' was all that Alice could bring herself to say. But those words from this kind nursing sister meant a great deal to her.

Suddenly there was a whole group of smiling faces, and Jane gazed at them all in amazement.

'Oh my, where do I start?' she exclaimed. Dorothy and Richard Stuart, who had been largely responsible for obtaining a place for Jane at Winchelsea Lodge, hugged her in turn, murmuring how pleased they were to be here today.

They then stepped aside so that Ted Grimshaw and his wife Maggie might have their say. 'You look a bit different today t' what you did when we first met,' Ted told her with a twinkle in his eye, and Jane's heart lurched as she looked again at this bluff, red-faced man who had played such a big part in her life for eight years. And she had to swallow hard as she kissed Maggie, remembering the many times she had been given a fairy cake or a sweet pastry straight from the oven by this homely wife of his.

Next, 'Oh Connie, my very first friend in the home!' Jane held her at arm's length. 'You're no longer fat and cuddly, and what happened to the pigtails?'

'You may well ask, an' I'd like t' know how come you've turned into such a graceful lady.'

'Perhaps it was all those cold-water washes,' Jane said as she gave this dear girl another big hug.

Connie was grinning like mad as she made way for Matron.

Tall and smart, Lillian Cooper, still smiling and finding time for her girls, stood in front of Jane and eyed her from top to toe. 'You are a credit to us,' she said softly. 'But then I always knew you would be.'

'I am so pleased to see you. Matron.' Jane told her, reluctant to let go of her hand, thinking how loath she had been to leave the safety of Winchelsea Lodge and the secure protection Matron had provided during all those years when she had felt she had no other family.

'And I you, Jane. As it's a party, maybe you could call me Lillian?' They both laughed and held each other close. Each one had memories that spanned those eight years.

Then came, Nellie Matthews, the cook who had taught Jane so much, especially in those two extra years that she had been allowed to stay on at Winchelsea Lodge. And now Patrick and Emma Carter were watching her with open mouths, utter disbelief showing on their faces.

'My, my,' Emma tutted at last. 'What a difference! I've never forgotten the day you were brought into our work-room. Such a little mite. Patrick reckoned you were over-awed by all the countryside and animals and that was why you'd lost your tongue.'

'Well, t' be sure it was true, wasn't it? Plucked from London and set down miles from home, what else did you expect of the lass?' Patrick asked, though not expecting to be given an answer.

'You certainly don't need me to find you clothing now,' Emma grinned. 'No one would describe you as a lost London lass today,' she murmured as she took in every detail of Jane's expensive beige suit. 'I couldn't be more pleased if you were my own daughter.'

'Oh, Emma, once you and Patrick took me in hand I became a well-turned-out child. You worked wonders for so many of us. You really did.'

'Not in the footwear department,' Patrick said, staring at Jane's tan-coloured leather court shoes. 'Never shod any of you well.'

'We helped a little there,' a gruff voice put in. 'Better introduce ourselves.'

But before the man could say anything more, Jane laughed heartily. How could she forget! She had practically fallen into this stout, jolly man's café when the sole of her shoe had parted company with its uppers. She'd eaten steak and kidney pudding with loads of vegetables, and apple pie and custard and a large mug of tea, all for the princely sum of one and tuppence!

Then there was his wife, Harriet, as thin as ever, wearing a great big smile. 'Sid's 'ere,' she said, pushing her brother forward. He was still a thin, weedy-looking man, but as before when he smiled his face was transformed, so much so that Jane had felt at ease with him from the moment they had met.

'An 'ow long did yer brown button-up boots last yer, gal?' Sid asked, a grin splitting his face from ear to ear.

'For a very long time,' Jane promptly told him as she grabbed hold of his hand. 'Largely due to the good polishing you gave them, I think. You'll never know, Sid, how many times I thanked you for those boots.'

'And 'ow about my thick socks that yer went off with?' Jack teased her.

'They were my lifesavers,' Jane replied seriously. 'And so were those meals you so generously provided for me.' Then she looked into the faces of these three ordinary working folk and quietly told them, 'I have never forgotten what you did for me. Those days were so bitterly cold and I felt utterly alone and unwanted by anyone. You truly were lifesavers to me.'

'Now, now, no tears t'day,' Harriet rebuked her. 'You ain't getting away with feeling sorry fer yerself. Looks t' me like you've 'it the jackpot with that good-looking 'usband of yours. You wanna know something? You're lucky you caught him before he paid us a visit, 'cos I knew the minute he set foot in our café that if he'd been footloose an' fancy-free, I'd 'ave upped sticks an' made off with him meself.'

'Oh! You would 'ave, would yer?'

Jane turned her head and stared in utter astonishment. It was Charles who had spoken, and she didn't know whether to laugh out loud or not. It was unbelievable to hear her Charles speaking with a cockney accent.

He came nearer and put his arms around Harriet's shoulders, then, looking first at his wife and then at the ring of onlookers, he smiled broadly and said loudly, 'Harriet, after you had served me with that Irish stew and dumplings I was yours to command, But . . .' He paused, giving his words a dramatic effect. 'It was that jam roly-poly that did it, and if only yer ole man wasn't a damn sight heavier than me I'd 'ave gorn off with yer there an' then.'

The silence that followed held for half a second, and then the whole room erupted into loud laughter. Mr Charles hadn't only invited cockneys to his luncheon do, he'd become one of them!

Jane looked from one to another, all these folk who had befriended her in more ways than one! It was beyond her, the lengths Charles must have gone to to find them all! The only person who was missing was Nancy.

Yet Jane had the strange feeling that she wasn't that far away. In fact she could hear her loud laughter and knew she'd be saying, 'See, gal, didn't I always tell yer that life's a gamble? And it seems t' me that one way an' another you backed a winner.'

This day was turning out to be something else! It was such a kind thing for Charles to have done. When this last group of people had been in her life she had been a lost soul. And that was no exaggeration. A poor mite indeed.

Now she was different, with a name that was her own. Not the name of some man who had married her mother but had not been her father. She was Jane Dennison now. A new person, a new woman in more ways than one.

She felt Charles take her hand and was so grateful that he had come into her life. That he had fallen in love with her had been something she could only have dreamed about.

Nothing that she or her mother had suffered in the past could be wiped out. But she could look to the future with high hopes. She had a mother and a father, because Wally Simmonds was that and more to her now. She had the dearest little brother. A mother-in-law who loved her and for whom she would go to the ends of the earth if needs be. And she had Charles.

What more could she possibly want?

Children of their own in the future? Please God.

Jane felt Charles put pressure on her hand. 'Stop daydreaming and come and enjoy the day. Stacked over there on those long tables is some of London's finest food. So, Mrs Dennison, shall we partake?'

When everyone had eaten their fill, a three-piece band was set up on the stage and a gentleman took a seat at the piano and struck a chord while the musicians took up their instruments. The music and the fun was about to begin.

The pianist was an elderly man but his nimble fingers flew over the keys and many guests were heard to say, 'Old Alf can really make that piano talk.' It was true, and he knew which songs to play to get the crowd going. He started off with a wartime tune, 'Tipperary', then moved on to songs from the music halls in the twenties. Marie Lloyd had died in 1922 but her songs and her reputation lived on, and these East Enders knew all the words!

'It's crowded, isn't it?' Christine smiled as she pushed her way through the mass of people to stand beside Jane.

'Yes,' Jane agreed. 'I still can't believe how Charles found all these folk and set this party up without me even knowing.'

'Well, besides finding everyone who had befriended you, I think he wanted to do something for your mother and Wally. They didn't invite many friends to your wedding and Charles saw this as a way to rectify that.'

Jane didn't answer, and Christine wasn't at all sure as to what she was thinking, so she said, 'The band is good, don't you think? But it's the pianist who's the real star. He knows exactly what songs to play to get the crowd in the party mood. I'm finding it a joy to watch all these people enjoying themselves.'

Jane was still feeling a little apprehensive. East Enders and what Christine would describe as the country set were certainly rubbing shoulders today.

Suddenly she looked at her mother-in-law and they both burst out laughing. A whole group of women had linked arms and gone to stand in the centre of the floor, where they were belting out 'Goodbye Sally I Must Leave You'. Hardly had they finished than the band struck up with the Charleston. This hugely popular dance had cut across all social boundaries, and these Londoners were enthusiastically giving it their all. Soon the pianist took over again, and this time he was playing black and white minstrel songs.

A hush fell over the audience as four of Wally's workmates walked on to the stage. Their faces had been blackened and white chalk used to draw a wide rim around their lips. The lights in the hall were lowered, and the men stepped forward and knelt down. No one spoke; even the children were quiet as the men put their heart and soul into an emotional rendering of 'Mammy, I'd walk a Million Miles'.

When the lights went up again, Wally turned to see his wife wiping tears from her eyes. 'Come on, you soppy beggar,' he laughed. 'There's no need for tears today.'

'I know, but it's because everyone is so happy that I'm afraid,' Alice said softly.

'Afraid! Of what?' Wally couldn't keep the disbelief from sounding in his voice.

'Everything is going so well. I can't help wondering if it can last.' Her voice now held a plea.

With a great show of tenderness, Wally took her into his arms. 'Alice, my love,' he whispered against her hair, 'you've known your share of dark days, and there isn't anyone here today who deserves happiness more than you and Jane. It might be hard for you to believe it, but trust me, you have Jane now, and she has you. Charles won't be taking her away from you. He worships her, anyone can see that, and if the pair of them are as happy as you and I have been, well, they won't go far wrong.'

Alice swallowed hard before wrapping her arms around Wally's neck. 'You're a good man, and I was so lucky when you took me on.'

'It takes two,' he smiled. 'And your daughter and Charles were made for each other, so will you please dry your eyes and come and dance with me.'

Alice took the handkerchief he offered and dabbed at her eyes. For a few minutes they watched as their young son held hands with a pretty curly-haired little girl and did his best to dance her around the edge of the floor as the band played a slow waltz. Meanwhile everyone clapped while Jane and Charles had the centre of the floor to themselves and eyes only for each other.

Alice looked up at her tall husband and managed a grin. 'I just love a happy ending, and those two coming together really is unbelievable.'

The rest of the day was so enjoyable, as Jane reminisced with old friends and danced with Wally's mates, who called her 'darling' and held her in a way that Charles's business partners would never dream of doing. There was no offence meant and none taken. They were proud, down-to-earth men who earned a living in the best way they knew how. Their wives were hard-working women to whom family meant everything, and they had taken Jane and Charles to their hearts.

Several times her eyes met those of her husband, and the unspoken message was *I love you.*

Jane felt safe and secure.

As the day drew to a close, she was thinking that she had the best of two worlds. Her own family, who lived in the East End of London, a place where she knew that she and Charles would always find a warm welcome. And their own beautiful cottage in Rye where they could close the front door and she could have Charles entirely to herself. And where Christine, who loved them both dearly, lived close by.

There was, in fact, absolutely nothing Jane would have changed about her life as it was now. As far as she was concerned, it was perfect.

TIME WILL TELL

Elizabeth Waite

Flame-haired Wimbledon girl Joan Harvey could not have chosen a worse time to fall in love with Matt Pearson. With no end in sight to the Second World War, and Joan discovering she is pregnant, a rushed marriage is her only option, despite her family's reservations.

Then, on a visit to Matt's family in the East End, a street accident results in Joan going into premature labour. As her baby is born, a bomb plunges the hospital into darkness, before Joan has even had a chance to look at her son . . .

No one is happier than Joan to see the end of the war. Finally she and Matt can begin to behave like a normal family, and bring up their son and two daughters. But then a call from a solicitor brings astonishing news, about the day Joan's son was born, that is set to change Joan's life for ever . . .

Other bestselling titles available by mail

☐ Skinny Lizzie	Elizabeth Waite	£5.99
☐ Cockney Waif	Elizabeth Waite	£5.99
☐ Cockney Family	Elizabeth Waite	£5.99
☐ Second Chance	Elizabeth Waite	£5.99
☐ Third Time Lucky	Elizabeth Waite	£5.99
☐ Trouble and Strife	Elizabeth Waite	£5.99
☐ Nippy	Elizabeth Waite	£5.99
☐ Kingston Kate	Elizabeth Waite	£5.99
☐ Cockney Courage	Elizabeth Waite	£5.99
☐ Time Will Tell	Elizabeth Waite	£5.99

The prices shown above are correct at time of going to press. However, the publishers reserve the right to increase prices on covers from those previously advertised, without further notice.

─────────── sphere ───────────

Please allow for postage and packing: **Free UK delivery.**
Europe: add 25% of retail price; Rest of World: 45% of retail price.

To order any of the above or any other Sphere titles, please call our credit card orderline or fill in this coupon and send/fax it to:

Sphere, PO Box 121, Kettering, Northants NN14 4ZQ
Fax: 01832 733076   Tel: 01832 737526
Email: aspenhouse@FSBDial.co.uk

☐ I enclose a UK bank cheque made payable to Sphere for £ . . . .

☐ Please charge £ . . . . to my Visa/Delta/Maestro

Expiry Date ☐☐☐☐   Maestro Issue No. ☐☐

NAME (BLOCK LETTERS please) . . . .

ADDRESS . . . .

. . . .

. . . .

Postcode . . . . Telephone . . . .

Signature . . . .

Please allow 28 days for delivery within the UK. Offer subject to price and availability.